The
KEEPER

The KEEPER

A Novel

Suzanne Woods Fisher

Revell

a division of Baker Publishing Group
Grand Rapids, Michigan

© 2012 by Suzanne Woods Fisher

Published by Revell
a division of Baker Publishing Group
P.O. Box 6287, Grand Rapids, MI 49516-6287
www.revellbooks.com

Printed in the United States of America

Library of Congress Cataloging-in-Publication Data
Fisher, Suzanne Woods.
     The keeper : a novel / Suzanne Woods Fisher.
         p.   cm. — (Stoney Ridge seasons ; 1)
     ISBN 978-0-8007-1987-6 (pbk.)
     1. Amish—Fiction. I. Title.
PS3606.I78K44 2012
813′.6—dc23   2011032011

Scripture used in this book, whether quoted or paraphrased by the characters, is taken from the King James Version of the Bible.

Quote on page 163 is taken from John Vivian, *Keeping Bees* (Charlotte, VT: Williamson Publishers, 1986), 82.

Represented by Joyce Hart of The Hartline Literary Agency

12 13 14 15 16 17 18   7 6 5 4 3 2

To the world's best sister, Wendy,
who is just the right blend of Julia's
and Sadie's best qualities.

Guess who inspired M.K.?

1

Spring came in a hurry. The wind had softened, bare branches were budding, and soon there would be the heavy green shade of the trees. Julia Lapp had already picked peas and spinach out of her garden, and set them, along with baskets of carrots and bunches of asparagus, on the produce table in front of the roadside stand.

When school let out for the year, Julia would get her youngest sister to watch over Windmill Farm's stand, but it wasn't necessary in late April. There weren't too many customers around, not the way it would be later in summer, once the corn started to sweeten up and the tomatoes ripened.

The day was overcast, but gardening was hot work and Julia had been up since five. She glanced in the mirror that she kept hidden against the back wall of the stand. It was a bad, vain habit, catching glances of herself in mirrors and windows, but she couldn't keep from looking. What did she see? A twenty-one-year-old face, with shiny mahogany hair and hazel eyes rimmed with black lashes, and nearly flawless white skin. She pulled herself away from the mirror, silently scolding herself for her vanity. But pleased, all the same.

She should get back to her chores before dinnertime. She placed the honor jar, along with the small chalkboard listing the prices, in the middle of the produce, then hesitated. A few minutes of rest wouldn't hurt.

Julia collapsed into a chair under the shade of an apple tree and sighed in appreciation as a light breeze swirled around her, lifting the strings of her prayer cap. She looked down at her hands and frowned at the dirt under her nails. She and her siblings had been trying to fill in for her father since his heart trouble had started, and she was already weary of plowing, dirt and dust, and the tangy smell of manure that she couldn't get out of her hair despite daily shampooings.

She glanced at the farmhouse and felt a wave of weariness. She hadn't even realized how rundown it was looking, not until Paul's mother pointed it out last month when it was the Lapps' turn to host church. How had it escaped her notice? An upstairs window was broken—a recent victim of her brother's poor aim with a softball. Black buggies awaiting repair littered the driveway in front of her uncle's buggy shop. The entire house was overdue for a fresh coat of paint. Edith Fisher was right—the house was in terrible shape. The whole farm was in terrible shape. There was so much to do before her wedding to Paul in November.

Her thoughts drifted to Paul. Soon, she would be known as Paul's Julia. She said it out loud, savoring each word and its delicious associations—wife-to-be of Paul Fisher. The words were ripe with a sense of promise.

The sound of a horse's footsteps made her look up. It was Paul's sorrel mare. She didn't expect to see Paul today! Her hand flew to her cap. Was it straight? She brushed the back of her hand across her forehead. Was she perspiring?

She needed a shower. Did she stink from the day's work? She hoped not.

Paul climbed down from the buggy, tied the horse's reins to a fence post, then approached the roadside stand. He stood, hands clasped behind his back, examining the produce.

"Paul, what a nice surprise!" Julia said, moving to the produce table.

"I was on my way home from work," he said.

She was beaming at him, positively beaming—she couldn't help it! She still pinched herself every morning when she first woke up and counted the days until their wedding on the first of November. Tall, slender, and elegant, Paul had honey-brown hair, shining azure eyes, milk-white teeth.

Today, his blue shirt matched his eyes. He was staggeringly handsome, Julia thought, but it was his smile that she loved best of all. It had a touch of sweet whimsicality about it that made her feel warm inside, as though they shared something private and precious.

Paul took off his hat and picked up a bundle of asparagus. "Most everyone else in April is still weeks from getting much of anything out of their garden. But yours is already producing."

"Helps to get a few things started in the greenhouse." But Paul knew that.

He sniffed a sprig of rosemary. "Sure will be glad when Amos's butter-and-sugar corn comes in. No better corn in the county."

She wondered where the conversation was going. It was not unusual for Paul to approach her like this, circumspectly, indirectly. "Looking for anything in particular?" She smiled. "Or did you just come by to talk wedding plans?"

Paul put his hat on the table. "Jules, we have to talk."

Well, hallelujah! she thought. Paul usually took time to circle up to his point. She often wondered when he was going to say he loved her. It was probably numbered among the rules that so carefully governed their lives—that moment when he could first say the words. There was a Stoney Ridge way of doing everything, Julia knew, and that included love. "So let's talk," she said.

Something was wrong. Paul's blue eyes were avoiding her. He straightened his shoulders and almost looked at her face again before he let his eyes slide down to the ground at their feet.

She sidled around the table and tilted her head. "Paul?"

He rubbed his forehead. "Jules, I have to tell you something and I don't want you to get upset. Just hear me out."

"What is it?"

Paul cleared his throat. "It's about the wedding. I've given this a lot of thought—quite a lot—and I've prayed about this and . . . well, we need . . . I think we ought to just put things on hold for a while." He swallowed hard, then whispered, "I need more time."

Oh no. Please no. Not again. This was some strange, cruel joke. Julia felt as if she was going to be sick. She gathered her breath to speak, but when she tried to find the words, there were none to be found.

"Please, Jules," Paul said. "Try to understand." He reached over to her, but she backed away. "Hold on. I know you're upset. Let me try to explain."

Outrage swooped in to displace her initial shock. "What is there to explain? Why do we need to postpone the wedding? Give me one good reason!"

He studied the ground and kicked a dirt clod away. "There's a number of good reasons."

"Name one."

He rubbed his temples, stretching his hand across his eyes. Hiding his eyes is what Julia was thinking. "There's that incident at church."

"That happened weeks ago! And besides, it was Uncle Hank's doing—it had nothing to do with me!"

"Sure, but you know as well as I do that a person marries an entire family. And you can't deny that your uncle lives up to his reputation as the town character."

Julia crossed her arms. She kept her voice low and measured. She was trying not to sound hysterical. "Sounds as if your mother's been influencing your way of thinking, Paul." She closed her eyes. "It's all because of that auction last summer."

He frowned. "I don't deny my mother has always worried about appearances. And I admit she's fretted quite a bit about us. But this isn't about the price your quilt fetched at the auction."

"I couldn't help that price. Your mother thinks I've gone proud over it, but I'm not. Not one bit!" She hadn't created another quilt top since Edith's criticism. She helped her friends with their quilts, but she had lost her desire to piece another one herself. To be accused of being proud—what could cut her more deeply?

Paul nodded. "I know that, Jules. But then your Uncle Hank pulls a stunt like he did last month, and it only added to Mom's perception that your family is a little . . ."

She glared at him. "A little what?" But she knew what he was struggling to say. She loved her family dearly, but she wasn't blind to their quirky ways. She waffled between feeling

11

fiercely protective of them and feeling . . . a little embarrassed. Still, she was a Lapp. This was the family God had
given to her.

Paul risked a direct look at her. "My mother's concerns
aren't the only reason I want to hold off, Jules. It's . . . we're
so young. We're both barely twenty-one. What's the rush?"

"That's what you said last year, Paul. So we waited, just
like you wanted to." She took a deep breath. "So now you
want to wait until . . . when? December? January? It can't be
past February because there's too much to do in the fields."
When Paul didn't say anything, she felt a chill run down her
spine. "Are you trying to tell me that you're not ready to get
married? Or you're not ready to get married to me?"

"I . . . don't know."

She was hysterical now, her breathing ragged, her tears hot
and salty; her eyes stung. "You don't know? You don't know?"

Paul took a deep breath. "No. I don't."

She couldn't believe how angry, how upset she was. Not
only was she humiliated, but bitterly disappointed. "This is
the second time you have postponed our wedding, Paul! The
second time!"

Paul reached for her and she surrendered. She buried her
face against his chest and started to cry. His shirt, his smell,
her Paul, she loved him so much. He was all she wanted, the
one she had always wanted. But she waited one minute, two
minutes, and he said nothing. He was shushing into her ear,
but he wasn't telling her it was all a mistake, that he was sorry
he upset her. It was true, the unthinkable was true! A promise
had been broken and it lay shattered at her feet.

She pulled back from him. "You have to go. Leave. I don't
want you here."

"Jules, you don't mean that."

"Don't call me that. Don't ever call me Jules again." Her own voice sounded strange to her. She turned from him and ran up the long drive that led to the farmhouse. If she had any pride at all, she thought, when she reached the top she would not look back to see if he was watching her.

She had no pride.

She whirled, but his horse and buggy were gone.

On the way home from school, eleven-year-old Mary Kate Lapp took a shortcut through the Smuckers' pasture. She didn't use this shortcut every day, only when she was playing hide-and-seek on the way home from school with Ethan and Ruthie. Before she jumped into the pasture, she shielded her eyes with her hand and scanned the woods behind her to see if her friends had caught up with her. No sign of them. That didn't surprise her. They had no detective skills whatsoever.

Running through the pasture cut the trip in half and it added a little danger to the day. To M.K.'s way of thinking, the time saved was worth the risk of getting charged at by Ira Smucker's mean and ugly goat. The goat was dirty yellow, with intimidating horns, and a long beard that dangled impressively from his chin. M.K. thought that beard was longer than the bishop's, just as straggly too.

She tiptoed quietly. On a normal day, as soon as she reached the fence, she would yell and yell at the goat so it would see her—she liked having it know she had crept through its pasture without permission—then jump the fence and take off for home. Today, she didn't have time to aggravate the goat. She had much on her mind, as she often did.

Sadie Lapp was idly scrubbing potatoes at the sink, gazing out the kitchen window to the end of the yard where her brother Menno's two bird feeders stood, their platforms heaped with sunflower seeds and cracked corn. The cardinal couple was there, the vivid red male perched on the peak of the roof, keeping watch, as his dull-colored wife was eating. Sadie let out a big sigh.

Even in the natural world, love was a wonderful thing.

Sadie glanced up when Julia came inside. "I saw you talking to Paul down by the stand," she said. "Did you remember to ask him what flavor wedding cake he wants?" She poured cooked and drained noodles into her Ham 'n' Noodle casserole. "I'm thinking that vanilla is safest. Everybody likes vanilla. Of course, it isn't my wedding. It's yours. Yours and Paul's. And you should pick the flavor *you* want." When Julia didn't answer, Sadie turned around. "Jules? Did you hear me?"

Julia had come into the kitchen and slid into a chair at the long harvest table. Her elbows were propped on the table, chin in her hands. "We don't have to decide for a while."

"Well, I just wanted time for plenty of practice. I want it to be perfect." She glanced at her sister. Julia's face was white and pinched. "Is something wrong?"

Julia didn't answer.

Sadie put down the wooden spoon she had been using to stir the casserole and sat next to Julia at the table. "There is something wrong, isn't there?"

Julia shook her head—vigorously; so vigorously, in fact, that Sadie's suspicions were immediately confirmed. Sadie laid her hand on her shoulder, gently. "Julia, you can tell me. What happened?"

Tears filled Julia's eyes. "Paul wants to postpone the wedding."

"Again? Not again!"

Slowly, Julia gave a slight nod of her head.

Sadie covered her face with her hands. "Oh Julia. Why?"

A tear leaked down Julia's cheek and she quickly wiped it away. "He said he didn't really know why, that he just needed more time. When I pressed him for a reason, he gave a vague excuse about the Incident."

"Uncle Hank and the root beer bottles? But that was a month ago!"

"I know, but you remember how upset Paul's mother was." The sound of popping corks in the basement had panicked the horses and caused a small stampede. Quite a bit of damage was done to buggies. What made things worse was that Uncle Hank had a buggy shop. It wasn't long before rumors started to fly that Hank Lapp might have done it on purpose, to drum up business for himself.

"But Paul's a reasonable fellow. He must realize that Uncle Hank is just being . . . Uncle Hank. That his . . . unfortunate incidents have nothing to do with you. With any of us. Surely he knows!"

Julia sighed. "Paul thinks that a family is a family. No one makes decisions alone. His mother thinks Dad could have done something to prevent the . . . the Incident." She smoothed out her skirt and pulled in her lips. "Maybe he's right. Dad lets Uncle Hank do whatever he wants."

"Uncle Hank may be a little eccentric, but he's the closest thing Dad has to a parent."

"Paul said he wasn't being influenced by his mother, but I find that hard to believe . . . why else would he have changed his mind?" Julia's voice broke on the words. A single tear fell and dropped onto her apron, followed by another and another.

Sadie got up from her chair and put her arms around her. Over Julia's shoulder she saw the cardinal husband lift his wings and swoop away, leaving his dull little wife behind. Maybe happiness, Sadie thought, was like a bird, fixing to take wing. Maybe it was never meant to stay.

⁓

Julia heard the little bell ring from her father's room. Amos Lapp rang it insistently.

"Dad's tea! I forgot to take it to him." Sadie jumped up from the chair to pick up a mug left on the counter.

"I'll take it up to him," Julia said, wiping her eyes with the back of her hand. The bell continued to ring as she hurried up the stairs with the mug of tea, trying to pull herself together. "You're supposed to be patient," she said as she walked into her father's room and found him sitting in a chair, engrossed in a game of checkers with his youngest daughter. "Where do you think the word comes from?" She set the tea on the table next to his chair. "How are you feeling this afternoon?"

"I'd be better if my children didn't keep me jailed up like a common thief," Amos grumbled.

"Doctor's orders." Julia leaned her back against the windowsill and crossed her arms. "Dad, you've got to do something about Uncle Hank."

Unruffled, Amos picked up a red checker piece and leaped over Mary Kate's black one. He collected the black checker and stacked it on the side of the board. "Uncle Hank is a fine old fellow." He looked over at her. "And he's kin. We take care of each other."

"I know, I know." This conversation wasn't a new one between Julia and her father.

"Jules, Hank is a man who has never worried about what others think of him. Few men can say that."

"That's just it! He doesn't even care that he makes us the laughingstock of Stoney Ridge! What happened last month at church was . . . outrageous!"

"Plenty of folks brew root beer," Amos said. He gave a mock scowl as M.K. double-jumped his checkers.

"But look at the aftermath . . ." Julia stopped short as she noticed that M.K. was listening. Listening hard.

"What aftermath?" Amos asked.

Julia looked away.

"Paul Fisher canceled the wedding," M.K. whispered to him.

Amos looked at Julia, shocked. "What?! When?"

"Postponed!" Julia hurried to amend. "Paul *postponed* the wedding. There's a difference." She glared at her sister. "You were eavesdropping on Sadie and me in the kitchen just now, weren't you?"

M.K. studied the checkerboard with great interest.

Amos frowned at M.K. "Why don't you go downstairs and help Sadie with dinner?"

"I happen to have some real interesting news I might be willing to share and instead I get sent away, like a dog," M.K. said glumly.

"What's your big news?" Julia said, eyes narrowed to dangerous slits.

Amos looked over at Julia. "Is it true about the wedding? Does Paul really want to postpone it?"

Julia tucked her chin to her chest. She gave a brief nod.

"And you think the reason is because of Uncle Hank and

the exploding bottles?" Amos asked finally, sounding pensive. "Paul's no stranger to Uncle Hank's ways."

"What else could it be?" Julia said. She turned to M.K. "What news did you hear at school today?"

M.K. shrugged. "I might have heard a few things. Got me to thinking . . . maybe . . ."

"Maybe . . . what?" Julia asked.

M.K. lit up like a firefly. "Jacob Glick called off his wedding to Katie Yoder. And Henry Stoltzfus broke off courtin' with Sarah Miller."

Julia tilted her head. "What? All of them? But . . . why?" She paused. "Oh . . . you don't mean . . . don't tell me!" She covered her cheeks with her hands. "He's back, isn't he?"

M.K. nodded, pleased to deliver the news. "He's back. The Bee Man is back."

"Ah," Amos said, leaning back in his chair. "That explains quite a bit."

"It's happening all over again," Julia said. "Just like last year." Her sadness over the postponed wedding dissipated. In its place was anger. Hot, furious, steaming-like-a-teakettle anger. Directed at the Bee Man.

Amos brightened. "Maybe it wasn't your Uncle Hank's fault at all that Paul wants to postpone the wedding!"

"He certainly didn't help matters," Julia said crossly. "And then along comes the Bee Man this week to really seal the deal."

"Or not," M.K. added helpfully.

2

$\mathcal{J}$f asked, folks would say that Sadie Lapp was solid and practical, on the quiet side, and that she was a fine example to today's youth. Or if they were feeling less generous, they said that Sadie was a girl no one ever had to worry about.

What they didn't know about Sadie was that she had a deeply romantic side that she tried to keep well hidden. She felt nearly as bad as Julia about Paul's perpetual cold feet. How could he do such a thing to her sister? Twice, now. After all, getting married was the biggest thing that could ever happen in a girl's life. A dream come true. To marry the man you loved. Sadie could hardly imagine how it would feel to be a bride—though she did try. She had such dreams for her own wedding. She'd already planned the menu, chosen her material for her wedding dress, added special treasures to her hope chest. She had everything ready and waiting.

Everything but the groom, M.K. frequently pointed out.

It was never too soon to plan for such a big event, Sadie would say in her defense. Weddings took a great deal of planning.

Sadie wondered how she would feel if she were in Julia's

situation. She thought it would be like an arrow had been shot through her from front to back, leaving her with pain, longing, regret. Julia had looked so sad during dinner and excused herself after eating only a few bites of casserole.

Sadie put her fork down and leaned back in her chair. She glanced at Uncle Hank, seated across the table, scraping crumbs of gingerbread off his plate with the back of his fork. He managed to put away a lot of dinner, despite the day's tragedy. He wanted seconds on everything except the Ham 'n' Noodle casserole. He had always reminded Sadie of a character from the Bible, a prophet, or maybe a shepherd, with his longish hair and untrimmed beard. She could see Uncle Hank was completely unconcerned about Julia's change of circumstances. So was Menno, Sadie's brother, who was preoccupied with helping himself to a second piece of cake. Uncle Hank held out his plate to Menno to be served.

Surprisingly, M.K. seemed to understand the gravity of the situation. She looked up the stairs and back at Sadie. "I could take Julia some cake. She likes your gingerbread."

Sadie brushed M.K.'s cheek with the back of her hand. "I think she just wants to be alone."

"Our Jules is better off without Paul," Uncle Hank said as he reached across Menno to grab the bowl of whipped cream. "Them Fishers always think they're something." He dropped spoonfuls of whipped cream on his fresh slice of gingerbread.

"Amen to that," M.K. muttered under her breath. "Especially Jimmy."

Sadie elbowed her to hush.

"Well, it's true," M.K. said. "In school today, Jimmy Fisher put a black racer snake in the girls' outhouse."

"That is pretty low," Menno said in his slow, deliberate way.

"You can say that again," M.K. said.

"That is pretty low," Menno repeated, ever literal. "That must have scared the snake."

M.K. stared at him. "The *snake*? It scared the living daylights out of me." She coughed. "I mean, out of the *girls*!"

Sadie cut the last piece of gingerbread cake—after all, why save it?—and slipped it on her plate.

———

Julia couldn't sleep. She was assaulted by an avalanche of thoughts, rolling, tumbling. How could life change so fast? This very morning she had woken earlier than usual, so filled with joy she could have burst. A taste of something unspeakably sweet—a wedding—and then, this afternoon, she had lost it. Paul took her dream and broke it like a fistful of spaghetti over a pot of boiling water. Snap, in half. Gone.

All thanks to the Bee Man.

Out of the blue, the Bee Man arrived in town and filled Paul's head with doubts. Paul had never been particularly confident. She knew that he had difficulty making even the smallest decision, let alone a firm decision about a wedding date. The Bee Man had a way of bringing doubts into Paul's mind—just enough doubts to convince Paul to postpone the wedding . . . again.

The bishop's sermon two Sundays ago was about the necessity of loving one's fellowman. Not only did Julia not love the Bee Man, she thought she might hate him. Wholeheartedly hate him! She knew it was wrong to hate anyone, but how could she love someone so despicable? How was it even possible? She knew that with God all things were possible . . . but this?

She couldn't get that exasperating man out of her head. After two years, the mental ledger of her grievances against the Bee Man had grown thick with entries. Finally, she decided to commit this big mess to prayer. She believed in prayer. Prayer worked.

She bowed her head and asked God to help her love the loathsome Bee Man and to give her the strength she lacked. "Amen," she said and snapped her head back, smacking the back of her head on the headboard of her bed. "Ouch!" She rubbed her head where it hurt. Really, wasn't this also the Bee Man's fault? Everything about that man created trouble—even thinking about him inflicted pain. Who was he, anyway? Where did he come from? She had always noticed how the Bee Man skillfully deflected questions about himself. Even her father—who knew him better than anyone in Stoney Ridge—was reluctant to ask the Bee Man anything of a personal nature.

Julia had known Roman Troyer—the Bee Man—for six summers. He seemed to be particularly fond of Windmill Farm and spent time with the Lapp family each year, and still she didn't know a single thing about him other than he went from town to town with his bees. And he was Amish.

What pleasure did Roman Troyer take in breaking up her engagement to Paul? Twice! What did he hope to gain from it?

The sounds of Sadie and M.K., as they changed into nightgowns and brushed their teeth in the hallway bathroom, drifted through the transom above her door. She heard Sadie remind M.K. to scrub her face because no boy would look at her twice with that milk mustache. M.K. answered back by saying she didn't *want* a boy to look at her, not even once.

Julia's eyes flew open. Suddenly, it dawned on her. Of course. Of course! How could she not have realized? It was all so simple—as plain as day. Roman Troyer was in love with Julia himself.

Too bad, Bee Man. I'm not interested. I never will be! She wasn't going to let Roman Troyer stand in her way with Paul Fisher.

Her thoughts drifted back to Paul, feebly telling her he wanted to postpone the wedding. What would Paul tell others? Her mind was racing—she felt deeply humiliated. But on the heels of her humiliation was an overwhelming sorrow. She loved Paul. Would he ever be ready to get married? Or would he always just like the idea of getting married?

She sighed. A more courageous woman would have told Paul to forget it. A tougher woman would have told him in no uncertain terms what he could do with this halfhearted plan to postpone. But Julia was neither brave nor tough. She just wanted Paul back. She wanted things back the way they were, yesterday, or last week. Before the Bee Man arrived.

Oh Paul. What was he doing tonight? Was he at home with his family, or out with his friends? He had to be missing her. He had to be thinking about her. He was in love with her! She was sure of it. Tomorrow, Julia decided, he would come to Windmill Farm and tell her it was all a big mistake.

Prayer worked, she reminded herself. And so she prayed. *Please please please please please please please.*

The last chore of the evening was to move the three cows out to the pasture with the creek flowing through it. It was usually Menno's job, but he told M.K. that he had something he needed to do first, and then he disappeared with a trowel in his hand.

M.K. opened the gate and pushed the rump of the first cow, Pizza. If she could get Pizza moving along, chances were good that Pepperoni and Linguica would follow behind her. They used to have thirty cows, a herd, and it was M.K.'s job to name each new calf. Her father had given her that task the year her mother had passed, and M.K. felt very important whenever a cow was due to calve. After her father's heart started to act up last year, he sold the dairy cows and sheep at an auction. It broke M.K.'s heart to part with the animals. "Just for a little while, M.K.," her father had promised. "Just until I'm back in the saddle, fit as a fiddle." He let her keep a few—her favorites—as long as she promised to care for them. And she did, most of the time, unless she forgot and then Menno would remember. Caring for the animals was the main thing on his mind.

Where was Menno, anyway? She hitched the lock on the gate behind Linguica and ran up the hill. Menno met her as she reached the barn, near Julia's garden. M.K. gasped. In his hands were Julia's prized pink Parrot tulips, dug up, with bulbs attached. Julia loved those tulips! This very morning, she had made the whole family come to the garden to admire them. They were in their glory. At their peak!

"Menno, *what* were you thinking?"

He looked pleased with himself. "Julia is so sad. These will cheer her up."

"Oh, they'll be sure to get a reaction out of Julia! If I were you, I'd hide out in the hills for a few days."

Menno looked confused and M.K. was just about to explain when she heard Sadie call out to them from the kitchen window. Menno spun around on one heel and headed toward the house, and M.K. shook off her shock and followed him. Let Sadie untangle this. Sadie made things clear to Menno. He walked into the kitchen, dropping clumps of dirt from the tulip bulbs wherever he went. M.K. came in behind him, stepping around the clots. Boys. So messy!

Sadie was at the kitchen sink, soaking the last few dishes from dinner. She caught sight of what was in Menno's hands and froze. She threw a questioning look—filled with horror—at M.K., who shrugged her shoulders.

"They're for Julia," Menno said. "To make her happy again."

Sadie put the dish towel down on the counter and exhaled a deep sigh. "Let's get those into a pitcher of water, Menno."

He walked over to the counter and placed the tulips down. "You fix 'em and I'll take them up to Julia."

Sadie found a glass pitcher and started to fill it with water. "She's sound asleep, Menno. Let's wait to show her the pretty flowers until the morning."

He tossed M.K. a smug look. "Mary Kate thinks I should hide in the hills."

"No, you shouldn't hide." Sadie cut the bulb off of each tulip stem. "Once Julia recovers from the . . . surprise . . . I'm sure she will think they're a lovely gesture."

And then she added, so softly that M.K. thought she might have imagined it, "I hope."

Gray light streaked the windows. Julia showered, turned off the water, stepped out, dried off, and ran a comb through her chestnut-colored hair. She'd always been secretly proud of her hair, thick and sleek and luxurious. She took a washrag and wiped the steam off the mirror. She didn't look too bad, did she? Tired, a bit frayed on the edges, but nothing that would frighten the birds off the trees, as her father used to say about people who didn't feel up to snuff.

Fooling yourself, her reflection said. Sore head, sore heart.

In the kitchen, Julia threw herself into a chair, bone-weary after a sleepless night.

"You look lovely, Jules," Sadie said, coming in from the other room with a basket of laundry in her arms. "You're the prettiest girl in our church. Paul will come to his senses soon." Sadie quietly folded the stiff, dry towels and piled them on the table.

Julia made herself smile at her sister. That was an interesting thing about Sadie, she observed. Sadie spoke with a quiet certainty as if she knew what she was talking about.

"I was just going to bring breakfast up for you. In case you'd rather not see anyone . . ." Sadie's voice drizzled to a stop as she fastened her eyes on Julia's face. "I only meant, you can take a day off, Jules."

Julia didn't want to talk, and Sadie—despite the subject of Paul Fisher hovering over the table like a hummingbird—wouldn't make her. Sadie knew that you didn't need to talk all the time. She had a great sense of stillness, making it very restful to be near her.

"I'm fine. Really."

Julia picked up a towel and started to fold it as Sadie poured a cup of coffee and handed it to her. Then she put bacon in the fry pan. The hot bacon sputtered and popped, so Sadie cracked the window open to fan out the smoke. Julia took a sip of the coffee and spit it out. Grounds were floating on top.

This time Julia had no trouble smiling. No sisters could be more different, Julia thought as she spooned out the grounds. Sadie had always been most like their father, a peacemaker. She was quite lovely in a round, soft sort of way, with curly light brown hair, a round face covered with freckles, and a shy, friendly smile, mild-mannered and dreamy. A listening person. She was of a fearful nature, but she knew that about herself and said it wasn't such a bad way to be because it led to so many nice surprises when frightening things didn't happen.

Julia glanced out the window. M.K. was having trouble coaxing the cows out of the barn into the paddock. The silly animals milled in a stubborn bunch, jamming the opening and squeezing her against the doorjamb.

M.K. would be twelve come winter. Too soon to tell what kind of woman she would grow into, but Julia thought M.K. took after their mother, at least in personality. Maggie Zook Lapp had been known as a woman who had a curious way of thinking.

Menno appeared at the barn door and pushed the cows through, rescuing M.K. Julia's heart ached sweetly as she watched Menno's gentle ways. Nearly seventeen, Menno had the body of a man, but his mind hadn't developed quite as far.

To an outsider, Menno seemed like any other healthy, handsome young man. But when he spoke, it was obvious that he was different. You'd know from watching or even talking with him briefly that something was unusual. The wheels of his mind turned slowly, cautiously. The doctors never could decide what exactly was wrong with Menno. The consensus was a lack of oxygen caused brain injury during birth.

Unless it was something he felt passionate about, Menno wasn't much of a talker, but he hummed. He was always humming from memory, and off-key, every tune that he ever heard. Uncle Hank had taught Menno to be a first-rate bird-house builder. He sold the birdhouses at Julia's farm stand and also at the hardware store in town. Menno loved birds. His favorite book was *Bird, Birds, Birds!* and he spent far too much time at the telephone shanty by the schoolhouse listening in to the Audubon Rare Bird Count. He loved all animals, dogs and birds best of all.

The one thing that defined Menno's life more than any other was his relationship with animals. He held them, raised them, loved them, cared for them, healed them.

Julia smiled as she saw Menno and M.K. race up to the house, like they always did, eager for breakfast.

As M.K. and Menno reached the kitchen porch and pulled off their shoes, the front door banged open.

"ANYBODY TO HOME?" boomed Uncle Hank, who always spoke as though he were addressing the deaf.

"Oh no . . . not this early." Julia sighed and rubbed her forehead. Uncle Hank had always been a sore trial to Julia, but the exploding bottle incident put him on very thin ice. Not that he was aware of it.

"Come on in, Uncle Hank!" Sadie said.

Uncle Hank stood in the doorway, grinning like he just tagged everyone in a game of hide-and-seek. In his hand was the lit stub of a cigar.

"No smoking in the house, Uncle Hank," Julia said. "You know the doctors outlawed it for Dad's sake." She put her hand out, palm up, until Uncle Hank forfeited the stub. Julia opened the kitchen door to throw it out. She turned and frowned at him, but he didn't seem at all offended.

"Still settin' to your breakfast!" he bellowed. "I had mine at 4:30!"

The entire town of Stoney Ridge was awake now. Julia filled a coffee mug and handed it to him.

"Say, Mary Kate, if I'd a knowed I'd see you, I'd a put my choppers in." Uncle Hank fumbled around in his pocket and pulled out a full set of fake dentures. They grinned out of his fist. Menno whooped out a big laugh. M.K. and Sadie started to giggle.

Julia shaded her eyes with her hand. It really was too early for this.

"Well, Uncle Hank, how are you today?" Amos asked, standing at the bottom of the stairwell. He was still in his pajamas, Julia noted. More and more often, there were days when he never changed out of them.

"Better'n you, Amos. You're gettin' to look more and more like a plucked chicken ever' time I lay eyes on you." He spied Julia and pointed at her. "That Fisher boy come to his senses yet?"

Julia thought, *Move on. New topic.* "Uncle Hank, was there some reason you came over so especially early this morning?"

His bushy eyebrows lifted on Julia in surprise. "Why, so I did!" He pulled an envelope out of his pocket and unfolded it. He hooked his spectacles over his ears and gave the envelope a close look.

"I've got news. I found somebody to help out while Amos is ailing." He glanced at the return address. "A lady named Fern Graber from Millersburg, Ohio."

"Is she Amish?" asked M.K.

Uncle Hank turned his spectacles on M.K. "Of course she's Amish!" he roared.

"What's this Fern lady like?" Menno asked in his slow way. "Can she cook five meals like Sadie?"

"No one can cook like Sadie Lapp!" Uncle Hank pounded his fist on the table for added emphasis and Sadie blushed.

M.K. had a sudden coughing fit and Julia elbowed her to hush up. Sadie was just starting to learn to cook when their mother passed. She had learned how to make five recipes and that's as far as she got. She didn't waver off those same five recipes: A big ham on Saturday night which gave them leftovers for Sunday, Ham 'n' Noodle casserole on Monday to finish off the ham, Haystacks on Tuesday, Tater Tot Casserole on Wednesday, Cheesy Chicken and Rice Casserole on Thursday, pizza delivered from a local shop on Friday if the budget allowed. If not, grilled cheese sandwiches. The family knew what day it was by what was being served for dinner. Julia, who never had much interest in learning to cook, wouldn't let M.K. or Menno complain about the lack of variety in their meals. She knew how much mastering those five recipes meant to Sadie. They were a link to their mother, just like quilting was for Julia. A reminder of life like it had been.

"How did you happen to find this woman?" Julia asked. She knew from experience that if she didn't immediately steer Uncle Hank back on course, she would be obligated to ride the path he started down, filled with infinite, unrelated details.

Uncle Hank drummed his fingers on the tabletop. "She must be reading my letters in the *Budget*. So she wrote and asked if we needed help." Uncle Hank was a *Budget* scribe and took his weekly letter writing seriously, filling it with all kinds of news—much of which Julia considered to be the family's private business. And then there was plenty of community news, adding his unique "Uncle Hank" spin on events, often irking many of the ladies in the church.

Amos walked over to the kitchen to fill a mug with coffee. He gave Uncle Hank a suspicious glance. "Just what did her letter say?"

"That it sounded like we needed help and she would be just the ticket!" He scowled at Amos. "The right price too, considering you ain't exactly rolling in greenbacks lately."

Amos ignored that observation and took a long sip of coffee.

"What's she like?" Menno asked, buttering his toast to the very edges.

Uncle Hank rattled the letter. His glasses slipped down his nose. "Says here she isn't fond of rules she hasn't made herself. She brooks no nonsense. She has strong opinions and she's not the kind who enjoys surprises. She expects brown-caked shoes to be left at the back door and for the family to don clean socks in the house. And she'll tolerate no muddy-bellied dogs in the house."

M.K. dropped her head on the table with a loud clunk.

Uncle Hank turned one eye in her direction. His eyes had a tendency to wander. "And she has a mustache, fangs, and eats ten-year-olds for lunch."

"Thank goodness I'm eleven," M.K. mumbled glumly.

"Out of the goodness of her heart, she is dropping everything and coming to this family's aid." He leaned over toward Amos. "I'd be a watchin' yourself." His face broke into a big toothy grin. "I smell a trap brewing!"

"We don't *need* help," Julia said crisply.

Peering over his spectacles, Uncle Hank looked around the room. Clutter was everywhere. The kitchen was the worst.

Countertops were buried underneath a motley assortment of newspapers and mail. Last night's food-encrusted dinner dishes were still piled in the sink. Even the pattern on the linoleum floor was hard to make out, littered with grass clippings that Menno had tracked into the kitchen and somehow managed to spread through the house. Furniture was shrouded under a white film of dust. They had worked so hard to get it all cleaned up before they hosted church, barely a month ago—that infamous morning when the bottles exploded. But since then, they had been working fourteen hours a day to get the fields ready to plant.

"We've been pruning the orchards and planting the crops and taking care of the animals and trying to get the roadside stand up and going . . . ," Julia started, but even she couldn't deny any longer that they were in over their heads. Her time passed in a blur of trying to get the farm ready for another growing season, caring for her sisters and brother, and tending to her father. It didn't help that Amos was an awful patient, ornery at being so confined, short-tempered and demanding. She fell into bed exhausted each night, woke in the morning, and started all over again.

"Maybe it wouldn't be such a bad thing to have a little help, Julia," Sadie said quietly. "Just until Dad is better."

"That's right, Sadie girl!" Uncle Hank boomed, right into Sadie's ear, and she cringed. "I'm sure Fern Graber is a fine housekeeper and a real good cook. And I'll do alls I can to help out in them fields too, when I get a little more caught up out in the buggy shop."

Julia had to bite her lower lip not to spit out the words that wanted to roll off her tongue: Uncle Hank could be counted on for one thing—he couldn't be counted on.

Uncle Hank circled behind Menno's chair and put a large hand on his shoulder. "But as for this beautiful spring morning, Menno and I have work cut out for us. We're gonna head to town and meet this Fern Graber at the iron horse!"

Menno looked at his father. "What's an iron horse?"

"It's an old-fashioned word for a train," Amos said.

Menno thought that over for a long moment, then threw back his head and barked out that single, joyous "Haw!" that distinguished his laugh from everyone else's.

"Let's be off, Menno!" Uncle Hank shouted. "But first things first. We'll swing by Blue Lake Pond to see if the croppy is bitin'. After all, spring is upon us!"

Menno jumped out of his chair and grabbed his straw hat off the bench. Uncle Hank tipped his hat to everyone as he held the kitchen door open for Menno. Amos looked longingly after them, watching the two men—one old, one young—head down the path with their fishing poles in their hands and a bucket of bait.

3

As M.K. drew close to the house on her way home from school that afternoon, the smell of something savory drifted her way from the open kitchen window. It was Tuesday, Haystack Day, but the smell coming out of the kitchen wasn't anything like Sadie's Haystacks. She eased into the kitchen, as quiet as a person could possibly be. A pot of beef stew simmered on the stovetop, filling the room with a savory aroma.

Her eyes landed on the most glorious sight in the world: On the counter next to the oven were thick chocolate chip cookies, cooling on a rack. M.K. grabbed a cookie and took a bite. Bliss! Which could only be improved upon with a glass of cold milk. M.K. reached into the refrigerator to get the milk pitcher.

"Get your hands out of that refrigerator!" a no-nonsense voice called out without so much as a *how are you today*. M.K. nearly jumped out of her skin. She spun around and came face-to-face with a tall, thin woman, with wiry hair the color of nickels and dimes, staring down at M.K.

"I'm Mary Kate," M.K. said timidly. "But you could call me M.K. If you like. That's what my family calls me . . ." Her voice drizzled to a stop. "You must be . . . Fern."

"I am," the woman said. She stood surveying the room. She was all business. Her eyes were a pair of pale-blue flints striking cold sparks, and she had a look on her face like she was sizing M.K. up and filing her under Trouble—a look M.K. was rather accustomed to from her schoolteacher. "New rule. No one is allowed in the refrigerator."

"But—"

"I spent the afternoon cleaning and organizing it. It was a disaster." Fern frowned. "And now the milk isn't in the right place. And the eggs. Why would anybody move the eggs?" She straightened everything and wiped the shelf with a dish towel. "They don't belong on that shelf!" A storm cloud seemed to form over Fern's head, threatening to shed cold sleet all over the room.

Talking around a mouthful of cookie, M.K. mumbled, "The eggs were in front of the milk."

Fern eyed the second cookie beside M.K.'s glass of milk. "One snack after school. Then nothing until dinner."

M.K. slid the extra cookie back on the cooling rack.

"And there's a smudge on the door handle!" Fern rubbed the handle of the refrigerator with her dish towel as if polishing fine silver.

The large kitchen suddenly began to feel small and confining as Fern's opinions began to take up residence. M.K. quietly backed toward the door while Fern's attention was focused on the smudge. She sat on the kitchen porch steps and finished up her cookie and milk. She dipped the cookie into the milk and took the last bite, savoring it because she knew she wouldn't be able to help herself to another. Fern was guarding them like a raccoon with her kits.

M.K. pondered Fern's no-one-in-the-refrigerator rule and

wondered if there would be more rules to follow. No one in the refrigerator? She would starve! She would grow weaker and weaker, languishing away, until she died from malnutrition. Tragic possibilities always lurked near the front of M.K.'s mind, just behind her common sense. "This is outrageous!" she hissed to nobody in particular.

M.K. didn't like change. In her eleven years, she had already discovered that when things changed, they always changed for the worst. Life as she knew it was over.

Sadie finished filling the water bucket for the buggy horse, turned off the hose spigot, and went to find Menno. She followed the tuneless humming that led to him, sitting in an empty horse stall that doubled as a maternity ward for his dog, Lulu. Menno's back was against the wall, and two yellow puppies were nestled in his arms.

Sadie leaned against the bars of the stall. "I'm amazed Lulu will let you hold them. M.K. said she won't let her near them."

"That's because M.K. moves too fast, Sadie," Menno said in his slow, deliberate way. "She's always in a hurry. She makes Lulu nervous. Lulu likes things calm."

"Are you going to put up a 'puppies for sale' sign down by Julia's stand?"

"No."

"Dad said you can't keep them, Menno."

"I know. But I need to find the right home for each one. And then I need to make sure the puppies are happy. Dogs pick their master, you know." He shifted a little against the wall. "Come, look at this, Sadie." He pointed his jaw at the puppy tucked in his elbow. "Does that eye look . . . ," he searched for the word, ". . . gummy?"

Sadie examined the puppy's eye. "Might just be a little sleep in its eye. I'll check it again later today." She didn't see anything wrong with the puppy's eyes, but there wasn't anything she would deny Menno. She adored him.

Sadie looked at her brother. Menno resembled Julia far more than Sadie—he was tall and slender, with thick, shiny, curly hair. He had Julia's hazel eyes rimmed with lashes so thick they looked like a brush. Not fair! Not fair that Julia and Menno took after their mother, while Sadie took after her father's side of the family. Short, round, bordering on plump, large-chested, and her honey-colored hair frizzed up on humid days like a Brillo pad. M.K. seemed to have features from both parents—small like her mother, snapping brown eyes like her father, hair that was colored lighter than Sadie's, but thick and satin-smooth, like Julia's. So not fair. And then she felt a pin jab of conscience.

The barn door slid open and M.K. flew in, feathers ruffled like an offended parakeet. True M.K. style. "Family meeting!" she shouted. "We need to have a family meeting! Right now! It's a dire emergency! Where is everybody?"

Sadie popped up so M.K. could see where she was. She held a finger in silence against her lips. "The puppies just fell asleep."

Menno was watching M.K. with an alarmed look on his face. "Is it Dad? Is he okay?"

"Menno, you know that M.K.'s dire emergencies are never real emergencies," Sadie said quietly, in a voice of one long accustomed to her little sister's fire alarms.

M.K. overheard her. "But it is! We are facing a *terrible* problem!"

"Calm down, M.K.," Sadie said. "Sit next to Menno and look at the puppies."

M.K. came into the stall and crouched down. As she reached out to touch a puppy, Lulu growled at her, so she drew back. She gave Sadie a pleading look. "Even the dog won't listen to me!"

Sadie's heart went out to her little sister. Her daily emergencies were casually dismissed by the family. Crying wolf, they said. Yet Sadie indulged her—she knew that M.K.'s enthusiasms were always genuine and passionate but seldom long-lasting.

Sadie put an arm around her. "You've got my full attention now, M.K. What's the emergency? Why do we need a family meeting?"

"Fern! Haven't you met her?"

Sadie and Menno nodded. "She made me a big lunch," Menno said. "It was amazing!" He cast a sheepish glance in Sadie's direction. "No offense, Sadie."

"None taken," Sadie said. "Why are you upset, M.K.?"

"She said no one is allowed in the refrigerator. Pretty soon, we won't even be allowed into the kitchen."

Menno scrunched up his face. "But how would we eat?"

"My point exactly, Menno!" M.K. folded her arms against her chest, satisfied that she had conveyed the critical urgency of her message. She pointed to the puppies sleeping in Menno's lap. "Dibs on the big one."

Menno shook his head. "You can't just say dibs, M.K. These puppies belong to me."

M.K. waved him off. "Menno, come with me. There's a pot of beef stew simmering on the stove and it is tempting me something fierce. Let's go see if we can sample a bowlful. Maybe Fern won't yell at you. Nobody ever yells at you."

Menno nodded solemnly at Sadie. "It's true. Everybody

likes me." He gently placed the sleeping puppies next to Lulu and scrambled to his feet to follow M.K. to the house.

Julia was having an awful day. Awful! She already felt fragile from yesterday's conversation with Paul, and now, Uncle Hank had invited a stranger to become their housekeeper. They didn't *need* a housekeeper. Well, maybe they did, but Julia should have been the one to choose her. *Not* Uncle Hank!

The woman who had arrived at their doorstep earlier in the day couldn't be any more of a mismatch for the Lapps. When Julia first met her, Fern Graber had a look on her face as if she had a kernel of popcorn stuck in a back molar. That was before Fern walked into the kitchen and actually gasped in horror. Within one minute of arriving, she was sweeping the floor and clucking her tongue.

And not only that—Fern Graber had ears on her like a librarian. She was already listening in to their conversations and offering up her opinion on serious matters. Unsolicited. Unwanted.

Just moments ago, as Sadie and Julia hung wet laundry on the clothesline, Sadie asked, "If you had three wishes, Julia, what would you wish for?"

Without thinking, Julia said at once, "I want Paul Fisher to marry me."

"If wishes were fishes," Fern said as she walked up to them with another basket of wet laundry, "we'd all have a fry."

What really irked Julia was that Fern was right. She had hoped for so much and ended up with so little. It seemed to Julia as if her future had been floating above her like a brightly colored kite, waiting to lift her away . . . and Paul had just ripped the kite string from her hand. She could only watch helplessly as her hopes and dreams to be Paul's wife slipped out of her hands, drifting up and out of sight as if carried off by the wind.

Julia sat down on the picnic bench near the clothesline. As she buried her head in her hands, she felt despair grip her. Her chest felt as if it were being squeezed by a giant fist, but she wouldn't let herself cry. If she did, she would never be able to stop.

"Juuu-Leee-Aaaa!!!!"

Julia swiveled around on the bench to see M.K. running toward her, her face in a panic.

"Fern says she's not making our dinner! She says she's here to help Dad and we're old enough to be on our own!" M.K. stopped as she reached Julia, planted her fists on her thin hips and stared at her, defying her to act. Sadie and Menno walked up to join them.

M.K.'s timing was impeccable. Julia needed something to think about other than her own miserable love life. And Fern nettled her. It wasn't unusual to have friends and relatives help out, even to move in, but no one knew Fern. And what was Uncle Hank getting at . . . that Fern was setting a trap for Amos? Was Fern after Julia's father?

Julia shook that thought off. Uncle Hank said all kinds of ridiculous things, all the time. More likely, he had misled Fern into what she was getting herself into. Well, Julia would clear things up. She hopped off the bench and headed to the kitchen to find Fern peeling potatoes at the sink. Sadie and M.K. trotted behind her. Menno sat down at the kitchen table, wide-eyed.

"Fern," Julia said in her most authoritative voice. "While

our father is recovering from his heart trouble, the rest of us are working long hours to get the farm ready for planting and harvesting. I'm very grateful you offered to help us, but Uncle Hank led us to believe that you would be helping all of us—not just Amos."

Fern's lips formed a thin, unhappy line, but she kept peeling potatoes. "I can't cook for the entire tribe of you. There's limits on what a person can do." She turned her head and looked at Julia, a long look. "How much is one woman supposed to do?"

Amen! Julia thought. Amen to that.

"If you don't want me to quit, you'll have to take care of yourself," Fern said.

Quit? She might quit? Maybe this was the exit door they were looking for. Julia grabbed a dishcloth and rubbed a spot on the counter. "If you need to quit and return to your home, we certainly understand." She turned to M.K. "Go get your piggy bank, M.K., and we'll pay Fern her wages."

M.K. lifted her hands, palms to the sky. "Why is everybody always asking me for money?"

"Because you're the only who has any," Menno whispered.

Fern's face flushed. Julia had called her bluff. Julia felt a tiny twinge of pity as she pulled six spoons, knives, and forks from the drawer. Just a twinge. "Of course, Sadie could always cook for the four of us while you tend to Dad. You don't mind sharing the kitchen, do you?"

Fern's thin eyebrows rose in alarm.

Julia gave the silverware to M.K. to set the table. "You have three choices, Fern. One . . . you certainly aren't obligated to stay. Two . . . you can let Sadie back into the kitchen." She took the napkins out of the drawer and started to fold them.

"Or, three, cook for all of us." She handed the folded napkins to M.K. "Just let me know what you decide."

A pregnant silence filled the room. Fern blew out a stream of air. "All righty, then. But you all will have to eat what I serve." She pointed to Sadie. "Even the overfed one."

Throughout the discussion, Sadie had been feeding steadily from a pan of brownies. She had taken a paring knife from the drawer and cut out a small piece, then evened out the cut by slicing another bite, then another and another. When she realized Fern was referring to her, she froze, midbite, and looked up, horrified.

"Fine. We'll eat whatever you make for us," Julia said. "No complaining allowed." She gave M.K. a look of warning.

M.K. raised her small shoulders as if to ask, "What?"

Fern scowled, but Julia's amiability took the fight out of her. "I don't want people messing up my kitchen."

Julia motioned to everyone to leave the kitchen. Sadie dropped the paring knife in the brownie pan in a huff.

Outside, Menno and M.K. ran to the barn to check on Lulu and the puppies. Sadie and Julia lingered behind, watching the sun slip behind the row of pine trees that framed Windmill Farm in the west, making for early sunsets.

Sadie turned to Julia. "Do I look fat?"

Julia put an arm around Sadie. "No. Not at all. Not in the least bit. Absolutely not." She pinched her thumb and index finger together. "Well, maybe just a little."

"I am! I'm fat!"

"It's just baby fat, Sadie. You'll grow soon and it will disappear."

"I stopped growing a year ago and I kept eating." She let out a soft sough. "I am. I am a fat girl. Fat, fat, fat."

"Sadie, don't let Fern Graber get to you. Fern is just . . . Fern."

Sadie took a few steps down the porch and turned back. "You're sure I don't look fat?"

"I wouldn't want you any other way than how you are right now, Sadie," Julia said truthfully.

Sadie smiled and crossed to the barn.

Julia walked over to the garden and examined the flowers along the front row. She loved her flower garden, small though it was. It had been her mother's garden, her special joy. And now the garden gave Julia constant pleasure. Julia had always felt a special kind of peace whenever she gazed around the garden. The crocuses, narcissus, daffodils, each blooming briefly, sometimes only for a day, then withering. She snapped off the dead blossoms every morning, though she hadn't that morning, so she did it now. When she finished, her hands were stained with yellow and orange from the crocus stamen. As the peaceful scents of the garden stole over her, she felt a peculiar excitement.

It felt good, being so direct and assertive with Fern. Really, really good. And yet to Julia's surprise, she felt relieved when Fern decided not to quit. Her father's heart trouble was taking a terrible toll on Windmill Farm. On all of them. Julia kept expecting her father to make a full recovery. Surely, any day now, his heart would regain its strength. The Lord knew they needed him.

And how Menno needed guidance. He was a strong boy and could work hard at times, but he needed to be told what to do and how to do it. He needed someone working alongside of him. Instead of providing daily instruction, Amos had been retreating from life. He stayed in his robe and slippers, staring out the window of his bedroom. The neighbors pitched in as often as they could, but they had farms to run too. Even with Sadie and Menno's help, Julia couldn't keep up with both the house and the fields. As March had turned to April—spring planting time—Julia often found herself fighting waves of panic. She was drowning in responsibilities.

But now, at the end of this day, Julia didn't feel quite as sad as she had a little earlier. Her spirits had lightened. She reached up to smooth out the furrows of a frown forming between her eyes. She didn't want to mar her complexion with needless worry lines. It was bad enough that she had a too-generous sprinkling of freckles across her nose that even a bucket of lemon juice couldn't fade.

Maybe . . . if she could handle Fern, she could manage anything. Maybe things weren't as bleak as they appeared. Maybe when life became difficult, it only meant one was facing a challenge, an obstacle to be overcome. She was only twenty-one years old, young enough to make changes. She was going to become the kind of person who took no nonsense from anyone. She could do it. After all, even Fern backed down!

She straightened her back and lifted her chin, a matter decided. How could she overcome Paul's reluctance to marry? How could she point him in the proper direction? Sometimes, a man like Paul only needed to be convinced of what he truly wanted. She was going to marry him, as planned. This very November. She would simply have to be more forthright.

Fern opened the one-hinged kitchen door and peered at the rusty hinge, as if wondering how it still remained. She shook her head and called to Julia. "Your Uncle Hank told me to tell you that the Bee Man is due in. Tomorrow or the next day."

Julia's new confidence popped like a balloon. She dropped

her chin to her chest, defeated, wondering how an awful stretch of days could turn even worse. It seemed like at some point you'd just run out of awful.

On her way to school the following day M.K. had much on her mind, as she often did. She made a mental list of Fern's new house rules. This morning, as she was lightly hopping down the stairs, Fern told her it sounded like a herd of mustangs were galloping on a concrete floor and that there would be no more running in the house. That, M.K. counted, would be Rule Number 436, right behind Rule Number 435: Do not sneeze indoors. She sighed, deeply aggrieved.

Every school morning, M.K. waited at the crossroads to meet up with her friends, Ethan and Ruthie. Ethan was only nine, but he was brilliant—nearly as smart as M.K. but not quite—so she was willing to overlook his youth. Ruthie was already twelve, kind and loyal, though she had a squeamish digestion that didn't tolerate anything too far out of the ordinary. Still, Ruthie was willing to hold a grudge against Jimmy Fisher for throwing a black racer snake into the girls' outhouse while M.K. was attending to business. Acts of such devotion had earned her a spot in M.K.'s heart.

Jimmy Fisher was a thirteen-year-old blight on humanity, a boy born with his nose in the air. Unfortunately, Jimmy wasn't bad looking. He was a tall blond, the tallest in seventh grade. Every girl kept one eye peeled on him. They looked at him all day long. It made M.K. disgusted and was added to her growing list: Why Jimmy Fisher Should Be Stuffed into a Rocket Ship and Sent to the Moon.

That particular list was started when M.K. was only five.

Jimmy Fisher, then seven, played a trick on her. He tucked a walkie-talkie under his dog's collar and told M.K. that he had a talking dog. M.K. believed him and carried on long conversations with the dog during lunch until Sadie found out and blew the whistle on Jimmy. Too late! Jimmy and his friends called M.K. Little Gullie—short for little gullible—from that point on. M.K. wasn't a girl prone to letting go of her grudges. And Jimmy Fisher topped the list of permanent grudges.

M.K. sat on the split rail of the fence, swinging her legs, when she spotted a horse and buggy coming toward her. She shaded her eyes from the morning sun and recognized the horse as belonging to the Smuckers. With any luck, Gideon Smucker would be driving the buggy to town. M.K. jumped off the fence and smoothed her skirts, then waved at Gideon. He pulled over to the side of the road.

"Hey there, M.K.! Need a ride to school?"

Drat! There was nothing she would rather do than arrive at school in Gideon's buggy. She'd love to see the look on Jimmy's face then! But she couldn't disappoint Ethan and Ruthie. "Thanks, but I'm waiting for some friends."

"How's everyone at Windmill Farm?" Gideon asked.

M.K. looked up into his face. He was sixteen or seventeen, tops, with freckled cheeks and a shock of red hair that flopped down on his forehead. Propped on his nose were spectacles that gave him, M.K. thought, a very learned look. Julia said he looked like he was peering at life through the bottom of two Coke bottles. Sadie, more kindly, thought he wore the look of an owlish scholar.

Sadie was the one he was really asking after, in Gideon's roundabout, acutely girl-shy way. He was frightened to death of girls his own age. M.K. thought it was a serious flaw in an otherwise perfect young man. Gideon adjusted his spectacles, acting nonchalant as he waited for M.K.'s answers.

"Everyone's fine. Just fine." She was being mean, but she enjoyed watching his ears turn bright red.

Gideon looked up at a crow cawing in a tree. "How's your father's heart? Improving?"

"Oh . . . about the same."

"And Menno? How's he doing?"

"You know Menno. He's always fine."

Gideon scratched his forehead. "And Julia?"

"She's . . . well . . ." What could she say? She was worried about her sister. Julia didn't complain or speak ill of Paul; she seemed distracted, preoccupied, sad. How could Paul treat her sister like that? Julia might be a little pushy and demanding, a tad overbearing, maybe a little vain . . . but she was also loving and kind and beautiful. She'd practically raised M.K. "Fair to middlin'."

"Edith Fisher paid us a visit yesterday. She told my mother that Paul canceled the wedding. Any idea why?"

"Paul's a dummy. That's why." All of those Fishers were dummies. With all that went on this morning, it nearly slipped her mind that she had a score to settle with Jimmy Fisher. The usual slimy slugs in the lunch pail never fazed him. She cast about for something that would.

Gideon grinned. His smile was dazzling. How could Sadie resist it? "Seems like Julia needs to shake Paul up a little. He doesn't know a good thing once he's got it."

M.K. rolled that remark around in her mind for a moment. Interesting!

"Mary Kate? I asked how Sadie is doing." Gideon was staring at her.

Lost in her thoughts, she hadn't caught what he was saying. She couldn't help but notice his ears had turned fire-engine red. "Oh! Sorry, Gideon. My mind got to wandering. Sadie's fine. Just fine."

"Well, if you don't need a ride, I'll be off then." Gideon made a clucking sound and his horse started off down the road.

M.K. hardly noticed he had left. Without meaning to, he had given her a whopper of an idea. She just might be able to fix two problems at once.

Yesterday, Jimmy had whispered to her that Paul finally came to his senses once he realized that M.K. would be his sister-in-law. When Paul made that discovery, Jimmy said, the wedding to Julia was off. "It would take wild horses to drag a vow out of Paul now."

M.K. thought that feeble remark deserved a response. She didn't know why Julia ever wanted to marry into that Fisher family. And to have Fisher babies! M.K. shuddered.

But Julia loved Paul, and love was a mysterious thing, sickening though it was. M.K. felt any Fisher would make a sorrowful choice for a husband, but she was willing to cook up a plan to help make that happen for her sister. She had a talent for involving herself in other people's business.

An idea took form in M.K.'s mind and a mischievous grin lit her face. At last she had a plan of attack pretty well worked out. Off she darted with wings on her heels to meet Ethan and Ruthie as they rounded the bend on the road. The whole day had brightened.

One thing Julia couldn't deny about Fern—quietly dubbed Stern Fern by M.K.—she was a get-it-done machine. Since her arrival, every closet, cupboard, and corner of Windmill Farm had been scrubbed and polished. Julia wasn't complaining. It was rather pleasant to have a well-run home, even if it did require effort to stay out of Fern's cleaning frenzies. And her cooking! It was *amazing*. This morning, she woke early to find Fern in the kitchen, flipping a tower of blueberry buttermilk pancakes for Menno and M.K.

Late in the morning, Julia came in from the garden to get something to drink. As she poured herself a glass from a container of iced tea, Fern walked into the kitchen and dropped a pile of mail on the counter. "I'd appreciate it if you'd stay out of the refrigerator. Everything's organized the way I like it."

Julia resisted rolling her eyes. "I won't move anything I don't eat." Fern was a monumental pain, but Julia was going to try to be more understanding. Sadie had scolded them all last night after she caught M.K. trying to slip a bullfrog into the refrigerator when Fern was upstairs. "Maybe if we weren't so snippy to her all the time," Sadie had said, "she wouldn't be so snippy herself."

Sadie had a point. They *were* snippy to Fern. Not Menno, but the rest of them were definitely snippy to her, even Uncle Hank. Yesterday, Uncle Hank wandered into the kitchen and Fern told him he smelled a little ripe. And when had he last bathed? Uncle Hank stomped away to his Grossdaadi Haus. Later, though, Julia noticed he had showered and shaved. Fern had moved in and had taken over, with plans to improve them all.

Julia wasn't sure why Fern had come to help them, but she was confident there was some tragic story behind it. For a woman her age—was she fifty? Sixty?—she was quite handsome in a plain way. But she never mentioned a family of her own, no children or husband. Most likely, Julia pondered, her heart had been broken. Remembering the pain of that particular ailment, Julia felt a small wave of empathy for Fern. She took a fresh tack. "Did you grow up in Ohio?"

"Yes." Fern pulled a mixing bowl from the cupboard.

Julia tried again. "Have you always worked as a housekeeper?"

Fern slapped the cupboard door closed. "I don't have time for idle chitchat. So much to do. Meals to prepare, beds to make, towels to wash. Then I need to get a head start on dinner."

"Someone took my bell," Amos said crossly.

Julia and Fern spun around to face Amos standing by the stairwell. "I took it," Fern said. "Got tired of hearing it ring every five minutes."

"Doesn't that defeat the purpose of a patient having a bell?" He pouted like a child.

Fern put her hands on her hips. "What do you want?"

"I'm hungry. I came down to make myself some lunch."

"I told you I'd make lunch."

"I'm not falling for that again. Yesterday I got a bowl of thin broth."

"And crackers and an apple. Stop being such a baby."

Amos scowled at Fern and turned to go upstairs, muttering halfway up the stairs until his breathing became labored and his coughing started up. Fern followed him.

As Fern's footsteps faded, Julia pondered the changes since she had arrived, just a few days ago. Fern had made herself thoroughly at home in Windmill Farm, rearranging furniture, dusting and sweeping and scrubbing the house as if it was as dirty as a pigsty. But as irritating as Fern was, she was exactly what her father needed. He had been so discouraged by his slow progress that he had stopped doing exercises. Fern would tolerate none of that self-pity. She had made him do his exercises every day since she arrived and ignored his steady complaining. And she was just as bossy with the rest of them—especially so with Uncle Hank and M.K. All but Menno. Him . . . she spoiled. Julia smiled as she heard Fern order Amos to get dressed and take a walk to the road and back.

Fern was a tyrant, a dictator, but not quite the bully she liked to think she was.

4

At the age of fifty, Amos Lapp felt as if he had just acquired a middle-aged mother in the size and shape of Fern Graber and he didn't like it. But then he didn't like much of anything or anyone these days, especially himself. He wanted all of this heart nonsense to go away.

Fern had just brought him a cup of coffee and it was decaf! He wanted real coffee. He waited until he heard the door shut to Fern's bedroom, then tiptoed downstairs. By the time Amos made it to the bottom step, he was wheezing. A year ago at this time, he was plowing fields and planting corn, sunup to sundown. Virtually overnight, because of his weak heart, he had turned into an old man.

Last summer, Amos was out in the barn on a warm afternoon, when he suddenly had trouble with shortness of breath and funny palpitations in his heart, as if his heart were a bubble ready to burst. At first he thought it was just indigestion from Sadie's dinner. The next thing he knew he was lying on his side on the barn floor. Menno came in, found him, and an ambulance was called.

His next memory was being in the Coronary Care Unit with oxygen lines in his nose, an IV in his arm, and hooked up to beeping monitors. Dr. Highland—a man who looked younger than Menno—came to visit him on rounds. He was the same cardiologist who had taken care of him in the emergency room.

"I guess this was serious?" Amos asked.

"Pretty darn serious," the doctor replied. He explained that Amos had suffered a major heart attack—something called idiopathic cardiomyopathy, a disease of the heart muscle.

Dr. Highland couldn't explain why it had happened. Amos wasn't in the high-risk category. He had never smoked, never used nonprescription drugs, was trim and fit from a lifetime of vigorous farming work.

After a series of tests, the cardiologist ended up implanting a mechanical device to assist Amos's heart, and put him on so many pills that he needed a chart to keep track of them all. Over the next few months, Amos's rebellious heart settled down, but during winter, his heart had weakened to the point of being in heart failure. He would become short of breath and fatigued when walking up stairs, taking a shower, or performing the simplest of chores. And always coughing. He couldn't take a full breath without coughing.

The doctor recommended retirement—the thought of which horrified Amos. He always wanted to drop in the harness. Then the doctor brought up the notion of a heart transplant. That stunned him too. His response was immediate and strong—no heart transplant for him. He wasn't afraid to die.

Funny, now that he looked back on that time, he had never felt any fear. His faith had stead him well, and he knew, with as much certainty as anyone this side of heaven can know, that this life was but a hint of things to come.

No, he had no fear of death. It was the thought of leaving his children behind that grieved him.

Amos listened carefully for a moment before tiptoeing into the kitchen. He didn't want to alert Fern that he was on the prowl for coffee. That would be cause for panic. First, Fern's. Then, his, when she started scolding him like he was a five-year-old.

The doctor told him panic was bad for his heart; stress of any kind could take a toll on him.

Amos felt as if he couldn't trust his heart—that it had become as fragile as spun sugar. And he was so tired. Most days, he stayed inside, in his bedroom or at his desk, bored to tears but too weary to do much about it. Some days, he didn't even get dressed.

When Amos reached the kitchen, he went straight to the coffeepot where he knew the real thing was brewing. He could smell it. The real stuff had a strong, genuine aroma—not like that pale liquid Fern tried to foist on him. He grabbed a coffee mug and frowned at the sight of his hands. Thin wrist bones protruded out of his pajama sleeves like knobs on the kitchen cupboards. And his fingers were trembling in a way that reminded him of his grandfather.

As Amos poured the coffee into the mug, he heard the plod of hooves and wheels of a wagon pull into the long drive. He peered out the kitchen window and the tightness in his chest alleviated a bit. The Bee Man was here. Amos was so happy that he wanted to shout to everyone, *Wake up! The Bee Man is here!* On the dawn of this spring morning. Instead, he remained quiet. It wasn't good to get too excited, the doctor had said. He closed his eyes and recited Psalm 23. It was amazing the way the words came to him.

After the episode with his heart, Amos had found solace in memorizing Scripture. The ancient words were like a balm, a salve. They eased Amos's weary soul.

The Bee Man looked exactly the same as he led his mule and wagon slowly up the drive and came to rest at the top of the hill. Amos would know him anywhere: that bushy head of salt and pepper hair on a young, smiling face. In the wagon were beehives, carefully protected inside of solid wooden boxes. The hum of the bees sang in the wind through the open kitchen window. Amos set the coffee down and went out to greet the young man.

"So," Amos said, pleased. "So, Roman Troyer, you and your bees, you're back. A sure sign that spring is here." He pumped the Bee Man's hand. "Good thing too. Overnight, the cherry trees blossomed out."

"Good morning to you, Amos Lapp," Rome said. "We're a little behind schedule this spring. Everyone wants my bees in their bloomin' orchards, all at once. We're plumb wrung out."

An amused look came into Amos's eyes. "I suspect the bees are a little more overworked than you might be."

"I think they would agree," Rome said, not at all offended. Rome was impossible to offend. Not that Amos would even try. He was fond of Rome, mystery man that he was. Everyone loved Roman Troyer and nobody really knew him. He was vague about where he had been, even more vague about where he was going. He and his bees traveled the country farm roads, somehow appearing right when the farmers needed him, on the dawn of a new day. He traveled at night when the bees were quiet. And he carted his bees away when the job of pollination was done. Rome wasn't typical for the Amish, who were connected to each other through intricate byways of cousinage that linked just about everyone with everyone else. But Amish Roman Troyer was, through and through.

"I happened to see Menno a few days ago. He's gotten tall. If I'm not mistaken, he's got some whiskers on his upper lip. Have you noticed?"

"I've been ignoring it." Amos clasped his hands behind his back. "So, my friend, how have your travels been this winter? Seen many changes?"

"Too many. Villages have become towns. Towns have become cities. The roads are squirming with traffic." Rome grinned. "Not easy to navigate a mule and wagon loaded with bees." He leaned against the wagon. "And you, Amos? How was your winter?"

"It was fine," Amos said. A pale, unenthusiastic answer, but it was all he could muster.

"Looks like your spring planting is a little behind."

Amos stiffened. "Got a late start."

Rome tilted his head in genuine concern. "I might have heard a thing or two about your ol' ticker giving you some trouble."

Amos waved his worries away. "You know the saying, 'Treat a rumor like a check. Never endorse it until you're sure it's genuine.' Don't listen to idle gossip. I'm just fine."

Amos saw Rome's eyes flicker over his clothing. He was in his pajamas. And if that weren't humiliating enough, Fern stepped out on the back porch and lifted an arm in the air. "Who left this on my clean counter?" In her hand was a coffee mug. She spied Amos and stared him down.

"Blast!" Amos muttered. "If my heart doesn't kill me . . . that woman surely will." He blew out a stream of air. "She's our new housekeeper."

Rome laughed. "Just point me toward the orchard where you want these bees, Amos."

Amos put a hand to his forehead. "The thing is, Rome, money is a little tight this summer."

Rome gazed around the farm. "Whenever you can pay is good enough for me."

"It's just that . . . ," Amos started, "with this drought going into its third year, I'm counting on those orchards. We need as much fruit as we can get out of them."

"I understand, Amos."

"I was thinking that maybe this next winter, you could leave your bees at Windmill Farm and we'll look after them. While you're off adventuring."

Rome thrust his hand out toward Amos. "Sounds like a deal."

Amos shook Rome's hand and stood a little taller, relieved. "Well then . . . cherries are in full bloom. And apricot and peach buds are swelling." He pointed to the north, beyond the cornfields with their small shoots of green. Amos sighed. The corn planting was over a month late. And what could he do about that? Julia, Sadie, and Menno had done what they could and finally, a few neighbors pitched in to help finish it up. *If only Menno were able—*

He stopped himself, midsentence, and shook that thought off. *What kind of thinking is that, Amos Lapp?* The Lord God knew what he was doing when he made Menno. A wave of deep weariness rolled over Amos. A nap sounded pretty good about now. He gave Rome a pat on the shoulder and slowly walked toward the house.

"Amos, before you go . . ."

Amos turned around.

"Have you heard about this brown bear?"

"The one with the cub? I've heard she's been poking around, looking for food."

"The carcass of Ira Smucker's old dog was found last night. Looked like it was mauled by something."

"Old Pete?" Amos looked disturbed. "Something got old Pete? Aw, that's a shame. He was a fine dog."

"You haven't seen any sign of bears in your orchards?"

"No, but . . . I haven't been out there too much this spring." He turned to head to the house.

"Uh, Amos?"

Amos stopped and swiveled around again.

"Amos . . . you might have heard a thing or two about me . . ."

Ah, so that's why the Bee Man seemed to be stalling. He walked back to Rome. "In fact, I did."

"Is Julia mad at me?"

"Frying like bacon."

"I didn't really mean to talk Paul into canceling the wedding. We just got to talking and one thing led to another—"

"I know, I know. You never do mean it, Rome, but you're starting to get a reputation. Some folks are calling you 'The Unmatchmaker.'"

Rome paled. "Paul and a few other fellows asked me what I liked about being unattached. On the move. About visiting places. That's all." He looked miserable. "And then I said that I sure did admire those fellas for knowing, at such young ages, that they had found the one woman they were going to spend the rest of their lives with. The one woman they would grow old with. Day in and day out, year after year, decade after decade. I told them I admired their commitment and resolve."

"Did you happen to stress the 'day in and day out' part?"

"I might have." Rome blew out a puff of air. "You must admit, Amos, that it is impressive. These boys are only twenty or twenty-one."

Amos felt his spirits lighten, talking to this young man. "Rome, I'm a man who believes that things have a way of working out the way they're meant to be." He patted Rome on his shoulder. "But I daresay you've always had a knack for getting Julia's dander up."

"Who's that with you, Amos?" Fern's voice shot through the air like a cannon from the window above the kitchen sink. "What's he got on that cart?"

Amos looked up at her. "It's the Bee Man. Those are beehives."

Out of the window came, "Beekeepers make a lot of money for doing nothing."

"Pretty much," Rome said agreeably.

"And just where does he think he's putting those hives?"

"Out in the orchards, Fern," Amos said in a longsuffering voice.

"Looks like he hasn't eaten a good meal in a fortnight."

Amos looked at Rome and raised his eyebrows, pleased. "I think that qualifies as an invitation." He turned back to Fern at the kitchen window. "Set another place at the table for supper tonight."

Rome waved off the invitation. "I don't want to cause you any trouble."

"I'm plenty accustomed to trouble around this place." She closed the window.

Amos turned back to Rome. "Don't pay Fern any mind," he whispered.

She opened the window. "I heard that, Amos Lapp!"

Amos ignored her. *That woman could hear a feather fall to the floor!* "You come on up to the house when you hear the dinner bell clang. I might not be up to our usual game of chess after dinner, but at least you'll see the family."

Rome wasn't listening. His eyes were fixed on the kitchen window. "What did you say your housekeeper's name was?"

"Fern Graber. From Ohio. Hank found her. She's only been with us a few days." Amos let out a deep sigh. "Feels like months."

Rome stilled, and an odd look came over his face. Amos noticed, and wondered what he had said to make the Bee Man look uncomfortable, but he had used up all his energy for now. He had to go lie down. "See you tonight, Rome."

Rome climbed back on the wagon and picked up the reins. When he looked up, Fern Graber was standing in front of his mule. "I'm not going near the back end with all those bees."

He glanced at the hives in the wagon. "They won't hurt you. Still too cold this morning. They won't be active for another hour, when the sun is on the hives."

She looked as if she didn't quite believe him, so he stepped down from the wagon and walked over to her. He crossed his arms against his chest. "So, Fern. How did you find me?"

"Wasn't easy."

"Maybe because I wasn't asking to be found."

"Gehscht weit fatt, hoscht weit heem." *Go far from home and you will have a long way back.*

He exchanged a long look with her. "Es is graad so weit hie wie her." *It's just as far going as coming.* He climbed back up on the wagon. "I'd better get those bees out to the orchards." He slapped the rein on the mule's rump and gave a curt nod to Fern as he passed. He tried to look dispassionate as he drove on, but the truth was, seeing her disturbed him. This was why he left Ohio in the first place. He didn't want any tethers to his past. Why couldn't she have just let him be?

Then his attention turned to Amos. The appearance of his friend added to his troubles. Amos's skin was the color of frostbite, tainted gray, even though it was nearly May. He looked positively wrung out. Yet, still, when he peered into his friend's weary face, Rome saw echoes of the lighthearted, carefree, and generous man he had once been. Rome wanted Amos to look the way he used to look, when he first met him, brimming with confidence, eager for another year of farming.

For the last six springs, Rome would wind his way to Windmill Farm to find Amos out in the fields, hanging on to a plow behind a gentle draft horse, or examining his green corn shoots for any signs of pests. Or playing games with his children—Amos was famous for his sense of fun. But maybe this winter had taken a toll on Amos. Maybe his heart was worse off than Rome had heard. Amos looked hopelessly burdened.

As Rome's wagon traveled along the path that led to the cherry orchard, he surveyed the weed-choked fields. It stunned him to see how quickly the farm had fallen into disarray. Chickens scratched in the dirt beneath an old maple in the front yard. Next to the barn, Amos's red windmill turned listlessly in the early morning breeze. Rome shielded his eyes and saw that a blade had broken. It seemed that nature was trying to reclaim the land. As he drove along the road, he passed Amos's north orchards. Some parts looked so jungly that you needed a machete to chop your way through. Only the well-fed horses and sheep in the pasture looked prosperous.

Every spring, Rome looked forward to his visits to Windmill Farm. It had always been one of the prettiest farms he'd come across in his travels. The house sat at the top of a gently sloping bit of lawn shaded here and there with maple trees. The house itself was a graceful rambling structure built of creamy white siding and a fieldstone foundation. Twin chimneys rose from the roof, and a galloping-horse weather vane turned lazily in the breeze. Bird feeders and birdhouses were everywhere. And he meant everywhere! From sophisticated purple martin houses on long poles to hollowed-out gourds and pinecones smeared with peanut butter, hanging off trees. It was all Menno's doings.

Off to one side, a windmill—red!—an expansive barn, and a white fence surrounding a pasture where livestock grazed. Since he had first arrived in Stoney Ridge with his bees, years ago, that red windmill spinning its wheels at the top of the ridge was like a beacon to him. And a metaphor. What kind of a Plain farmer—other than Amos Lapp—had a red windmill? But Amos was like that—he had a love of life that was infectious. And Rome had grown fond of the entire family—irascible M.K., kindhearted Sadie, prim Julia, earnest Menno.

As he passed the vegetable garden, he smiled. Now *this* was the Windmill Farm he remembered. The garden was neatly tended; flowers bookending tidy rows of young vegetables. There was a sense of peace here, of order and tranquility. It looked the way Windmill Farm should look—could look—if Amos were well. This garden . . . it had always been Julia's domain, her pride and joy. It looked like a quilt top.

And then he saw her, bent over, at the far end. Up so early! She didn't seem to hear the thud of hooves and the jangle of the mule's harness. He could have just hurried the mule along and vanished into the orchards, but he had to face Julia, sooner or later. This seemed to be the chosen morning for facing hard things; now was as good a time as any other. He stopped the mule and tied it to a hitch post. He watched her for a few moments, bracing himself for . . . for what? He doubted Julia would outright yell at him. More likely, she would be frosty. Well, he could handle frosty.

He put his straw hat back on, fitting it snugly. Then he hopped over a few rows of spring onions to catch up with her. "Hello, Julia."

She popped up from leaning over a row of asparagus, slicing spears at ground level and laying them gently into a basket. She looked at him for a moment, deciding something. "I suppose it wouldn't be spring without the Bee Man." She put the basket down and crossed a few rows until she reached him. She came up so close to him that he could see little sweat beads on her upper lip. She wiped the sweat away with the back of her hand. "Hello, Rome. Looks as if life is agreeing with you."

He felt more than a little surprised at Julia's calm demeanor. He wasn't quite sure what to expect, but he didn't expect calm. He wouldn't have blamed her if she threw some asparagus spears at him. It was a rotten thing he had done, even if it was accidental. "No complaints. Did you win any prizes for your quilts this winter?"

She stiffened and looked very uncomfortable. "I don't have time to do much quilting anymore."

Rome was puzzled. Why was that such a bad thing to

ask? Last summer, Julia's quilt had been auctioned away in a fundraiser for a clinic benefit. That one quilt raised three times as much money as any other quilt auctioned off that day. Folks talked about it for weeks afterward. He had figured quilting was a safe topic, but her face had a tight look on it, like she had just tasted something bitter. Rome decided to try a fresh tack. "I just saw your father."

"Really? Was he outside?"

Rome nodded. Julia's face brightened with that piece of news, which told Rome that Amos must not be getting outside much. That explained the neglected condition of the farm. "That's good. He has been a little . . . under the weather this winter."

"So I heard."

Julia lifted her palms. "But of course. The Bee Man knows all."

The silence between them lengthened. Rome braced himself. Here it was . . . he was in the eye of the storm and he hadn't even realized it. "Julia, I didn't set out to talk Paul out of the wedding."

She took her time answering. "Again. You forgot to add the word 'again.' You didn't mean to try to talk Paul out of the wedding *again*."

"It just happened. One minute we were talking about how well his hens were laying eggs this spring, the next minute we were talking about—"

"About thinking of marriage as a ball and chain. About a man taking time to enjoy his freedom. About seeing the ocean. And traveling. "

Rome winced and rubbed his chin. "That's . . . about right."

"Well, once again, you have influenced Paul to postpone the wedding."

"Julia," he started tentatively, "it wasn't like that—"

She put up a hand to stop him. "Rome, I think I understand something about this situation. Something about you. It suddenly became so clear. Two springtimes in a row, you arrive in Stoney Ridge, you hear whispers about my engagement to Paul—and you convince him to postpone the wedding."

"That's what I'm trying to explain." He pushed his hat off of his forehead, uncovering a hank of thick salt and pepper hair. "I didn't set out to change his mind—"

"I realized why you're so intent on making sure I don't marry Paul." She looked away, a faint blush on her cheeks. "I hope you don't mind if I speak plain."

Rome nodded, curious. "Please do."

She glanced down at her hands and paused for several long moments, as if collecting her thoughts or her wits or both. When she finally looked up, her eyes were simmering with emotion, but he could not tell if she was deeply embarrassed by what she was about to say or if she simply found it uncomfortable to share it. What could be so hard to say?

Her dark-fringed eyes were cast down modestly. "I realized that you might be . . . sweet . . . on me yourself."

Rome choked on the piece of peppermint gum that had been lurking in the corner of his mouth. Julia ended up pounding him on the back. Unfortunately, she pounded like she was hammering a stubborn nail, and he was sure he felt a rib crack. Maybe two. When he got his breath back, he coughed out a weak, "Pardon?"

Emboldened, she looked him straight in the eyes. "It

makes perfect sense. After all, I'm the only girl in this town who is immune to your charms. Maybe the only girl in Pennsylvania. I certainly understand why that would be . . . a . . . challenge . . . to you." Her cheeks flamed a deeper pink, reminding him of the blush on the yellow apples just before harvesting.

"But—" He felt dizzy. Part of it might have been his busted ribs, but most of it was trying to get his mind to make the connection between Julia Lapp—Amos's eldest girl—and this bold young woman who stood before him.

"I should have realized it sooner. I mean . . . I'm aware that you've always been attracted to me."

"Wait. What?"

"But my heart is set on Paul. I suppose if I were in your shoes, I'd be feeling a little . . . threatened myself."

"Attraction?" Was that his voice? It sounded squeaky. He cleared his throat. "Threatened?"

"Thank you, Rome, for letting me clear the air on this sticky situation."

Rome was speechless. "Julia, there might be some kind of misunderstanding . . ."

She gave him a pitiful smile. "Trust me, I know it can hurt to be rebuffed. But I felt I had to be truthful with you." She patted him on the arm like a child. "You'll be fine. Really." She brushed past him, cap strings dancing as she jumped a row to reach the spiky asparagus.

Rome stood there for a moment, thoroughly flummoxed. What just happened? Although the words coming out of her mouth seemed ridiculously . . . naïve. Absurd! He was shocked by her forwardness. So bold! So audacious. After all, Julia was four or five years his junior. A child, really. Still, there was a willful tilt to her chin that surprised Rome. She was a woman and a girl at the same time. He looked at her in a new way, as if he had seen her for the first time. His mouth lifted with the beginnings of a new smile.

How had he never noticed? She was darling.

5

Sadie had been working indoors most of the day, ironing for Fern. Before dinner, she wanted to sneak off to see the cherry orchards in bloom. She walked between the long rows of cherry trees and finally sat down in the middle, under her favorite tree, and lay on her back to look up at the sky through the pale pink blossoms. If she squinted her eyes, it seemed as if the blossoms were like a lace tablecloth that covered the cerulean sky. She drew in a long breath, inhaling the woody scent laced with a subtle fragrance of sweet cherry flowers.

For just a moment, she could pretend that everything was fine, that her father was getting better, that Fern would return to Ohio, that life could go back to the way it was. And that Sadie would find something she was good at. Was everybody born knowing what they were good at? She wasn't good at anything, not really. Julia could do everything well. Menno had a way with animals. M.K. was smart as a whip. Sadie was . . . what? Polite? Even-tempered? A friend to all? *Boring.*

She saw Julia cross from the garden to the house. Julia had chestnut-brown hair, smooth and shiny as a satin curtain, and a twinkly smile. Her body was tall and slim and perfect. Best of all, most important, Julia could talk to anybody, parents or boys, and everything that came out of her mouth—the words and the sound of the words—was always just right. It was hard to believe that she and Julia were related. She was flat where Julia was curvy, large where Julia was small. Usually when Sadie got upset about her appearance—which even her own sisters described only as "nice"—she reminded herself to be grateful for her good features: a pair of very nice blue eyes, thick lashes, and a peaches-and-cream complexion—give or take a few zillion freckles.

She knew she shouldn't feel jealous of her sister. Her mind drifted to a proverb Julia would tell her when she was in a funk: "Compare and despair." Or had she said, "Despair and compare?" It was difficult to remember these things when there were so many proverbs jostling in her head, eager to spout advice. Was meh as zwee wisse, is ken Geheimnis. *Three are too many to keep a secret.* Wammer Dags es Licht brennt, muss mer nachts im Dunkle hocke. *Burn the candle by day and you'll sit in the dark at night.* . . . so on and so on and so on. All of these sayings were undoubtedly true and just as easy to dismiss—until the moment you found yourself doing the very thing that the proverb warned you against.

She heard someone call her name and she popped up. *The Bee Man!* She didn't know that he had arrived in Stoney Ridge. Her heartbeat kicked to double time. He'd still had the same effect on her that he'd had since she was nine. And now Roman Troyer was less than eight feet away from her. *Eight feet!*

"How are you, Sadie?"

Roman Troyer walked right up to her and offered her his hand to help her stand. The Bee Man was talking to her! She scrambled to her feet. She wheezed for air, choked, and started to cough. He waited patiently. Her eyes began to tear. She pressed her fingers to her throat, trying to clear the air passage. No words came out of her mouth. Seconds ticked by. Sadie had to say something. Anything! But she couldn't adjust to having the man she'd had a crush on since she was nine years old stand in front of her.

Finally, somehow, Sadie managed to squeeze out a wheezy, "H-hello."

"I've brought my bees," Rome said. He pointed to a towering stack of wooden beehives, humming with life, situated in the center of the orchards. "Found just the right spot for them. There's a water trough nearby, and they'll get full sunlight in the morning. The sooner the hives warm up in the morning sun, the sooner they'll get to work." He wiped the sweat off his forehead. "What are you doing out here?"

Her eyes went wide. Her mind reviewed several witty responses, but in the end she could only seem to spit out, "I . . . I don't know."

"You don't know?" Rome looked at her as if she might be somewhat addle brained.

She took a deep breath. "I'd better go." She ran down the long corridor of blossoming cherry trees that led to the barn, mortified.

❖

Although Julia considered herself a mild-tempered person, quick to make allowances and slow to anger, she felt indignation rise within her when she heard that her father had invited the Bee Man to stay for dinner.

Earlier this morning, it had taken every ounce of grit and determination Julia could muster to try to act nonchalant when the Bee Man found her among the asparagus spears. The *nerve* of that man. How dare he act as if he was apologetic about Paul's decision to postpone the wedding. Everything seemed to be progressing so nicely, right on schedule—and then along came Roman Troyer, with his buzzing bees and his silver tongue and that way he had of convincing a fellow that his life of freedom and independence was the best possible life. He may not have meant to instigate the breaking of her heart, but intention was irrelevant. Once a heart was broken, the words "I didn't mean to" afforded little relief.

And now she had to see Rome again for dinner, thanks to her father. Amos had a fondness for the wandering Bee Man, as did so many girls in their church. Julia had never understood what made people go to such great lengths to befriend Rome. Mothers washed and mended his clothing like he was a long-lost son. Fathers invited him home for dinners to meet their eligible daughters. Julia was always amused at how eagerly her friends gazed at Rome, making fools of themselves. Young boys followed him around and picked up his swagger, imitating the way he wore his hat slightly tilted over his forehead. Close to looking like a cowboy hat but not enough to draw the attention of the ministers.

That was the way with Rome. He stayed safely within the Amish framework but lived a solitary life. And rather than raise controversy, folks tried to think of ways to please him, to entice him to stay. Julia saw that on the first day, six years ago, when Amos found Rome camped out at Blue Lake Pond.

As Rome was with her in the garden this morning, she had tried to study him objectively. His was a handsome face, with its thin blade of a nose and strong cheekbones, and a wide mouth that held a certain wild charm. And his eyes—the

71

color of a cup of Fern's rich coffee. His hair was the same hue as a winter storm, and it curled a little over the back of his collar. But none of that mattered to Julia. What bothered her about Rome—what had always bothered her about him—was how he kept himself detached from others, uninvolved, unencumbered. Julia thought the only things Roman Troyer might truly love were his bees.

Last summer, when Rome first influenced Paul to postpone the wedding, Julia's feelings about Rome turned from mild disdain to downright dislike. To her way of thinking, Rome Troyer was a blight on the landscape, a pox on their district. And still, people welcomed him with open arms.

Well, she was not going to let Roman Troyer get to her. Nor would she let him distract her from her objective—convincing Paul to keep the wedding date. She was sure that once she and Paul married, all of those silly doubts of his would disappear. She wasn't quite sure how to make that happen, but one thing her father had always said, "First the vision, then the plan."

When Julia heard Fern clang the dinner bell that hung by the kitchen door, she closed the roadside stand for the evening. She walked up to the kitchen, carrying the vegetables and early cherries that hadn't sold, plus the honor jar, in a woven basket. Rome was coming in from the orchards and met her halfway along the drive. He took the basket out of her hands. "Looks like you didn't have too many customers."

She shrugged. "It's early in the season." She picked up her pace.

Rome kept her pace. "What would you think if I sold some honey at the stand while I'm here? I've started making beeswax candles too."

She didn't respond.

"I was thinking, maybe I'd give you ten percent. You know, for the trouble of selling them."

If anyone else had offered her this, she would have readily agreed, just to be kind. But there was something about Rome's manner that made her act as stiff as Fern. As starchy and prickly as a boiled shirt. "60/40," she said curtly.

He stared at her for a long moment, then opened his mouth to speak. Shut it. Opened it again. She watched the muscles in his throat work as he swallowed. He was obviously surprised. She could almost read his thoughts: He thought she would be grateful to receive a ten percent cut. He thought he was doing her a favor. "Once folks hear you're selling my sweet honey, they'll come from miles around. Why, they'll be lined up, all the way to town!"

"Excellent point." She started up the hill. "50/50. That's my final offer." Why, she was even sounding like Stern Fern.

"Highway robbery," he muttered. "Fine." Rome hurried to catch up. "Julia, I am sorry. About Paul. Maybe I could talk to him. Get him to change his mind."

She stopped abruptly. "Roman, you give startlingly bad advice. Why would I ever want *you* to try and convince Paul to keep our wedding date?"

He seemed a little puzzled. "Maybe I could talk to Edith Fisher. You know, sweet-talk her a little. So she isn't quite as standoffish toward you."

Julia looked at him as if a cat had spoken. "No. I do not want you to talk to anyone about me." She spoke in a tone as if she were addressing a very young, very dense child.

M.K. came flying down the drive with Menno right behind her. She ran behind Julia as Menno tried to grab her. "M.K., what did you do to Menno?" Julia asked.

"I didn't do anything!" M.K. said.

Menno pointed at her. "She threw a water balloon at me!" His shirt was soaked.

"No, I didn't!" M.K. peered into the basket in Rome's arms. "Dibs on the leftover cherries."

"You can't just call dibs, Mary Kate," Menno scolded. He looked woefully at Rome. "She puts dibs on everything."

Something at the house caught Rome's eye. "Look up there, Menno. There's your water balloon culprit."

Their gaze turned to the Grossdaadi Haus, an apartment-style house above the buggy shop. Uncle Hank was leaning over the windowsill with a red water balloon in his hand, the size of a softball, aiming directly for Fern as she hung some dish towels on the clothesline.

"Uncle Hank! No!" Julia shouted. "Don't do it!"

Too late. The small red water balloon hurled through the air, splattering on the lawn after barely missing Fern's head. She didn't miss a beat. She finished clipping the wet dish towel to the line and crossed the line to head to the house.

"Well, well," Rome said. "Good to see Hank is still the same."

Julia sighed. "He's the biggest child in the neighborhood."

And then, because Uncle Hank wouldn't be satisfied with just one balloon, he wound up his arm to toss another at Fern. Again, it missed and splattered at her feet. She stopped, looked at his window, and calmly said, "You, Hank Lapp, have terrible aim." She walked up the porch stairs to the kitchen, cucumber calm.

Julia thought Uncle Hank seemed a little disappointed that he didn't get a more flustered reaction out of Fern.

Menno cupped his hands around his mouth. "Uncle Hank,

you shouldn't do things like that to Fern. She's not used to us yet. And she's trying to help us."

Fern spun around on the porch and pointed to Menno. "No wonder that boy is the pick of the litter. He's the only Lapp male with a lick of sense."

"She's right," Menno said earnestly. "Uncle Hank gets in as much trouble as M.K."

"Hey!" M.K. said, arms on her hips, a little general.

"I heard that, young Menno! Try and catch this!" Uncle Hank tossed a balloon in Menno's direction, but at the last second, Rome pushed Menno out of the way. Unfortunately, Julia was behind Menno. The balloon hit Julia right in her midsection and burst, showering her with cold water. After the initial shock wore off, she seared Rome with her gaze.

A cackling sound like dry leaves floated down from the porch. It was Fern, laughing.

The family went ahead with supper as Julia went upstairs to change into dry clothes. She hadn't said a word after getting hit by the balloon; she just glared at Rome as if he had engineered the entire incident.

Rome had been thinking about Julia a lot today, maybe because he felt more than a twinge of responsibility for Paul Fisher's decision to back out of the wedding. But he was also thinking about Julia because it baffled him that she didn't seem at all interested in impressing him. It was odd being with a woman who wasn't interested in him. Odd and appealing. Oddly appealing.

When she came into the kitchen, she avoided any eye contact with Rome; he was invisible to her. The only time she even acknowledged his presence was when M.K. mentioned that she had heard at school today that two more courtships had been broken and that the bishop considered there to be an epidemic of broken promises among the young people.

"Bet my last dollar we're going to be getting a sermon on it next week," M.K. said glumly.

Rome squirmed uncomfortably at M.K.'s remark—those same two fellows had been standing with Paul Fisher the other day when he had that infamous conversation about getting married.

"In Ohio, young people keep their courting business to themselves," Fern said.

"It's supposed to be that way here too," M.K. said, "but everybody knows, anyway."

"What has happened to courtships?" Fern asked, shaking her head.

"Ask Roman Troyer, why don't you?" Julia said in a rather schoolmarmish way as she joined them at the table.

All eyes turned to Rome. He occupied himself with buttering his bread.

"Maybe there's a good reason for a man to change his mind," Amos said quietly.

"Dad!" Julia looked horrified. "You're defending him?" She meant Rome.

This evening wasn't going well. Rome suddenly wished he were anywhere but at the Lapps' dinner table.

"I'm only saying . . . ," Amos started, "that sometimes a man just has to do what he thinks is right. Even if he might be wishing things were different." He looked at Rome. "Isn't that true?"

Rome had no idea what Amos was getting at. Did Amos

think Rome was sweet on Julia too? He hoped not. Julia Lapp was an intriguing girl, and she was pretty great to look at, but he wasn't the settling down type. Not by a long shot.

Fern had served Amos a special plate of food—low sodium, she said, and jumped up if he needed anything, as if she was afraid he might keel over. Just how sick was Amos? Rome would have to find out more, though since Julia wasn't exactly talking to him, he wasn't sure whom he could squeeze that information out of. He glanced at Sadie, sitting across from him, wondering if she might know more, but he doubted it. Sadie was looking down at her plate, a little stunned. She had filled her plate to overflowing, a double helping of mashed potatoes and four pieces of chicken. Fern snatched it away from her and set in its place a plate with one skinless, boiled chicken breast, and two sprigs of broccoli—even less substantial than Amos's plate.

Menno noticed too. "Why isn't Sadie eating what we're eating? Does she have a bum heart too?'

"No," Fern said. "She's got an overfed problem."

Sadie's head jerked up.

Julia straightened, stiff as a poker. "Fern, Sadie is fourteen years old. She should be allowed to make her own decisions."

"Almost fifteen," Sadie said, casting a sideways glance at Rome.

"She already has a substantial figure," Fern said flatly.

"She's big-boned, is all!" Julia said.

"Bones don't jiggle," Fern said.

"Now, Fern," Amos said, poking at his plate and frowning. "This isn't exactly a meal to get excited over." He looked longingly at Menno's plate, loaded with fried chicken next to a cloud of mashed potatoes with a pat of butter melting in the center. "I thought I smelled fried chicken. I only came downstairs because I thought I smelled fried chicken."

"You did," Fern said. "Just not for you. You're on a low-to-no-sodium diet. And you're supposed to lose weight so that your heart doesn't have to work as hard. I've been reading up."

"I haven't had a good fried chicken in years," Amos said, releasing a martyred sigh.

"That's not the point, Dad," Julia said. "Sadie shouldn't be told what she can and can't eat."

Rome glanced at Sadie to see how she liked being talked about in the third person. Sadie's mouth was a tight little pucker, and her freckled nose twitched like a rabbit.

"That was our agreement," Fern said firmly. "If I cook for all of you, you eat what I give you. Especially that one." She pointed at Sadie. "She's as plump in the middle as a Christmas turkey."

"She has a friendly softness!" Julia said.

"I am right here," Sadie reminded them.

"Actually," Rome said, "I need to shed a few pounds myself. I'll join you in eating light, Sadie." He picked up the broccoli bowl and helped himself to a few sprigs. Sadie looked at him adoringly.

Julia's gaze shifted from Sadie to Rome. He couldn't quite tell what she was thinking. "Fine. I'll join Sadie too." She put back a roll into the breadbasket.

"Not me," M.K. said, reaching out to grab the roll. "Dibs on the rest of the mashed potatoes."

"You can't just call dibs on everything, Mary Kate," Menno scolded. "Can she, Dad?"

Everyone looked to Amos for an answer, but he didn't have one. He looked suddenly spent, as if he had used up all of his energy.

Fern hopped up. "Maybe that's enough excitement for one day."

As she helped him upstairs, Rome heard Amos mutter, "You treat me like I'm an invalid."

Fern snorted. "You're not exactly plowing up fields by moonlight."

"You're no spring chicken yourself."

Their voices, engaged in gentle sparring, drifted into silence. Something about it felt strangely familiar, comforting to Rome. As they walked away, a wisp of memory tugged at him . . . His mother bringing his father soup in bed one day when he was sick with laryngitis, and his father trying to squeak out a thank-you in such a way that they all laughed and laughed.

Had it really happened, or was it something he'd dreamed?

As soon as Fern was out of sight, Julia jumped up from the table and disappeared without offering up an excuse. As Rome was dumping milk into his coffee, he saw Julia drive off in a buggy as if she was heading to a fire. Rome thought it might not be a bad idea to say his goodbyes before Fern came back downstairs. He wasn't particularly worried that Fern would press him with questions while they were in the midst of the Lapp family, but he had no interest in finding himself alone with her. He gulped down the last swig of coffee and stood to leave. As he whirled around to pluck his hat off the wall peg, Fern beat him to it. She stood there, holding his hat out to him. How had she appeared so suddenly? This day was getting stranger and stranger.

"Seems like you and Amos know each other pretty well," she said.

"I'd say so," Rome said.

She folded her arms across her chest. "Where are you holing up while your bees are doing their business?"

"Oh, here and there," he said.

"He's very mysterious," M.K. whispered to Fern. "That's why Julia calls him Roamin' Roman."

Fern rolled her eyes. "Mystery, schmystery. A man who roams is looking for something."

"I do all right," Rome said, a little peeved. He wondered what Fern had up her sleeves. She seemed to have settled quickly into her place in the Lapp household, wanted or not. Good. As long as she was preoccupied with them, maybe she would leave him alone.

Fern rubbed her chin, thinking for a long while. Then she jumped into action. "You three," pointing to Menno, M.K., and Sadie. "We've got work to do." She turned to Rome and pointed a long finger at him. "You. Meet us back here in two hours. Before sundown. Don't be late."

<hr />

During dinner, Julia decided that Rome was right about one thing: Someone should talk to Paul. Someone like Julia's best friend Lizzie. Lizzie knew Paul pretty well; she might be able to help sort things out between them. As she drove the buggy down the drive, she saw a stranger standing by the roadside stand, a young lady. She looked up at Julia. It was Annie—the granddaughter of a neighboring Swartzentruber farmer M.K. had dubbed "gnudle Woola," *curly wool*, making fun of his long hair and untrimmed beard. Julia hadn't seen Annie since last summer. Then, she was a gangly girl, as slender as a willow reed, as dainty as china. Now, she was a young woman, with generous curves. Pretty too.

Julia pulled the wagon to a stop. "Can I help you, Annie?"

"Menno told me about Lulu's puppies. He told me to come and see them sometime, so that's why I'm here."

"When did you see Menno?"

Annie's face turned crimson red. She shrugged. "He might have stopped by once or twice." She spoke in a small, breathy voice. "Menno's been very nice to me."

Menno? When would he have stopped by Annie's farm? "You might be able to find him up at the house. The puppies are in the barn, in an empty horse stall. I'm sure Menno wouldn't mind if you wanted to look at them."

Annie started walking up to the house.

A spike of concern rose in Julia. She had to force herself to speak calmly, naturally. "Annie . . . you know that Menno is a special child, don't you?"

Annie tucked a loose curl behind her ear. "I know he's special." She spun around and kept walking, hips curving as she walked.

Julia felt time slowing down a bit, all her senses growing more alert. Menno wouldn't be sweet on a girl, would he? The thought of Menno getting involved with someone never even occurred to Julia. He'd always been so childlike to her; she thought he always would. Things were so different these days she could hardly understand them.

She wished she could have a conversation with her father about this, let him do the worrying, but then she thought twice about it. The last thing she wanted to give him was something else to fret over.

The horse nickered and Julia turned her thoughts back to her errand. She flicked the reins and the horse lurched the buggy forward before settling into a smooth rhythm. She was eager to talk to Lizzie. She was sure Lizzie would agree with Julia that the blame for Paul's reluctance could be pinned directly on Roman Troyer. It took everything she had to be polite at dinner. She tried to remember if Lizzie had been one of Rome's adoring fans. So many girls were. Even her own sister. Sadie stared at Rome during dinner as if he held the moon in his hands. Julia wanted to scold Sadie, to kick her in the shins, to warn her it was the same smile he gave everyone. Rome Troyer might not be hideous looking, but he was effortlessly charming, far too confident—he thought he was something. At least she was glad that would be the last dinner she'd have to share with Rome Troyer this year.

As she turned onto Rose Hill Farm, she saw that Lizzie already had a visitor. A familiar horse and buggy rested at the top of the drive. It was Paul's buggy and sorrel mare.

She stopped the horse, heart pounding, then turned the buggy around and left.

Sadie and M.K. hurried to gather a list of things Fern wrote down: buckets, brooms, mops, Clorox, ammonia, and rags. Fern told Menno to harness his pony to the cart, and the girls piled everything on the cart. Then Fern added more things: towels, sheets and pillows, a blanket or two, and rag rugs.

"What do you have on your mind, Fern?" Sadie asked, but Fern wouldn't answer.

She led them out to a small cottage on the far edge of the property. It had been the original house. Amos's great-grandfather had been born in it. Later, his grandfather built the large farmhouse closer to the hilltop because he liked the view. Amos added the red windmill.

Fern took an old key from her apron and jimmied the door open. She walked in, swatting cobwebs. The others tentatively followed. Fern walked around, examining the cottage.

Fern told Menno to get the supplies out of the pony cart and bring them in. The four of them spent the next two hours sweeping out dirt and more than a few dead mice, dusting, scrubbing, washing windows. She sent Menno back up to the house for more supplies, including a bed frame and mattress from the attic.

When they were done, Fern looked it all over, gave a satisfied nod of her head. "It'll do just fine."

"I'm just not sure Roman Troyer is going to want to live here," Sadie said. "He likes being known as the wandering type. What's this going to do to his reputation?"

"His reputation will just have to survive," Fern said decidedly.

* * *

At seven o'clock, Rome walked in from the orchards, washed up at the hose spigot, and was suddenly interrupted by Fern.

"Come with us," she said. Ordered was a better word. And how did she always seem to appear out of thin air?

M.K. ran out the kitchen door and leaped off the porch, landing by Rome's feet. She was nearly beside herself with excitement.

"Don't you tell, Mary Kate," Menno warned as he joined them.

"I won't!" M.K. shook her head, dimples flashing.

M.K. grabbed Rome's hand and pulled him along, down past the fields and through a wooded area. She chattered like a magpie the entire way, pointing out bats and lightning bugs and owls. Sadie was on his other side, quiet, looking so pleased she might burst with happiness. Fern and Menno brought up the end.

When they reached the top of a hill, M.K. couldn't contain herself any longer. "Look, Rome." Then, more impatiently, "Look!" She pointed down the path. He almost missed it. A small, weathered cottage, made out of clapboard.

Pine needles dusted the shingled roof and four spindly candlestick posts held up the rickety porch. The once-white paint had grayed and the shutters had faded to a dull green. It was really old-fashioned, with firewood stacked on the porch. The fireplace was the house's best feature; it was made of stacked fieldstone. The windows glowed with yellow lantern light.

M.K. ran to the porch and stood by the door. Rome saw that there was no knob on the door, just a string latch arrangement.

"Hurry, hurry, hurry," she said. "Open it!"

He eased up the latch, and the door swung open. They walked into the living area, which had bare wooden floors and two windows. The main room had little furniture: an overstuffed sofa topped with a quilt, a painted three-drawer chest, and a table holding a kerosene lamp. A potbellied stove sat in a corner. Rome peeked into the bedroom. There was a charming bed with a curlicue iron headboard covered in chipped white paint.

"Fern thought the kitchen could be the room for your honey equipment, since it's got a door to the outside," M.K. said. "There's good sunlight and the linoleum floor can be easily washed."

"In case it gets sticky, Fern told us," Menno said.

Rome looked around the kitchen. A table and two chairs. A shelf with some cans of food. Pegs on the wall, and a blue coffeepot on the stove. He walked from room to room, first once, then twice.

Finally, M.K. couldn't stand it any longer. "Will you stay? Oh Rome, will you stay?" Her small face was shining with excitement.

He gave a nod; he didn't trust his voice.

"Fine, then," Fern said. "Everyone, clear out and let the man have some peace and quiet." Before she left, she added in her dictatorial way, "You'll take your evening meals with us."

Rome stood out on the front porch, watching the four of them head up the path until they reached the top and disappeared down the other side. It was so quiet.

His heart hammered.

This was home. "Dibs," he said softly.

6

Six years ago, Roman Troyer was almost twenty, a typical Amish farm boy. Born and raised in Holmes County, Ohio, where his father owned a sixty-acre dairy. The farm had originally belonged to Rome's grandfather, then his father, and Rome grew up understanding it would one day be his. He was his father's only son, the eldest, with four younger sisters. Rome's mother was the beekeeper in the family. She had several hives of brown bees that she nurtured and protected. Folks drove long distances to stock up on her sweet clover honey. It was the best, the very best.

Two months before Rome turned twenty, his family hired a van and driver to attend the wedding of Rome's uncle, his father's eldest brother, who was finally marrying at the age of fifty-one. His bride was marrying for the first time too, late in life. The two had exchanged letters for over two years before meeting face-to-face and then waited another six months to marry. They were cautious types, his uncle had said. The wedding was a distance, at the bride's house, so Rome volunteered to stay home and take care of the dairy cows. His family and his uncle were on their way to the wedding when a recreational vehicle had skidded on ice and sideswiped the van. They crashed into the guardrail. It wasn't anyone's fault, the highway patrolman explained when he came to tell Rome what had happened. It was wintertime, and the roads were icy. It was just one of those things, he told Rome.

But it wasn't fair how things happened without warning. Rome had woken up that morning to life as usual. Someone's vehicle skidded on ice, a family was wiped out, and his whole reality was changed forever. Rome had lost everyone. He was left orphaned, although that wasn't really a word he wanted to attach to himself. He was, after all, nearly twenty. An adult.

After the funerals, Rome sold off the dairy cows and other livestock at an auction—even his favorite buggy horse. No attachments, not even to a horse. The only things he kept were his mother's beehives. He built a specially designed wagon to hold the beehives, leased the fields to a neighbor, bought a mule to pull the bee wagon, locked the house up tight, and left it all. He ended up in Lancaster County, though it wasn't by design. All that he knew about Lancaster County was that there were plenty of crops needing bees and plenty of Amish, and that no one knew him.

Amos Lapp found him one April day. Rome was camping out by Blue Lake Pond, after an early fishing trip. He had made a small campfire to cook his breakfast. The morning fog hugged the lake's surface. The trees weren't leafed out yet, but blossoms were starting to swell. Out of nowhere, Amos tapped on his shoulder. "You lost?"

Rome jumped up, spilling his coffee into the campfire. "No. No, I'm not."

But the words rang uncertain and Amos cocked his head to one side, taking a step closer, his fishing pole and line dangling at his side. "Those are your beehives?"

"Yes. They are."

Amos sat down beside the campfire.

He watched Rome with a deepening frown, then his eyes rounded upward in a wise, tender curve. "That hair of yours could fool a fellow. You're awfully young."

"I'm not so young," Rome answered, and Amos leaned closer, smiling slightly, as if he were trying to figure him out.

Amos looked at him, looked at the beehives, and said, "Are you and your bees looking for work?"

Rome didn't even think about it. "Yes, we are. I mean, I am."

Amos wrinkled his forehead. "You wouldn't happen to know how to play chess, would you?"

"I do. My father taught me."

Amos nodded. "None of my children have any interest in the game. It's a sore trial to me." He yanked his hat off and ran a hand through his dark hair. "When was your last home-cooked meal?"

Rome looked away. "Awhile back."

And those were the only personal questions Amos had ever asked of Rome. He fit his black felt hat snugly on his head. "Well, come on then." He seemed to trust Rome, intuitively.

Rome followed Amos to Windmill Farm and met his family: fifteen-year-old Julia, eleven-year-old Menno, nine-year-old Sadie, and five-year-old Mary Kate. It was the first time he'd had a chance to look at a mirror too. During those winter months of wandering, his nearly black hair was now peppered with white. It shocked him at first, and then, it suited him. He had been marked. A sign of grieving.

Amos gave Rome his first job in the orchards and quietly spread the word to others about his fine bees. Rome soon found himself booked out for months, traveling from county to county with his bees. Whenever he moved the hives, he had to travel more than five miles away or the bees would get confused and swarm, not returning to the hives. He worked from early March until November, taking his bees from orchards to fields, selling honey from his wagon. In the winter months, for the first few years, he would do construction work or find a temporary job. But the last two years, he asked himself why he was saving so much money when he really had few needs. Instead, he found an Amish farmer who would let him leave his hives on a remote corner of his farm—sheltered from wind—in exchange for honey. A fair exchange!

Rome would wrap the hives with tarpaper to keep them dry. The bees stayed in their hives in the winter months, forming clusters to keep the hives at a steady 99 degrees. As long as they had enough honey and pollen to eat, the bees could overwinter by themselves. Even heavy snowfalls weren't a concern—the snow acted as insulation. As soon as Rome sold off the mule each year, he was free to travel during those coldest months, via Greyhound bus. Once to Florida, to see the ocean. Another time to Washington D.C. to walk through the Smithsonian museums—each day a different one. Another time to Kentucky to the Creation Museum. It was a good life and he was content. He owed much of it to Amos Lapp.

May could be a changeable month in southeastern Pennsylvania. Though it was warm and sunny today, two days ago the temperature flirted in the low forties. Julia crossed from the greenhouse to her garden, carrying a flat of lettuce seedlings. *The Farmer's Almanac* called for rain—even though the sky was bright blue—and she hoped to get these seedlings in the ground, just in case. After two years of drought, she treasured the rain as God's good gift from above and didn't want to waste a single drop.

Suddenly, Roman Troyer was at her side. "Just how sick is your father?"

She stopped abruptly. "Where did you come from?"

Rome pointed vaguely in the direction of the orchards. "What exactly is going on with his heart? I've noticed everyone just talks around it, like a coupla bears dancing 'round a beehive. Last night, Amos moved as slow as I'd ever seen him. He limped out of the kitchen and up the hall. That's not like your father. I'm asking you straight, Julia. How bad is it?"

As she considered how much to tell him, she gazed at the cheery May sunshine and thought what a contrast it provided to this sad topic. "It's not good." She set the flat on the ground, picked up her trowel, bent down on her knees, and started to make holes in the dirt for the seedlings. "He has a condition called idiopathic cardiomyopathy. His heart is damaged. The doctors have tried to see if the condition might reverse itself with some treatments. Sometimes, that can happen."

"Is he getting any better?"

She shook her head and stabbed at the ground. "As the problem gets worse, his heart is growing weaker. His heart has to keep working harder to pump blood through the body, so it tries to make up for this extra work by becoming enlarged. In time, the heart works so hard to pump blood that it simply wears out."

"What then?"

She paused, holding the trowel in midair. "I don't know."

"There's got to be something they can do. He's only fifty!"

"The only cure would be a heart transplant. But Dad won't even consider that."

"Well, what about a transplant list? He should be on it, at least. Maybe he would change his mind."

She shook her head. "Dad won't even consider it."

"Julia, you can do something about this. You need to persuade him to consider a heart transplant."

What Rome didn't know was that she had tried to persuade Amos to at least get his name on the National Transplant List. The doctors had tried. The bishop, ministers, and deacon had tried. He refused. "I can't do that."

"Why not?"

"A number of reasons. First of all, he believes his ailing heart means it's his time to die."

Rome blew out a puff of air. "What else is stopping him?"

She shrugged. "The money."

"You can't be serious. He'd let money stand in the way? The church would help. I know they would."

"They already have. His hospital bills have been astronomical. But it's more than that. He just can't accept the idea that someone would have to die for him to live. He thinks the cost—the sacrifice—is too high."

Rome shook his head. "That isn't right. He must know that person's time was up, anyway. He had nothing to do with that—that's in God's hands."

"That's how he feels about his own illness. It must be his time. He said that it's not such a bad thing, to know and recognize what you're up against."

Rome was quiet for a long moment. "Have you thought

about what you're going to do? You'll be left alone to run this farm, raising your sisters and brother. To manage your Uncle Hank. You can forget about marrying someone like Paul Fisher and starting a life of your own."

Julia sat back on her knees and looked around the farm, at the weeds that were overtaking the orchards, at the cockeyed rows of corn that Menno had planted. Before her father became ill, she had thought she knew just what her life would look like: she would marry Paul and they would buy a farm of their own. She would be known as Paul's Julia, rather than crazy Hank's grandniece—and she couldn't deny there was a part of her that longed to be a Fisher, no longer a Lapp. She would move on and start a life of her own.

With her father's illness, that scenario seemed unlikely, if not impossible. It was going to be just like Rome said. She had pondered the notion of talking Paul into moving to Windmill Farm to finish raising M.K. and Sadie. As for Menno, she had no idea what the future would hold. Maybe working with Uncle Hank at the buggy shop? No, that would be a disaster. They would spend all day, every day, fishing or hunting. She would have to find someone else he could work side by side with, someone who could keep him directed on a task. She knew he would never be able to live by himself.

Rome cleared his throat and she realized her thoughts had drifted away from the topic of the heart transplant. He looked at her, expecting an answer to his questions. Had she thought about what she was going to do? Had she realized she would be left alone? Her dad worried her mind the whole day. Did Rome really think she hadn't thought all these things through?

She stood and walked a ways out into the side yard. The

house and fields were set on a clearing at a high point; below it were other farms. She pointed to a white farmhouse, tucked against a hill, with a willow-lined stream that wove in front of it like a ribbon. "There's Beacon Hollow. My mother grew up there. Now her brother lives there." She pointed to another house, far in the distance. "That's Rose Hill Farm. My friend Lizzie lives there with her parents. Last winter, we had a work frolic and finished off the Grossdaadi Haus for Lizzie's grandparents, Jonah and Lainey, to move into because Jonah needed to live in a one-story house—he has a bad back." She pointed in the other direction. "If you look hard, you can see the glare of the sun off of a big pond. My cousin Mattie and her husband Sol live on that farm. You couldn't get better neighbors than Mattie and Sol." She turned back to him. "That's the difference between you and me, Rome. I'm not alone. My future may not be what I thought it was going to be, but I'm not alone." She tucked a loose strand of hair inside of her bandanna. "Besides, maybe Dad will get better. Maybe this new treatment will work." She looked at Rome and read his mind. She knew he didn't think that was very likely. Her father was weaker each week.

"The children don't know how serious this is, do they?"

"No. There's no need. Not now." She looked at him. "And I'd appreciate it if you wouldn't say anything."

"I won't. You can count on it. But I hope you won't mind if I try to talk Amos into considering a transplant. I've known a few folks—Plain folks—who have had kidney transplants. One with a heart transplant."

"Feel free. But I thought you were moving on soon."

He lifted his dark eyebrows. "Oh—didn't you hear? Fern set me up in the cottage."

Julia had returned home to an empty house last night and went straight to bed. "Here? That spooky old cottage near that stand of pine? But it's . . . so run down."

"Fern and Menno and Sadie and M.K.—they spiffed it up after dinner."

"So you aren't . . . moving on?"

"I'll be sticking around," he said, smiling broadly. "Just for the summer. In exchange for some work around the farm."

Julia felt as if she'd swallowed a chicken bone.

❖

On an overcast Saturday morning, M.K. tagged along with Fern on an errand in town. Fern took her time at the hardware store, looking for a list of supplies Amos had given her. M.K. wandered off with a promise to return in thirty minutes. She walked down to the farmer's market that set up in front of the Sweet Tooth bakery for a few hours every Saturday morning. She heard someone yell her name loudly, and turned to see Paul Fisher waving to her. He was selling fresh eggs at his family's booth and motioned to her to come over.

"Want to earn some spending money, Mary Kate?"

"I'm always open to making money," she said.

"I need someone to man the booth for a spell while I run home and get more eggs. It's busier this morning than I thought it would be."

Mary Kate was just about to say "Sure!" when Jimmy returned to the booth, chomping on a green apple. He glared at her as he chewed and she squinted her eyes back at him.

"I'll go back to the house for the eggs, Paul," Jimmy said between bites. "We wouldn't want Little Gullie to miss her afternoon nap."

Jimmy! So obnoxious! M.K. fought the urge to throw an egg right at his belly. Instead, she spun around and stalked off. She made her way through the stalls, looking at the fruits and vegetables that sat on the vendor's tables. Carrots, spinach, lettuce, peas, cherries, a few peaches. None looked as good as what came out of Julia's garden.

She stopped to watch a small dog performing tricks for dog biscuits. A man wearing a panama hat stood next to her for a while, laughing along with her at the dog's somersaults. M.K. noticed the hat because Ruthie's older brother was old enough to run around, and he wore a panama hat every Saturday night when he went into town. It made his mother crazy. After the performance, the owner picked up the dog's leash and walked around the crowd with him. "Shake hands with the puppy for a dollar." In his hand was a jar to hold the money. The owner brought the dog to M.K. The dog sat in front of her and held out his paw for a shake.

M.K.'s felt her cheeks flush. "I'm sorry. I don't have any money."

The man in the panama hat handed her a dollar. "Go ahead. That pup wants to shake your hand."

She looked up at the man. He had a kind face and warm brown eyes that reminded her of her father. She stuffed the dollar in the jar and bent down to shake the dog's paw.

When she stood up to thank him, the man in the panama hat was gone.

⁂

While Fern was in town with M.K., Sadie was at work in the kitchen, hot and airless as it was on that May afternoon. She missed cooking. No, that wasn't true. She liked Fern's food

95

and was happy not to have to clean up the kitchen afterward. But she did miss feeling needed. And she missed the feeling of being connected to her mother that she felt whenever she was working with her mother's recipes. If Sadie closed her eyes, she could still see her mother cooking in the kitchen, bustling around, humming slightly off-key. Maggie Lapp was always humming.

Fern Graber didn't hum.

A few days ago, Sadie had watched Fern make snicker-doodles to take over to a comfort knotting and she decided to try to make a batch. She found the recipe in Fern's recipe box and set to work, mixing butter and sugar, eggs and flour. She dusted the mounds of dough with cinnamon, just the way Fern had done, and put them in the oven. As she waited for the cookies to bake, she planned to clean the dishes and dry them, putting them away so Fern wouldn't suspect anything. But then she got distracted with the contents of Fern's recipe box.

Just as she pulled the last cookie sheet out of the oven, Menno came into the kitchen. He hopped up to sit on the counter, just like he used to, before Fern had arrived, to keep company with Sadie as she cooked. And to sample the offerings.

"These are good, Sadie," he said after his third cookie.

"Menno, do you think about Mom very much?"

He grabbed another cookie. "I think about her every day." He swallowed a bite. "Before I get out of bed in the morning, I ask God to tell Mom hello for me if he happens to see her walking by in heaven that day."

Sadie smiled at her brother. His simple faith was so pure, so complete. Sometimes, she thought he lived with one foot on Earth and the other in heaven.

But thoughts of eternity were forgotten in the next moment. A buggy came to a stop by the kitchen door, and Sadie saw Fern hop out, sniff the air, and clutch her purchases to her chest. "Someone's been cooking in my kitchen!"

Sadie gasped. She hadn't expected Fern back for a while longer. Every workspace in the kitchen lay covered with cookie sheets and cooking utensils. Egg yolk ran down the front of a cabinet door. The sink was stacked with a motley assortment of bowls and dirty dishes. Fern's recipes were spread out all over the kitchen table. Two hours ago, this room was spotless. How had it become such a mess? She had tried to be so careful!

"Uh-oh," Menno said. He pocketed three more cookies and dashed upstairs.

Whenever M.K. could slip away from Fern's watchful eyes, she would find Rome and pester him to let her help him with the bees. Beekeeping fascinated her. She wanted to learn everything she could about bees. Rome wouldn't let her out near the stacked supers—the portion of the hives where the honey was stored—in the orchards, despite her begging. She promised to bundle up in protective clothing, like he did, but he refused. "I know my bees," he told her. "I know when they're angry or feeling threatened. I know when they smell a predator in the orchard. I know when they're calm and getting ready to swarm. I don't want you getting stung."

"Have you ever been stung?"

Rome laughed. "More times than I can count. The truth is, beekeepers want to get stung a few times each year. We build up antibodies so the stinging isn't serious."

"Well, then, I think you should let me go out to the supers with you and bring back the frames. I can handle a few stings."

But he was adamant. She was to stay away from those hives—at least twenty feet away. He did finally relent to teach her how to extract honey from the frames back in the cottage kitchen. He showed her how to warm up the uncapping knife in a dish of steaming hot water, then slice the caps open by running the knife down along the honeycombs. Then the frame would be put into the extractor, hand cranked, to spin out the honey. First one direction, then the other, to empty each side of the comb. M.K. loved watching the honey sling out at the sides of the extractor and drip down to the bottom, ooze out the honey gate, into a waiting bucket. Then Rome would filter the honey with cheesecloth before pouring it into clean jars.

"What makes bees want to swarm?" she asked Rome.

"Lots of reasons," Rome said. "In springtime, beekeepers keep a close eye on their colonies. They watch for the appearance of queen cells. That's usually the sign that the colony is determined to swarm. It's not a bad thing to swarm. It can be healthy for the colony to split the hives. And before leaving the old hive, the worker bees fill their stomachs with honey in preparation for the creation of new honeycombs in a new home. That's one of the ways I can tell that they're ready to swarm. They're so gentle that I don't even need gloves or a veil. All that's on their mind is a new shelter."

She opened her mouth to say that maybe she should help him get the frames out of the hives while the bees are ready to swarm, when they were gentle and quiet, but he read her mind and gave her a warning. "You are not to go near those hives. Understand?"

She sighed. "But how do the bees know it's time to swarm?"

"Nature's pretty smart. The bees might be feeling like the hive is getting too crowded. Time for a change. Time to move on."

M.K.'s head bolted up so fast that her capstrings danced. "That's like you, Rome. Maybe you're a beekeeper because you think like a bee."

He grinned. "You might have something there. Though there is such a thing as a solitary bee. It lives on its own, not in a colony."

"So you're a solitary bee." She rolled that over for a moment. "Fern says you can't just go taking your bees from place to place forever."

"She does, does she? Well, you can tell her I've got lots of time left."

"Not really. You're practically elderly. After all, you've got gray hair."

He laughed out loud at that.

Why was that so funny? M.K. would never understand boys.

7

The next week slipped by quickly. One afternoon Sadie sat on the back porch step by the kitchen door with a large bowl of green beans. She was snapping the ends off of them as Rome came up the steps. "Hello there, Sadie."

She froze.

"What are you up to?"

"I'm napping sbeans. Beaning snaps." She shook her head. "I'm snapping beans." She felt her face flush beet red.

An awkward moment of silence followed, before Rome said, "If you don't mind moving just a little, I was planning to go inside to ask your father a question about the orchards."

Mortified, Sadie jumped up to get out of his way. The bowl went flying, spilling beans everywhere. Julia stepped out of the kitchen as Rome tried to help Sadie pick up the beans. "Go on in, Rome. Dad's inside at his desk. I'll help Sadie with the beans."

Sadie waited until Rome disappeared, then slumped down on the top step. "Did you hear that brilliant conversation?"

"Some of it."

"I'm an idiot."

Julia sat down next to her. "Don't worry. He's used to it. He's handsome and he knows it."

"You've pegged him all wrong, Julia. He's not just handsome. Why, he's . . . he's fundamentally good. I just know it." She thumped her fist on her chest. "Deep down."

"Sadie, Rome is more than a dozen years older than you!"

"True love knows no age." She snapped the ends off of a bean and tossed it in the bowl. "I just wish I could say two words that actually make sense when I'm near him."

M.K. came outside and sat on a step, leaning against the porch railing to face her sisters. "Most girls get tongue-tied around Rome Troyer. Not me, of course, but then again I'm not prone to getting the vapors like most girls do when they get around good-looking men."

Sadie threw a snap bean at M.K., and she grabbed it midair and put it between her lips, pretending it was a cigarette.

"Mary Kate, were you ever a child?" Julia said in an exasperated tone, yanking the snap bean from her mouth.

"Just for a year or so," M.K. said. "So . . . our Roman Troyer is really only twenty-five? I figured him to be Dad's age, with that gray head of hair."

"Fifty?" Julia laughed. "Hardly! His hair just turned gray prematurely."

"I love his hair," Sadie said dreamily. "So thick and crisp. And those bold, dark eyebrows."

"He needs a haircut. His hair is curling over his collar," Julia said, clearly annoyed. "And he's not *our* Roman Troyer. He's not *anybody's* Roman Troyer. I never knew anyone so determined to hold himself apart from other people. He uses his charm to isolate himself. It's like he's afraid if he starts caring too much about anybody, he'll lose something."

"But knowing how old he is does change the picture a little," M.K. said thoughtfully. "He sure has nice features. And I like that cleft in his chin."

"He has wonderful features!" Sadie said. "That straight, confident nose. And don't you wonder why he has that small scar in his eyebrow? Even his teeth are beautiful—so strong and square and white."

Julia rolled her eyes. "Listen to the two of you. Mooning over the Bee Man."

"You can't deny he is unbearably handsome, Julia," Sadie said.

"It's a fact, Jules." M.K. reached for another snap bean out of Sadie's bowl. "Why are you so hard on him?"

"Julia has taken a strong dislike to Rome," Sadie explained to M.K. "On account of his influence over Paul and the other boys."

"That's not the only reason!" Julia said. "Rome represents everything I don't like in a man—he swoops into town and goes through girls like potato chips. Why, look at how he's encouraged our Sadie to fall in love with him—"

"He hasn't needed to encourage me, Jules," Sadie said solemnly. "He's been a perfect gentleman to me."

"—and then he swoops out of town . . . heading to who-knows-where and leaving all of those broken hearts to mend. Roman Troyer is as slippery as a fish. Impossible to grasp. He is living a thoroughly self-indulgent life." Julia crossed her arms against her chest.

Uh-oh, Julia's climbing up on her high horse. Here comes the lecture. Sadie exchanged a brace-yourself look with M.K. Julia had a tendency to think she knew everything, even if she didn't.

"He has no responsibilities to anyone. He never mentions any family, he avoids any and all attachments to others . . . why, he doesn't even have a dog! Just that mule and those bees—they work for him and they don't have any opinions. They're the perfect partners for Rome."

"Bees can have strong opinions," M.K. said. "I know that from personal experience."

"Besides, Paul Fisher manages to avoid attachments too," Sadie said quietly.

"That's not true!" Julia said. "Paul is very loyal to his family."

"Especially his mother's feelings about not wanting to be related to Uncle Hank, you mean," Sadie said.

"Can you blame her?" Julia said.

"I like Uncle Hank," M.K. said. "He keeps life around here interesting."

"You can say that again," Julia muttered.

"It's a mystery to me why you'd want to marry into that Fisher tribe, anyway," M.K. said. "They're standoffish and have their nose in the air. They think they're too good for us Lapps. Edith Fisher isn't just against Uncle Hank, Jules. She's against you too. She says you're not up to scratch as a daughter-in-law. Jimmy told me so."

Julia looked as if she had just been slapped. Sadie's heart went out to her. How could M.K. have repeated such a thing?

Julia straightened her back. "I'm going out to the green-house."

Sadie and M.K. watched her go. Sadie gave M.K. a look.

M.K. raised her palms. "What? I'm just speaking the truth! Dad's always telling us to speak the truth."

Rome opened up the squeaky kitchen door. "It might

depend, M.K., on whose truth it belongs to." He tapped her gently on the top of her bandanna and went back into the house.

Sadie scrambled mentally backward, wondering how much Rome had heard. She turned to M.K. "Think he heard everything? Even the part where Julia was saying why she didn't like him?"

"I think so."

"And the part where we were talking about how handsome he was?"

"Probably."

"Even about his white and straight teeth?"

M.K. nodded. Then she brightened. "We were just speaking the truth!"

Sadie handed M.K. the snap beans to finish. *Mortified*. She was positively mortified.

Rome went back inside and found Amos at his desk in the living room. "The cherries are in full bloom, just like you said. The peaches are going to be blossoming out in a week or two, and plum and apricot buds are starting to swell. I'm concerned about the weeds in the orchards, though. Too many dandelions blooming. The bees will forage the pollen from the dandelions instead of those trees. It's the pears I'm most worried about. You know that pears need more bees than other fruit flowers."

"Why's that?" Fern said. She brought in two cups of coffee and handed one to Rome.

"Thank you, Fern." Rome looked her right in the eyes. He still wasn't sure how she ended up at Windmill Farm, but she wasn't pestering him with questions or demands to return to Ohio the way he thought she might. He felt a grudging respect grow for her. Maybe it was true—that she just wanted to check up on him. If so, check away! He had nothing to hide, because he had nothing. "Pear flowers produce only a small amount of nectar, which is low in sugar."

Amos looked troubled. "I thought I told Menno to keep the orchards mowed."

"He needs directing," Fern said. "He can't think of those things on his own, especially when he's distracted by those pups." She turned to Rome. "I'll be sure he gets out there today."

It was strange and yet comforting to Rome to see how Fern fussed over each member of the Lapp family. In a short period, she seemed to have a sense of each person's strengths and weaknesses. How had she done it so quickly? "The hives are out there, so Menno needs to wear light-colored clothing," Rome told her. "Both shirt and pants. If he doesn't have light-colored pants, he can borrow a pair of mine. Bees are soothed by lighter colors." He turned back to Amos. "I don't want Sadie or M.K. out in those orchards for a while. While bees are getting accustomed to a new area, that's when they're most dangerous."

"Fern tells me you're staying out at the old cottage. That's good news. Until I'm back on my feet, I'm grateful for every pair of extra hands."

"I'm staying at the cottage for that very reason, Amos. To see if I could help. Can I help?"

Amos nodded. "I won't refuse you."

"Better not," Fern added. "Alle Bissel helft, wie die alt Fraa gsaat hot, wie sie in der See gschpaut hot." *Every little helps, as the old woman said when she spat in the sea.*

Amos heaved a ponderous sigh. "Geblauder fillt der Bauch net." *Talking won't fill the belly.*

"Oh no! My muffins are in the oven!" Fern sailed to the kitchen.

Rome waited until Fern was out of earshot. "Amos, I thought I saw some bear scat in one of the orchards." When he saw the alarmed look on Amos's face, he waved it off. "Never mind. I might have been mistaken. Don't worry yourself about it."

Rome wasn't mistaken, though. He had seen quite a bit of evidence that a bear and her cub had passed through Windmill Farm. Broken branches, scat, the remains of a small animal. The bees weren't the only reason he wanted the girls to stay out of the orchards. Brown bears were common in Pennsylvania, and under normal conditions, they didn't engage with humans. But these weren't normal conditions. After two years of a severe drought, he knew wild life grew even wilder. Especially when a mother bear was trying to forage for food for her hungry cub. He was worried enough that he decided to use a solar-powered electric bear fence—three strands of wire fenced around the hive, connected to insulated posts. A curious bear would get a shock on its nose and that would be enough to send it packing.

Bears were a beehive's biggest natural enemy. They could devastate a hive—tip it over, tear it apart, chew the comb, carry off parts. It wasn't just the honey they were after—they needed a high protein diet and bee larvae fit the bill.

He heard the creak of Fern's bedroom door and thought he'd slip out while Fern wasn't in the kitchen. As he left Amos and walked to the kitchen door, Fern cut him off at the door. She handed him a manila envelope, fat with letters. "Here. You've got a decision to make. It's time."

Julia had an idea. If Rome offered to help out this summer, why not take him up on that offer? Regardless of his shortcomings, and there were many, he was an able-bodied male and the price was right: free. She actually felt a small tweak of gratitude for Fern for finding a way to keep Rome beholden to them for the summer by setting him up in the old cottage.

In the greenhouse, she grabbed a pad of paper and a pencil and started writing. She had to hurry. She kept one eye on the house, waiting to catch Rome after he finished talking to her father. When she heard the squeak of the kitchen door, she rushed out of the greenhouse and across the lawn. "Rome!"

He stopped when he saw her running toward him. Lulu, who had been roaming around the yard sniffing for squirrels, bounded over to him, her red ball in her mouth. Rome took the slimy thing and tossed it across the lawn.

When Julia reached him, she drew herself up to her fullest height. Roman Troyer was a tall man and could be intimidating, but she wouldn't let him have the upper hand. "I always think it's better to clear up things right from the beginning, don't you agree?"

He looked amused. "We're clear enough for now."

"I have a list." She thrust the list out in front of him. It was three pages long, filled with undone work to do around Windmill Farm. Fences to mend, hay to be cut, leaky barn roof to be patched, a window to be replaced. She hadn't even finished the list, but it was a start.

Rome studied the list intently, page after page. "Fine. I'll have to squeeze the tasks around my bees, but I'll get to them."

She eyed him suspiciously. "There's more. I didn't finish."

"Fine." He waited patiently.

"I'd like all of those jobs done before you disappear . . . wherever it is you disappear."

"Fine."

That was it? Just . . . fine? She felt a little disappointed. She expected him to be taken aback, to start making noises about the need to move on. "Well, then, you'd better get started." She brushed past him to return to the greenhouse. She wanted to add more things to the list. *This list will never end!* she decided with a catlike smile. One way or another, the Bee Man would move on.

Rome watched Julia march back to the greenhouse. Despite her order-giving, he found himself intrigued by her. As she pushed the list—three pages long!—into his face, her little chin shot up, her shoulder levered back, and those full lips set in a stubborn line. He pretended to study the list just so he wouldn't laugh at her feigned boldness. Then she pushed past him, nearly knocking him over as she swept by, and his amusement changed to fascination.

At that moment, Rome's enthrallment with Julia Lapp was official. *Boom!* A blow to the heart. She had a way about her that riled him right down to his toes.

This bee season might just turn out to be more fun than he'd had in a long time.

At his cottage, Rome sat at the kitchen table with the manila envelope. He tore the first postmarked envelope open, dated over a year ago, and read the letter.

Dear Mr. Troyer,

We haven't met, but I would like to make you
an offer to buy your farm in Fredericksburg,
Ohio. I'm prepared to offer you $5,000 per
acre—as is. No improvements necessary. A
simple, clean transaction.

Roman (may I call you Roman?), I hope
you'll accept my offer. I think you'll agree
it's a pretty good deal. You can contact me
at P.O. Box 489 in Fredericksburg.

Waiting to hear,
R.W.

Then Rome read the next letter, and the next. They were all the same. The only change was that the purchase price kept going up. An offer to buy the farm out from under Rome's feet? For twice the going price for land? From a mystery man named R.W. Outrageous! Insulting.

Intriguing.

───────❖───────

It was a few weeks later and Julia's first tomatoes—grown in the greenhouse—were ready for picking. She had a way with tomatoes, which she trained way up high on stakes. They were big monster beefsteaks, big as a softball. You could make a meal out of them.

One night Fern said, "Mary Kate, skin up the road to Annie's house and give her this box of tomatoes."

"I'd rather not," M.K. said. "Annie's grandfather is mean. And it's getting dark. Too scary. I'll get lost and eaten by that bear that's prowling around."

"You could scare off any bear," Fern said, holding out the box to M.K.

"That's not true. Edith Fisher said she's sure she's heard that brown bear and her cub prowling around her hatchery, helping itself to a hen or two. More than twice! She said she doesn't go anywhere without a shotgun. It's true too. I've seen it with my own eyes. She walks around everywhere with it in the crook of her arm."

"That is ridiculous," Fern said.

"I'll keep an eye on her," Menno said, grinning ear to ear.

M.K. found a Kerr quart jar and punched holes in the lid. "For lightning bugs," she told Menno. "In case we need to see our way home." She waved the jar in front of her. "I call it an Amish flashlight."

Menno rolled that over a few times before letting out a "Haw!"

M.K. had only been to Annie's house once or twice before. It was the sorriest excuse for a farmhouse that she had ever seen. Paint peeling off the tired-looking clapboards. The porch roof sagged on one side. One puff of wind might blow it over. There were no flowers bordering the house. Only the barn looked slightly cared for—painted a dark red color. A dim light shone from one downstairs window. Nobody seemed to be around when they went up on the porch to leave the tomatoes.

"HEY, BOY! WHAT BUSINESS HAVE YOU GOT HERE?" A voice sailed out of a downstairs window.

Every hair on M.K.'s head stood up.

"I SAY WHAT BUSINESS HAVE YOU GOT ON MY PORCH?"

M.K. walked a few feet to see a wispy-haired man with a

long scraggly beard peering at her through a grimy window-pane. Annie's grandfather.

"Tomatoes. I mean, TOMATOES!" She held one up for proof and set the box on the floor. "THEY'RE FOR YOU AND ANNIE."

The man turned his glare toward Menno. "I RECOGNIZE YOU. ARE YOU THE SAME BOY WHO THREW EGGS AT MY BUGGY WINDSHIELD?"

"NO. I'M MENNO LAPP. ANNIE'S FRIEND."

M.K. stepped out of the shadows. "The boy who threw eggs at your buggy windshield was Jimmy Fisher. JIMMY FISHER." She assumed her most docile expression, the one that had never fooled Fern but seemed to do the trick with Annie's grandfather.

"M.K.," Menno scolded. "You're telling tales again."

"It's true! Jimmy bragged about it at school."

"Daadi?" Another voice floated out from another window. "Who are you talking to?" It was Annie. When she saw Menno, her face broke out in a big smile, matched only by his own.

Annie invited them in for some peach pie, but M.K. wanted to get home. She couldn't stand another moment of yelling at Annie's grandfather so he could hear. And why did he yell back? She wasn't deaf! Menno wanted to stay, so M.K. ran home as fast as she could. Those bear stories gave her vivid imagination too much fodder to chew on. She was sure she was hearing bears at every turn.

She burst into the farmhouse at Windmill Farm, face flushed and breathing hard, and pounded up the stairs two at a time to reach her father's room. As soon as she could catch her breath, she asked him, "Is Annie's grandfather poor?"

"Poor in worldly goods but rich in faith," Amos said.

"But you said they're Amish."

"They're Swartzentruber Amish. Low people."

"What does that mean?"

"Humble. Humble to a fault, some might say. Ultra-conservative."

"They have outdoor plumbing. And Annie's grandfather was smoking. And Menno said they practice bundling."

Julia walked in the room at that. "He said *that*?"

M.K. nodded. "What's bundling?"

Julia paled. Amos frowned.

8

The most puzzling thing had just happened. Rome had just mailed off a package to a beekeeper in western Pennsylvania who had heard about his strain of brown bees. In the package was a screened box of sweetly humming bees, including a new queen. It was a lengthy process to ship a living thing like a bee, and the postmaster had been very patient with him. She picked up the package and peered at it with a curious look. "Bet this will move along quickly and get where it needs to be." Rome turned to leave, but she called him back. "I'm guessing you're the Bee Man. I got something here that looks like it was sent by pony express." She took the bee package into the back and returned with a letter.

She slid the letter across the counter to him. It was addressed with a now-familiar spidery handwriting to: *The Bee Man, Windmill Farm, Stoney Ridge.*

```
Dear Roman,

Just imagine—with the money I'm offering
you, you could move to Sarasota, Florida.
```

No more cold winters. No more lugging bees
from one county to another. My offer stands.

>   Sincerely,
>   R.W.

P.S. You can now write to me at the post office in Stoney Ridge, P.O. Box 202.

Who was this R.W.? How did he know Rome was in Stoney
Ridge? Rome folded the letter and looked around him. Was
R.W. here? Was he watching him, right this minute? Just in
case, Rome balled up the letter and tossed it in the garbage
can out in front of the post office with a large thud.

Rome pondered the mysterious letters as he drove down
Stoneleaf Road, passing by the Fisher farm on his way home.
He saw Paul struggling with an overturned wagon filled with
hay and pulled the buggy to the side. "Could you use an extra
pair of hands?"

Paul gave Rome a sheepish grin. "Got myself into a jam
here while I was taking some hay out to feed the cows." He
gave a gentle swat to the mule, who was now tied to a fence
post. "This gal decided to take too sharp a turn and the wagon
didn't seem to agree with her way of thinking."

"I'll help," Rome offered. He tied his own horse to the tree.
He picked up one side of the wagon and Paul picked up the
other. On the count of three, they heaved and uprighted it.
Paul tossed Rome a hayfork and they both started to rake
hay back into the wagon.

It didn't take long. When they were finished, Paul placed
both hayforks on top of the hay and leaned his back against
the wagon. "That's the Lapp buggy, isn't it?" He took a jug
of water from the front of the wagon and offered it to Rome.

Rome took a swig of water and wiped his mouth with the back of his hand. He handed the jug back to Paul. "It is. I'm staying in an old cottage on the Lapp farm this summer. Trying to help out when I can. Amos isn't doing too well."

Paul nodded. "So I heard."

Rome took out a handkerchief and wiped sweat off his forehead and neck. "Paul, when I first got here, and we had that talk about getting married, I surely didn't mean to imply you should call off your wedding to Julia."

A look of shame covered Paul's face. "You didn't. I mean—I was already waffling, and you sort of drove the point home."

"What point?"

"About how young we were to make a lifetime decision."

"But Paul—that's not necessarily a bad thing. I was just saying I admired how you could make a choice about one woman at your age."

"See—that's the thing. I haven't really decided on Julia. Not entirely. In fact, I don't even remember proposing to her. One time the subject of marriage came up—one time—and suddenly, she was talking about a wedding. The whole thing just got carried away!" He blew a puff of air from his mouth. "I was able to slow it down last year, but then she started up again this spring. Talking again about setting a date in November. I kept waking up in the night in a cold sweat. That was when you rolled into town and convinced me to call it off."

Rome rolled his eyes. He didn't try to convince *anybody* to do *anything*. Would he ever live that down? "Are you saying you don't love her?"

Paul rubbed his face. "There's the rub. I do. I do love her. But . . . I'm just not settled that Julia is the one and only for me. Julia . . . she just . . . she's so sure we're meant for each other. She's been that way since we were ten. Don't get me wrong—Julia's a wonderful girl. But she's headstrong and opinionated and bossy . . ."

Odd. Those were the very qualities Rome had been admiring in Julia lately. A person knew where he stood with her. He shrugged. "I guess you know her better than I do."

". . . well, suddenly I feel as if I'm no longer in charge of my life."

Now *that* made Rome want to laugh out loud. With a mother like Edith Fisher, when had Paul *ever* been in charge of his life?

"Here's an example: Julia brings me samples of wedding invitations—she's kept all of her friends' invitations. Doesn't that seem like a crazy thing to do? To save those pieces of paper? Anyway, she asks me which one I like best. I told her they all look alike. *What?* she says. How could I even say such a thing? It was like we weren't looking at the same things!" He shook his head. "Women tend to confuse me."

"How much of this doubting has to do with Lizzie?" Rome had heard a rumor or two about Lizzie and Paul.

Paul's eyes went wide. "But how did you—? When would you have . . ." He sighed, and a look of abject misery covered his face. "Plenty. I think I love Lizzie. I love them both."

Rome was relieved. Julia's fizzled engagement wasn't his fault, after all. "Call me crazy, but I don't think you love either one."

"Of course I do," Paul said. "I definitely love Julia. And with Lizzie—well, Lizzie is special. I love Lizzie. There's no other word for it, although I feel differently about Julia than I do about Lizzie. But they both feel like love." He was

obviously torn between the two—marrying one meant giving up the other. "The reason it's a problem is that I don't
know what to do."

"If you were going to marry Julia, you would have done
it already. But you haven't. And if you were that taken with
Lizzie, you would have ended things clean with Julia so you
could start courting Lizzie. I stand by my word. You don't
love either one."

Paul ran a hand through his hair. "Maybe you're right.
Maybe I don't love either of them."

But Rome knew Paul was only agreeing with him to be
agreeable. That was the thing about Paul. He was a very
likable guy. He didn't make waves. He didn't offend anyone.
Sometimes, Rome thought Paul was like . . . that strange
block of tofu that Fern served for dinner last night. Flavorless.
Instead, he assumed the flavors of the people closest to him.

Paul Fisher just didn't know his own mind.

Amos opened one eye and stared out the window. The
sun was just rising above the ridge that surrounded the town
like an embrace. Shards of pink light pierced the predawn
darkness. It was going to be a glorious day, he thought, slid-
ing out from under a quilt his Maggie had made when they
were first married. When had he last noticed a sunrise? Why
did it take the threat of dying to truly notice how exquisite
a sunrise or sunset could be?

No place on earth was as dear to him as Stoney Ridge.
He couldn't imagine living anywhere else. Unlike others—
Roman Troyer came to mind—who felt the need to travel,
Amos felt no such need. Everything he wanted was already

here in this small town he so dearly loved—good friends, caring neighbors, and a land filled with soft rolling hills, gentle streams, and rich soil. Living in Stoney Ridge was one of the many blessings he made sure to thank God for each morning upon rising.

His stomach rumbled again and he glanced at the clock. Breakfast wouldn't be ready for a while, so he decided to risk venturing downstairs, taking care not to alert Fern. Hers was the only downstairs bedroom and she had ears on her like a bat. He stopped for a moment, winded, trying to suppress that blasted cough. As he moved soundlessly past her door— quiet as a church mouse—into the kitchen, the early-morning sunlight flooded the room, infusing the room with a sense of warmth and serenity. He felt his heart leap with praise and thanksgiving. And there was the coffeepot on the stove top, filled, ready to go. *Thank you, Lord, for favors big and small.*

He opened the refrigerator, looking for something delicious to snack on before the family woke up. He spotted a Tupperware bowl, carefully lifted a corner of the lid, and took a sniff. Horrors! It smelled like the compost pile on a hot day. Not much of a chance of his stealing a bite of that or anything else. He hastily patted the lid in place and pushed it aside while yearning for the good old days—chicken potpie, meat loaf, potato salad, cheesecake covered with whipped cream—all of which Fern referred to as "Off Limits to Amos Lapp" food.

That woman had turned into the resident nutritionist.

A few days ago, he had his head in the refrigerator, searching for something worth eating, when Fern caught him red-handed. He thought she was safely off to town on an errand, but no! She had already returned. Her arms were filled with an assortment of cookbooks bearing such titles as *Heart*

Healthy Food, Eating Your Way to Health, and *No-Fat Recipes That Taste Great.* Fern dumped them onto the counter with a thud. One slid off and crashed onto the floor on the opposite side, near Amos's feet. *Fat-free Delights.* That one, Amos thought, was an oxymoron.

He found something that looked more like a loaf of birdseed than a loaf of bread, but it was all he could find. He cut two slices and popped them in the toaster. Then he found butter—real butter!—hidden behind a large bottle of V-8 juice. He hoped Fern didn't plan to spring that on him today. Last week it had been prune juice. His digestive tract was still off kilter.

He slathered his toast with enough butter to clog several main arteries, filled his coffee mug, and looked around the kitchen to cover his tracks. All clear. Not even a crumb. He picked up his well-worn Bible from his desk and tiptoed slowly upstairs to his room.

———◆———

Fern was in a hurry to get some new cookbooks at the library one afternoon and didn't notice as M.K. slipped off toward the magazine and newspaper section. M.K. plopped in a chair and picked up a magazine that boasted a headline: *10 Ways to Get Rich Quick.* She sat down and turned to the article. Someone eased into the chair next to her and she shut the magazine tight and braced herself for a lecture from Stern Fern about the evils of wealth. When the lecture didn't begin, she opened one eye, then the other. It wasn't Fern who had sat down. It was the man in the panama hat!

"Hello," the man said to M.K., smiling broadly. "Have you shook any puppy's paws lately?"

"Not hardly. I still don't have a dollar to spare."

He pointed to the magazine cover. "Are you in need of money?"

"I've got a plan to help someone in my family, but I need to figure out a way to pay for it."

The man in the panama hat rubbed his chin. "I might have an idea for you."

* * *

Three days later, the Lapp family was sitting in the kitchen having dinner when Annie stopped by. Julia invited her to join them, so Sadie made a place for her at the table and Fern filled a plate for her. Annie sat in her chair, prettily. Her laugh tinkled like wind chimes. She moved more food around her plate than she ate. The sparkle of her gaze played back and forth over everyone, always ending to linger on Menno.

Julia kept a close eye on Menno's behavior. She noticed that he often rubbed his chin—probably to make the point that he shaved. Normally, he stood quietly at the edge of a conversation. Tonight, when M.K. asked him a question, he pitched his voice way down below his bootlaces. He was too bashful to chance a look at Annie, but he drank in her every word. He was wide-eyed with wonder.

At one point, Annie reached out and touched Menno's wrist. Julia didn't draw a breath until Annie's hand slipped back in her lap. Menno stared at his wrist where her fingers had been. Julia saw it and didn't like it. She noticed how red his cheeks had become. As red as a ripe tomato! Who could miss them? They were on fire.

* * *

It was lunchtime at the schoolhouse, and the sun was high in the sky overhead. M.K. waited until the big boys were involved with a softball game and motioned to the girls to follow her behind the girls' outhouse. Mary Kate explained she had a new game to teach them. A secret game.

M.K. placed three small seashells on the top of a sawed-off tree trunk.

Alice Esh, a timid thirteen-year-old who spoke in a whisper, was first in line.

"Cross my palm with silver," M.K. told Alice, holding her hand up.

"What?" Alice whispered.

"Gimme a nickel, Alice," M.K. said.

She put Alice's nickel next to one of her own, and then placed a dried-up pea under one of the shells. "Watch the shell that's got the pea, Alice."

Alice nodded, wide-eyed. M.K. moved the shells around and around until Alice looked cross-eyed. Then M.K. stopped. "Okay. Pick the one with the pea."

Alice pointed to the one in the center. M.K. pulled it off with a flourish. Nothing! Alice, who was naturally pale, went even paler. M.K. covered Alice's nickel with her palm and slipped it into her shoe. "Next!"

Later that same day, M.K. and Menno were in the barn, watching Lulu and her puppies. The door slid open, letting in the feeble light of an overcast afternoon, and in walked Rome. Lulu scampered across the floor and flung herself at Rome, knocking him off balance in her exuberance so he nearly lost his hat.

"She doesn't usually take to strangers," Menno said. "You should feel real good about that."

Rome bent down to scratch Lulu behind the ears. "I do. I surely do." He looked up at Menno. "Fern's looking for you. Said you were supposed to be weeding the peach orchard."

Menno nodded. "I started. But then I thought I'd better check on Lulu." He set off toward the orchard at a leisurely pace.

Rome went over to Amos's tool bench and scanned the wall pegboard. "I'm looking for some tools to get that broke window fixed." Lulu followed behind him and sat by his feet.

M.K. sidled up to him. "I have a favor to ask you."

Rome looked at her, amused. "And what would that be?"

"I need some help." She held out a heavy bag of nickels. "And I'm willing to pay you handsomely for your time."

"What kind of help are you talking about?"

"The romance kind. I need you to make Paul Fisher jealous. Over Julia."

Rome folded his arms across his chest. "Call me crazy, but it sounds like you're meddling. Or getting ready to meddle."

"Not at all!"

"M.K., I'm a believer in letting nature take its course."

"I am too. But sometimes nature needs a little help."

He was silent for a while. Then he picked up a hammer and a wedge. "Just what do you have in mind?"

She jumped up on the workbench. "I'm thinking you take her home in your buggy after Sunday church. So word gets around that Julia has a suitor."

"Is this your idea?"

She nodded, pleased with herself.

"Why me? There must be plenty of fellows who'd be delighted to take your sister home in their buggy."

"There are! Plenty. First, I thought you were too old on

account of your hair is gray. But then Julia told me that you aren't so very old at all!"

Rome held back a grin. "There are some who find my gray hair to be distinguished looking."

M.K. shrugged, unimpressed. "So once I started giving you some serious consideration, I decided you were the ideal candidate." She held up two fingers. "Reason number one. You and me, we understand each other."

Rome held back a grin. "You mean, trouble knows trouble."

M.K. waved that off. "I meant we both like to fix problems for folks." She picked up a screwdriver. "That's what you're doing, right now. You saw we needed some help around the farm and you're pitching right in."

"What's reason number two?"

"You are just the fellow to make Paul green with envy. You have a history of being admired by the ladies. You've given a buggy ride to just about every pretty girl in the district . . . maybe two or three districts . . . and if Paul thinks you're finally getting serious about his girl, he'll be in a hurry to marry Julia before she changes her mind and falls in love with someone else."

"Now, you bring up a serious concern. What if Julia falls crazy in love with me? That's a very real danger."

Boys! So unobservant! "Not a chance. She's only got eyes for Paul. And besides . . . you deeply annoy her."

Rome rubbed the back of his neck. He stayed silent for a moment, then said, "So what makes you think she'll go with me on this important buggy ride? That could be uphill work."

"You leave that to me." She hopped off the bench. "Do we have a deal?" She stuck out her hand.

But Rome wasn't quite ready to seal the deal. "I was under the impression that you were not a fan of Paul Fisher."

"Aw, Paul's all right. It's his brother Jimmy that I take a serious objection to."

"What's so bad about Jimmy?"

"What's so bad about Jimmy?!" She started to sputter. She felt her face turn a shade of plum, but she couldn't help it. "Why . . . he's horrible, that's what's so bad about him! He's the kind of fellow you should never *ever* let turn a jump rope because he'll trip you sure as anything. He takes the girls' lunches and throws them high in the trees. Why, it's practically a holiday at school when Jimmy's home sick. It just doesn't happen often enough."

"That does sound like a fellow to avoid." He tried to hold back a grin. "But you'd give Paul a chance to turn the jump rope?"

"I suppose." She shrugged. "Julia says she loves Paul. That's all that matters. So . . . deal?" She stuck out her hand again.

Rome looked at her open palm. "I need to think this over before I agree. And I want you to make one thing absolutely clear. I'm not hiding anything from Julia. No deceit."

Uh-oh. M.K.'s eyebrows shot up. She hadn't expected Rome to be a rule abider. Why, he sounded as straight an arrow as Julia! This created a problem. If Julia found out M.K. had cooked this up, she would be facing a year of extra choring on top of her current never-ending round of chores. "But . . . she doesn't have to know that I'm a part of this, does she?"

"You don't think she could figure that out?"

"Julia doesn't know everything. She just thinks she does." Rome laughed and shook her hand.

M.K. walked to the barn door and turned back to Rome

as she pulled it open. She lifted up the nickel bag. "And there will be a bonus in there for you if Paul sets a wedding date and sticks to it."

"M.K., I have to ask. Are you coming by this money honestly?"

It was a scandal how the finger of blame pointed to M.K. on a regular basis. "Absolutely! I'm working myself to the bone for it." She slid the door to a close, but just before it shut, Rome called to her.

"M.K., wait! Why is it so important to you that Julia get back together with Paul?"

She took a deep, dramatic breath. "'Cuz we're sisters," as if that explained everything. "You should be glad you haven't got any sisters. They are a continual worry."

How to explain about Julia? Rome had known her for five or six years; she was a face that belonged at Amos Lapp's farm. If he'd seen her on the street or in a crowd, he probably wouldn't have noticed her. So many women tried to catch his attention, how was he supposed to notice the ones who didn't?

He had never even thought her particularly beautiful. Yet in the last few days he thought she was the most striking woman he had ever known—tall and slender, with thick and shiny chestnut hair that refused to stay tightly pinned. On any other woman, her full bottom lip would have been petulant, but on her, it was . . . well, he had trouble keeping his eyes off of those lips of hers. Rome was finding that he couldn't get Julia Lapp out of his mind.

Surprised by the mere possibility that he might ever find

her appealing in any way, he wasn't prepared to pose the question to himself of why he found Julia's opinion of him so important. Why did it matter? He would be moving on in a few months, anyway.

It was just that Julia had taken such a powerful dislike to him, which was more than a little disconcerting, since she was female and he was . . . well, he was Roman Troyer. He wasn't puffed up with himself as she often accused him. It was just a fact, the same kind of fact that he was six feet tall, with dark eyes and gray hair. He seemed to have some kind of effect on women that made them predisposed to him, with very little effort on his part. It had always been so and he never understood it, though it had some distinct advantages. A steady supply of offers for home-cooked meals, clean and mended laundry.

He thought about M.K.'s proposition. He would never take her bag of nickels—the thought of how earnestly she offered it to him made him smile—but maybe she was on to something. Julia had always been single-focused about her devotion to Paul, too single-focused for her own good. And here Paul was seeing Lizzie on the sly. Maybe Paul needed to have a dose of his own medicine—to realize what he might be losing. M.K.'s plan might work. At least he could try to help.

Still, to him, only one course of events made any sense— Julia should forget about Paul Fisher. He wasn't worthy of Julia Lapp. But Rome also knew that people rarely did what made sense, especially when it came to matters of the heart. Wasn't he a prime example of that? Wasn't there a pressing matter in his own life that he couldn't make sense of?

Later that evening, he sat down to write a letter.

Dear R.W.,

If we are going to carry on this curious
conversation, I would like to ask you a question. Why do you want my property? You have
never mentioned any reason.

Cordially, Roman Troyer

9

Even though the May heat was thick enough to make the brim on M.K.'s bonnet curl and her sweaty legs stick to the buggy seat, she was happy. Happy to not be in school, happy to be headed to Sunday church, happy and excited because she would see her friends today.

A fly buzzed a lazy figure eight in front of M.K. She sat in the place that she always occupied with her sisters, in the middle of the room and at the end of a bench. A good spot from which to observe the congregation. She saw a mouse scamper along the edges of the kitchen. She stole a glance at Jimmy Fisher, who caught her looking at him and stuck out his tongue at her. She wished she had her peashooter with her so she could send a pea flying right into that boy's open mouth. Maybe he would choke to death, she thought wryly, and then immediately took back the uncharitable thought, remembering where she was. People were singing the second hymn, the *Lob Lied*, slow and mournful. She had been thinking, allowing her mind to wander, and had not noticed that the ministers had come in. She bolted to her feet and made an effort to follow the service once it began, but there seemed to be so much to distract her, and after a while she abandoned her attempt.

Fern jabbed her in the ribs and M.K. straightened up, stiff as a rod.

"Hmmm," Fern said, in that way of hers.

Fern. So everpresent. She was putting a crimp into M.K.'s life. Friday noon, Fern had shown up, out of the blue, at the schoolhouse. She found M.K. playing her shell game behind the backstop. Fern had the nerve to put her hands on the two outside shells and held on tight, staring M.K. down. Somehow she knew that the pea had been dropped in M.K.'s lap. M.K. quietly packed up her game. Fern led her to a big shade tree, far from the schoolhouse. Then Fern told her that gambling was wrong, wrong, wrong.

"I didn't know it was gambling!" M.K. told her. "I just thought it was a game."

Fern sighed. "When money is at stake, it's always gambling." She raised an eyebrow. "It seems to me that somebody as smart as you would have enough sense to figure that out for herself."

It seemed that way to M.K. too.

"Where'd you learn that game, anyway?"

"A man at the library taught me while you were busy looking for cookbooks. He never said anything about it being a gambling game!"

There was a slight twitching at the corner of Fern's lips. Her expression softened a little. After a long pause she spoke. "Don't tell me anything more. I don't even want to know."

Surprisingly, Fern never told Amos that M.K. had been gambling. Of course, she also didn't offer up how she knew about it in the first place, but Fern seemed to have a disturbing knack for knowing things.

The morning sun beat down on her head. Julia was placing produce from the garden out on the shelf at the roadside stand. She put the carrots on a plate, then in a mason jar, then stood back to look at it, frowning. This was the hardest part for her, the presentation. She had no idea how to display the produce so it looked appetizing. She knew it was important to create an eye-catching display to entice those who stopped by, so each day she tried something new. But it never looked the way she wanted it to look. She couldn't get it right and she hated anything that made her feel incompetent. She heard a deep sigh behind her, an exasperated soughing sound that was becoming all too familiar.

Fern.

"What?" Julia said.

"Seems like a girl who spends hours ironing her clothes and prayer cap, and another hour getting her hair pinned just right . . . could figure out how to put together a good-looking produce table."

Julia crossed her arms against her chest, defensive, then dropped them with a sigh. "I know. I can do it with quilt tops, but I just have no imagination for a produce table."

"You don't say." Fern shook her head, then pulled out a roll of twine and scissors. She grabbed a bundle of carrots and tied them gently with the twine, making a neat little bow. Then she placed the bundles in the basket.

She handed the twine and scissors to Julia and turned to leave.

That one little thing looked . . . charming. Absolutely charming. "Wait! Any other ideas?" She waved a hand in front of the shelf. "I'm open to suggestions."

Fern sighed. "I have to do everything around here." She squinted at the table, seeing something Julia couldn't see. "Run to the house and get a checkered tablecloth." By the time Julia returned, the table had been transformed. Mason jars were filled with flowers. One with sweet-smelling roses, another with brightly colored zinnias. A small chalkboard was propped up against the honor jar, left in the center of the table. In colored chalk, the prices for the day's offerings were listed, and a note: *Everything picked fresh today. Please leave the money in the jar. Thanks and blessings from Windmill Farm.* Even the scripted handwriting was neat, elegant.

It looked exactly the way Julia had hoped it would look but could never actually create it. "Fern, you are a wonder!" Julia was truly astounded. "What would we ever do without you?" She reached over and gave Fern a loud buss on her cheek.

Patting her hair back in a satisfied way, Fern said, "You'd do exactly what you were doing, which wasn't much."

Sadie walked up to the stand to see what was going on. In her hand was a half-eaten blueberry muffin. "The table looks amazing!"

"Fern did it," Julia said proudly. "Why, she's got all kinds of talents we're just finding out about."

Fern didn't pay her any mind. Instead, she took the muffin out of Sadie's hand and replaced it with a carrot, top still on, from the produce table. Then she turned and walked to the house.

The weather turned unseasonably hot for the month of May. One afternoon, after Rome had finished a few chores from Julia's endless to-do list, he sat in the shade of a tree near the barn, his arm draped across Lulu, who'd fallen asleep with her nose resting on his thigh. The dog didn't stir as Menno approached.

"Lulu isn't much of a watchdog," Rome said.

Menno chuckled and lowered himself beside him. "No. I guess not. But she's young still. She was only a pup when I found her rootin' around in the alley behind the Sweet Tooth bakery." Menno plucked a blade of grass and began to chew on it. "I've noticed you spend a lot of time with Lulu."

"Lulu spends time with me, not the other way around."

Menno removed the blade of grass from his mouth. "I was thinking that maybe you'd like to have one of Lulu's pups for your very own. They'll be ready for a home pretty soon."

Rome shook his head. "Thank you, Menno, but no."

Menno looked confused. "I won't charge you. It would be a gift. You could have the pick of the litter. Well, Annie got first pick. But you could pick second." There were only two pups.

Again, Rome shook his head, more vehemently than before. "I appreciate the offer, Menno. But I'm not a man who wants a traveling companion."

Menno rose to his feet. "It's just that . . . I think dogs have a way of knowing who they want to be with. Seems like Lulu thinks you'd be a good choice for her pups. She's picked you."

"I'm sorry." He was too. Menno seemed hurt as he left. But Rome wasn't about to waver from his "no attachments" policy. It had stead him well for six years. Why change it now?

Sadie came into the kitchen after working in the garden and saw that Fern had set hot fruit scones on a rack to cool by the window. She noticed one scone was a little larger than the others, so she broke off a corner. Then another corner to even it out, so Fern wouldn't notice.

Her mind drifted off to church yesterday. Julia, Paul, Lizzie, Rome.

Love. It was all so complicated. That was probably why you didn't get to the good kind of love until you were older.

She looked at the scone and realized it now seemed as if it had two bites taken out of it so she nibbled delicately around the edges and soon the fruit scone disappeared. She still felt a little hungry—after all, she had worked long and hard in the garden this morning. So she ate another. She slipped one more in her pocket, in case she got hungry before lunch, and she carefully spread the scones out so that it didn't look as if three—or was it four?—were missing.

Tomorrow, for sure, she would stop eating sweets. That very morning, she had noticed that her apron seemed too small. She struggled briefly to pin it around the small paunch that, since her fourteen birthday, had begun to inflate like a rubber raft around her middle. She retrieved an apron from Julia's laundry hamper, but it was too small around the waist. So she decided to skip an apron altogether yesterday.

She grabbed one more scone, for later, licked her lips, brushed crumbs off of her face, and hurried outside before Fern found her in the kitchen.

Later that afternoon, Sadie waited for M.K. to come home from school and met up with her at the Smuckers' goat pasture. When she saw her, she waved her home so that M.K. would join her. "I need to borrow some money."

M.K. looked at her suspiciously. "Why?"

"I need to get something from town."

"What?"

Sadie frowned. "Why do you need to know?"

"Because you want my money! What makes you think I have extra to spare, anyway?"

"You always have money."

"You tell me what you've got on your mind, first."

Sadie crossed her arms over her chest and lifted her chin. "If you must know, it's to buy a Spanx."

"What's that?"

"It's . . . a body shaper. Something to help me hold my stomach in."

M.K. looked puzzled. "Like a corset?" She made a face. "Does Dad know?"

"Do you need to know everything?"

"Yes. I do."

"Fine. Yes, Dad said that if it was so important to me, go ahead and get one. So I need to borrow forty dollars." She held out her palm. "I'll pay you back in a week or two with an extra dollar thrown in."

M.K. shook her head, but she pulled off her shoe, yanked out the lining, and pulled out two twenties. "Make it two dollars extra."

Sadie snatched the money out of M.K.'s hands and ran to the horse standing hooked to the buggy.

She drove into town and parked at the department store, looked carefully to make sure she didn't recognize anyone, made her purchase, and hurried home. She ran to the bathroom and squeezed into the body shaper. It definitely made her belly flatter. Her bottom too. But it wasn't easy to move around or to sit down. She felt as if she had a yardstick down her back. She blew out a puff of air. This was a small price to pay for a flat belly.

As the afternoon carried on, Sadie felt as if her middle section was in a vise, getting tighter and tighter. She had a hard time getting full breaths of air. And it was itchy. She kept scratching herself and it sounded like a cat scratching a brick wall. She couldn't think, couldn't move, couldn't breathe. She was a sardine in a can! A stuffed sausage! She hated this girdle. Hated, hated, hated it. Finally, right before dinner, she couldn't stand it for another second. She ran upstairs, took off the body shaper, and threw it out the window as far as she could, furious with herself for wasting money.

But ahhh . . . relief! She felt free!

By the time she got back downstairs, everyone was seated at the table. Rome walked in the back door, holding up the girdle. "Does this belong to anyone? I was minding my own business and this came flying at me, out of the sky."

"That's Sadie's new corset," Menno volunteered. "Mary Kate told me about it."

Sadie gasped, mortified, ran upstairs, and threw herself on her bed. She would never eat again.

Why did every encounter with Roman Troyer seem to turn her into an idiot? What must he think of her? Just last night, she was peeling a carrot for the dinner salad when Rome came in to ask her father a question or two. While he was there, just a few feet away from her, talking to Amos, Sadie dropped the carrot peeler for the third time. Rome bent down and picked it up, handed it to her, then nodded toward the carrots she'd just peeled. "Are you expecting a family of rabbits as dinner guests?"

He was standing so close to her that she could smell his

shampoo and see dark hairs glinting on his forearms, above the rolled-up sleeves of his shirt. She blinked and looked to see what he was talking about. Instead of peeling just a few carrots for a salad, she'd peeled the entire pile that Julia had brought in from the garden. A small mountain of carrot peels. Enough for a dozen salads. Idiot!

After a while, Fern had come into her room and sat on the bed, patiently waiting while Sadie had finished her weeping. Then, she said quietly, "Sadie girl. We have got to find something for you to do. You need more on your mind."

M.K. and Jimmy Fisher met on the way home from school, not entirely by chance.

Jimmy blocked her path. "You told! You told Old gnudle Woola that I egged his buggy windshield!"

"You did egg his buggy! I heard you bragging about it to Noah."

He scowled at her. "Now I have to wash every window in that crummy old farmhouse. Plus the buggy!"

"Too bad for you." She tried to get around him, but he kept blocking her.

"You'd better watch your step, Little Gullie. I'm going to get even with you."

M.K. stared at Jimmy. Then something came over her and she stomped on his foot so hard that he let out a big "OUCH!" and doubled over to grab his foot. M.K. took off as fast as she could, just in case Jimmy had recovered.

Before crossing the small stream that separated the road from the Smuckers' wheat field, she glanced behind her and didn't see any sign of Jimmy. She bent forward as she scrambled up the steep embankment and headed toward the woods that lay just past the field, another useful shortcut to get to Windmill Farm. She stopped for a moment behind a tree, resting her hands on her knees to catch her breath. It was supposed to be a sin to hate, M.K. knew, but she had trouble not hating Jimmy Fisher. It was probably also a sin to allow her mind to dwell on such thoughts, but M.K. often wondered why God chose to afflict Stoney Ridge with such a vile boy as Jimmy Fisher.

The bushes crackled behind her. Ears straining, she stared hard at the tangled thicket of blackberry bushes.

A breeze came up, stirring the leaves on the bushes and trees above her, rustling, whispering, crackling . . . it sounded like a creature. A bear creature!

She let out a shaky breath. It was only the wind.

But she sure didn't want to meet up with any she-bear and her cub. She wasn't afraid of many things, but so much talk of bears lately gave her the willies. She liked it better when she knew the bears were snoozing away the winter. She ambled on down the trail, relaxing a little. A squirrel scampered ahead of her, disappearing into the trees, tail twitching.

As she neared the edge of the wood, the bushes rustled again. M.K. looked up at the treetops, but this time there wasn't any wind. Could it be Jimmy, playing tricks on her? She wouldn't put it past him, especially as she was about to walk past a small graveyard, tucked in the corner of Beacon Hollow, the Zooks' farm, with gravestones jutting crookedly out of the ground like buckteeth. Is this what Jimmy meant by getting even with her? Out of habit, M.K. hurried past the scary graveyard with just a quick glance. She had to dash through a cornfield to reach Windmill Farm. She tensed as the crackling, rustling noises came again, followed by a low growling sound. Every small sin she'd ever committed in her life passed before her. She broke into a run and made it home in record time.

That night, M.K. slept with three lamps in her bedroom.

— 10 —

It was late May. Off-Sundays in spring were some of Julia's favorite days of the year. The weather was usually perfect, like it was today, and neighbors often gathered in a nearby meadow to enjoy fishing in the stream, a softball or volleyball game, and a picnic. On this sunny afternoon, Julia drove Menno, Sadie, and M.K. over to the field and decided to stay when she spotted Paul's mare and buggy. She hadn't had any chance to see him in the last few weeks and hoped he might slip off on a walk with her, like they usually did on lazy afternoons, while the others were involved in a game of softball.

Menno and M.K. hopped out of the buggy to join the game, already in progress, and Julia watched for a moment as she tied the horse to the railing. Ever since her father had taken sick, Julia had a hard time watching these games. Amos Lapp was one of the few men who put himself in the game. He'd ask a little one for some help at bat, then together they'd hit the ball and Amos would swing the child into the crook of his arm, bobbing and weaving around the bases. If he were running the bases alone, he'd always let himself get tagged out. But with his heart ailing, the doctor wouldn't even let him attend church anymore. No crowds, the doctor said. Too high a risk of infection. Julia wasn't sure what crushed her father's spirit more—missing church or missing those softball games. Both, probably.

Out of the corner of her eye, Julia noticed Rome. She didn't know he would be here. He hadn't asked for a ride. Why was he here? She saw him walk up to a picnic table where a young woman, Katie Yoder, was scooping homemade ice cream into cones. Katie laughed at something Rome said, and he gave her an answering smile so charged with effortless charm that Julia could almost see Katie fall in love. Infuriating! Exasperating. It was like watching a predator swoop down on its prey. Why were girls so blinded by charm and good looks?

But then she saw Paul. He was on the other side of the softball field. Julia started to make her way in his direction, moving casually and nonchalantly, as Menno took a turn at bat. She stopped to watch, then cheer when he hit the ball past the outfielders. Unfortunately, he got so excited that he started running in the wrong direction, but M.K. was running from third base to home, grabbed Menno midway there, stepped on the home plate so her run would count, and set Menno off in the right direction. Sadie joined Julia and they cheered for Menno, only stopping when he made it safely to first base.

Suddenly, Julia felt so childish. She felt as if Paul would think she was . . . that she was so pathetically eager to see him again that she was making all this noise so he would know she was here!

And that was true.

Julia gripped Sadie's arm. "Paul's over there, all alone. Walk with me a little so it looks like we just happened to bump into him."

As they turned to go, Paul's mother, Edith Fisher, a large boxy woman, stood ahead of them in their path and fixed her eyes on Julia with a discouraging stare. "Don't let her intimidate you, Julia," Sadie whispered.

Edith gave Julia one of her thin, wintery smiles as they approached her. "Hello, Julia, Sadie."

Julia braced herself. "Hello, Edith. And how are you?"

"I've hardly had a chance to see you since Paul canceled the wedding." There was something triumphant about Edith's expression.

"*Postponed* the wedding, Edith," Julia corrected. "Paul wants to wait a few months. That's all."

Paul was now walking alongside Lizzie over by the creek. Edith noticed too. Julia's heart sank. She could feel her face flush with warmth. She turned to Sadie to leave, but her sister was looking intently at Edith Fisher.

"Paul is young," Sadie said. "But Paul is a good man."

"He's a fine man," Edith Fisher said. "A fine, fine man."

Sadie nodded. "And good men have room in their hearts for more than one person, you know. They can love their mother and their wife." She put a hand on Edith's arm. "Julia would never let Paul forget you."

Julia heard Edith Fisher breathing, a slightly raspy sound, her eyes fixed on Sadie. Then Edith drew herself up tall and turned her attention back to Julia. "Folks are saying that Amos Lapp isn't long for this world. And what will happen to you when he dies? Menno can't take care of the farm. You'll have to sell it."

Sadie's eyes went wide. "What? *What?*" She looked at Julia with panic in her eyes. "Dad is . . . dying?"

Julia put an arm around Sadie. What could she say to

that? "Dad is trying some new treatment and it's just going to take a little time to help him get stronger." She pointed to the field. "Menno's up to bat again. Will you make sure he runs toward first base?"

Sadie gave her a wobbly smile, threw a dark look at Edith Fisher, and walked back to the softball game.

After Sadie left, Julia turned to Edith. "Only God knows what lies ahead for my father, Edith. But I do know we are not selling Windmill Farm."

"Well, I hope you don't think you can talk my Paul into managing Windmill Farm! I count on him to manage the hatchery."

Julia looked over at Paul, still deep in a conversation with Lizzie, who gazed at him with adoring eyes. Julia couldn't blame Lizzie for being infatuated with Paul. It wasn't just his dark blond hair, blue eyes, and easy smile that made him irresistible. It was his entire Paul-ness. She turned back to Edith. "I'm not counting on Paul for anything right now."

Suddenly, Rome was at her side. "There you are, Julia! Here's the ice cream cone you wanted." He handed her a cone, dripping with melted ice cream. "Don't forget that you promised to ride home with me today." He grabbed her elbow and steered her to the bee wagon before she could object. He practically pushed her into the buggy. He hopped into the driver's side and flicked the reins to get the horse moving. "You don't have to thank me."

Julia looked at him, baffled. This man's head was full of kinks. "For what?"

"For saving you from Edith Fisher. She's one of those people with whom there simply is no dealing." He pointed out the window past her. "And you don't have to thank me for that, either."

She looked where he was pointing. It was Paul, watching Rome and Julia, with an odd look on his face. A shocked look.

Julia sighed—relief, happiness, elation!

"Paul Fisher is no match for you."

Slowly, she turned to glare at Rome. What did *that* mean? Did he think Paul was too good for her? How rude! Rome was abominable.

And he was oblivious to her indignation. "Julia, when are you going to realize there are other men in this world than Paul Fisher?"

She regarded him primly. "Like you, for example?" She blew out a puff of air. "We discussed this when you first arrived. I am not interested, Roman Troyer."

He wore a strange, bemused look on his face. "Well, I'm terribly flattered, but I'm not exactly the settling-down sort." He gave the reins a small shake as the mule had slowed to a crawl.

Julia snorted. "You mean, the settling-for-anyone sort. You want to have your cake and eat it too."

"I'm a pie man, myself. Cherry pie." Rome gave a sly grin. "I was just trying to help out."

"And why would you go out of your way to help me?"

"Well, excuse me for being a compassionate and caring human being."

Julia rolled her eyes. "As much as I appreciate your misguided help, I have the situation covered."

"So what exactly is your plan to win Paul back?"

She lifted her chin. "I am going to overcome his reluctance. I am going to be more forthright."

His eyes opened wide in surprise, then he started to laugh.

"You? You think you need to be *more* forthright?" Laughter overtook him, so much so that tears rolled down his cheeks.

She should have been insulted—she *was* insulted—but at the same time, an urge to laugh had come over her. Rome was so arrogant! And he was also right. Sometimes, she was too bossy. Some of the fire left her. "I really would like to know why you would go out of your way to help me."

He took a few deep breaths to get himself back under control. "All right. You win. The truth? Even though I didn't intend to make your endless engagement to Paul even more endless, I did you a disservice." He glanced over at her. "My folks raised me to believe that every wrong should be made right."

"And where exactly were you raised? Nobody seems to know where you're from, or who your family is or how many brothers and sisters you have." She looked at him expectantly. "And why bees? Of all things, why bees?"

"I'm touched, Julia—to think that you have so many thoughts about me."

She stiffened her spine and looked straight ahead. "It's flattering yourself to think I have any thoughts about you at all."

His face broke into a smile, and she couldn't help smiling in return. The moment seemed to last forever, even as Julia heard the crack of a softball leaving the bat. Then she realized that people were shouting and waving their arms. She looked around and up . . . and saw the ball sailing, a high arc through the air.

"Look at that!" Rome said. "Your brother just hit one that's headed over the fence!" He shouted out to Menno and waved to him. Menno stopped running to see who was calling him, so M.K. ran out on the field and dragged him around the bases.

Rome seemed so genuinely pleased about Menno's accomplishment that something inside Julia melted a little, right along with the ice cream cone in her hand. She quickly licked it before it dripped on her dress.

She wrinkled her nose. So what if Rome was slippery and elusive, not to mention too charming for his own good? He seemed genuinely sincere about helping her win Paul back. Maybe it was time to rise above her dislike.

Rome glanced at her. "You've got ice cream on your nose. Never gonna catch a fella with those kinds of table manners."

Julia gasped and rubbed her nose with her dress sleeve. She promptly yanked back her imaginary olive branch toward Rome. He was incorrigible!

Still, Julia felt curiously elated. She knew it came from the emotion she had felt when she saw the look on Paul's face. That, she felt, could only be a wordless affirmation of the fact that nothing had changed. Paul still loved her, she was sure of it. How strange. How wonderful.

Later on that night, though, doubt returned as Julia was sitting at the kitchen table, glancing through the *Budget*.

Sadie sat down beside her with two cups of herbal tea. "Try this. It's made of a combination of dried herbs from the garden. It's supposed to help digestion. Or maybe it's a cure for a headache." She shrugged. "One or the other. Maybe both."

Julia took a sip and tried not to cringe. It tasted like something made from rancid garbage. "Really . . . tasty, Sadie."

Sadie took a sip and spit it out. "It's awful. Needs more mint to camouflage the taste." She pushed the mug aside. "Paul was watching as you left the game with Rome. He was obviously bothered by the idea of you spending time with Rome. That's encouraging. I really think he's coming around."

Julia propped her chin on her hand. "Then why don't I feel encouraged?"

When Paul first saw Julia drive off from the softball game with Rome, he felt strangely disturbed. But the longer he thought about it, the more it seemed like an opportunity in the making. If Roman Troyer was after Julia, then Julia would let Paul go. He wouldn't have to be known as a heart breaker. It was a free pass! He could start courting Lizzie. He planned to tell her the good news on the buggy ride home.

But as soon as the words came out of his mouth, the smile slid off Lizzie's face. "No," she said. "I can't do that to Julia. She's my friend."

"I already told her that I wanted to postpone things. I thought I'd give her time to get used to that. Next, I'll tell her that you and I are seeing each other."

"Paul," Lizzie said, shaking her head sadly.

"What?"

"Go to Julia and take it all back," she said.

"Are you saying you don't want me?"

"It was just a few kisses, Paul. And now someone's gotten hurt."

In late March, Lizzie had needed a ride from a singing on a Sunday evening. Paul had agreed to drop her off—he passed right by Rose Hill Farm—and they started talking. And talking. Then something happened between them as he helped lift her out of the buggy. It started slowly. One kiss, another kiss, more kissing. He couldn't stop thinking about those kisses with Lizzie. They were nothing like the kisses he shared with Julia. Not even close. He dropped by Lizzie's house every chance he got, hoping there would be a chance for more kisses. So far, no such luck.

"Just go to her," she said. "I'm not coming between you and Julia. You should be with her. I'm just a friend, Paul. That's all I'll ever be." She jumped out of the buggy before he could stop her.

He listened to her footsteps crunch across the loose gravel. What had happened? How could this be? This was too much: to lose them both.

Monday morning arrived and Uncle Hank arrived with it. He was sitting at the kitchen table when Julia came downstairs with a load of sheets in her arms. "JULIA!" he bellowed. "I told you I would help get those weeds in the orchards. I've got a plan all worked out!"

Julia stopped by the kitchen table. "Let's hear it." She slipped into a chair beside Sadie and Menno and braced herself for the news.

"I got to talking to Ira Smucker. He said he would loan us his herd of goats. I just need to set up a wire fence. Something I can move around that could be goat proof."

Rome appeared at the kitchen door while Uncle Hank was explaining his idea. He took a seat at the table. Fern brought both of the men a cup of coffee and sat down herself.

Uncle Hank was delighted to have an audience. He turned to Rome. "What do you think, Bee Man?"

"I've seen a lot of folks using goats to get rid of under-growth," Rome said. "Only thing is that they'll eat the blossoms right off the trees. They'll eat anything they can get their mouths close to."

"That's the beauty of my plan!" Uncle Hank said. "They're pig goats! Little tiny things!"

"You mean, pygmy goats?" Rome asked.

Uncle Hank banged on the table with his fist. "That's it! That's their name. Why, you've never seen such cute little critters—"

"Hank Lapp, just when were you supposed to get that goat-proof fence up by?" Fern asked, looking out the window. "Because your goats are heading this way."

Uncle Hank bolted out of his chair and stood behind Fern. Ira Smucker and his son, Gideon, were heading up Windmill Farm's driveway with a horse pulling a trailer full of small goats. "Blast! What day is it, anyway?"

"Monday," Rome said, looking out the window.

"Double blast! I didn't think Ira meant this particular Monday morning. I thought he just was talking about some Monday morning in general."

"Some of us live in reality," Fern said. She looked at Uncle Hank with an arched eyebrow. "And others live in their *own* reality."

Uncle Hank huffed, thrust the coffee cup in her hand, and went outside to meet Ira Smucker.

"Hurry with your breakfast, Menno," Julia said. "Our morning just got rearranged."

"I'll help," Rome said. "You don't have to, Julia. Menno and Hank and I can handle the job."

Julia gave him a sharp look. "I thought you had honey to collect today."

Rome gave a half shrug. "Tomorrow is as good a day for honey as today. I'm here to help."

Footsteps came thundering down the stairs as M.K. flew into the kitchen with Amos's breakfast tray. She passed it off to Fern and ran to the door. "Sadie! Gideon Smucker is here! He's so sweet on you he can't put two words together in a sentence." She waved her arm like a windmill. "Come on, Sadie! Let's go see his ears turn red when he tries!"

"Oh, M.K. Schtille," Sadie said. *Quiet.* But she smoothed out her hair and dress and followed behind M.K. Menno hurried to join them.

"Well, well, maybe Sadie might be willing to consider other fellows besides Rome, after all," Fern said.

"Rome doesn't mind sharing one devotee," Julia said, picking up the laundry basket of sheets. "There's plenty of other girls to take Sadie's place."

Rome wasn't paying any attention to them. He was frowning at Amos's breakfast tray. "He hardly ate a thing."

Later that day, M.K. hurried home from school. She had told everyone at school about the pygmy goats and couldn't wait to see them. She ran through the kitchen to drop off her lunch pail and grab a snack. Fern caught her, gave her a large white bucket, and told her to pick some cherries as long as she was lollygagging in the orchards.

Lollygagging? Fern! So bothersome. As if M.K. *ever* lollygagged.

She slipped through the wire fencing that Rome and Menno and Uncle Hank had fixed up and walked among the small goats. There were goats of all colors, and they looked up at M.K. with mild interest before turning back to their weeds. She picked a favorite—a small black-and-white female goat

149

with peaceful eyes—petted her for a while, then took her white bucket to start picking cherries. The bucket was about a quarter of the way full when she heard laughing sounds, like a hyena. Or jackals. Or . . . ! She jumped off the ladder and scanned the orchard for the source of that hideous noise—it came from Jimmy Fisher and his sidekick, Arthur King. They were laughing so hard they had to hold their sides.

She stomped over to them and called over the fence. "What's so funny?"

"That!" Jimmy said, pointing behind her. She turned around to see a large goat that stood out from the rest. He surveyed his new home with an air of disdain and shook his head.

She knew that particular billy goat! "You stole Ira Smucker's goat, Jimmy!"

"Didn't steal him," Jimmy laughed. "Just borrowed him!"

M.K. pointed at him. "Don't you know that the ninth commandment says 'do not lie'?"

Jimmy nudged his friend, Arthur. "Loss dich net verwiche, is es elft Gebot." *"Don't get caught" is the eleventh commandment.*

M.K. heard a bleating sound and her head swiveled in its direction. Ira Smucker's yellow billy had lowered its head and was charging right at her. M.K. darted to the nearest cherry tree and climbed it. The goat bumped his head against the trunk of the cherry tree several times for good measure. Each time, Jimmy and Arthur's laughing fit started up again. M.K.'s outrage nearly choked her, and she could barely hold on to her temper. She was trapped in a tree with a mad billy goat underneath her, and Jimmy and Arthur were enjoying her humiliation at a safe distance.

Boys! So horrible! She broke off branches and threw them down at the billy, but he only chewed up the branches. He gazed at her with his weird yellow eyes as if to thank her for the snack.

Finally, the yellow billy returned to the rest of the herd who had continued eating, unconcerned with the big intruder. M.K. slipped carefully down the tree. She knew she had to get that pail before the billy goat ate up her cherries. She tiptoed over to the pail, bent to get it, heard another bleating sound, and turned to find the billy charging at her with lowered head. She didn't have time to get to a tree, so she took the pail and jammed it on top of the billy goat's head. He shook and shook his head, trying to get that pail off of him. If M.K. weren't so furious with Jimmy and Arthur, she might have even enjoyed the ridiculous sight. As it was, she lost her cherries and her pail. The other goats milled around, curious, and finished off the cherries that scattered on the ground.

Then she picked up a big stick and eyed Jimmy and Arthur, tapping it in her hands a few times. They started backing up and took off running. M.K. ran to the fence, bent over to slip through, when a big arm scooped her up. The arm belonged to Rome, and her legs were dangling in the air like riding a bicycle. "Let me at 'em!"

"They're halfway home by now, M.K." He set her down and took the stick out of her hands. "Using a stick is no way to get even with those two."

She stomped her foot. "They're the scum of the earth! The worst of the worst!" She started to take off after them, but Rome grabbed her shoulders.

"Now you just calm down." He waited until she stopped

struggling, then released her. "You stay put while I go get that billy." He pointed his finger at her in a warning way as he jumped over the fence. She saw that he had a rope with him. He looped it around the billy goat's neck and carefully pulled the bucket off the goat's head.

He led the yellow billy out through a makeshift gate into an empty pasture, then returned for her. As they walked back to the house, Rome said, "Jimmy is hoping he'll get you upset, M.K. You'd have the upper hand if you didn't always overreact to him."

M.K. scowled at him.

"Have you thought about just trying to let it go?"

"Let it go? Let it go?" Her voice rose an octave.

"This will just keep getting worse. Jimmy does something mean to you. You do something mean right back to him. Why not try something different? Don't work out a plan to get even with him. Maybe . . . turn the other cheek."

M.K. knew where this was heading. Hadn't she been in church for her whole entire life? Before Rome could start in on a lecture about loving your enemies, she cut him off at the quick. "That might work with some folks. But the problem with Jimmy Fisher is that by the time you've turned the other cheek a couple of times," she patted her face, "you start running out of cheeks."

— 11 —

Sadie had borrowed Julia's hand mirror while she was in town. Lately, Sadie studied herself in mirrors as she hadn't before. She wasn't overly encouraged by what she saw.

"You look better today than you did a week ago," Fern said.

Sadie whipped around. Fern was leaning against the door-jamb with some freshly ironed prayer caps in her hands. How long had she been there? Sadie was mortified! Fern came into Sadie's room and opened a bureau drawer to tuck away the prayer caps. While Fern's head was down, preoccupied with the messy condition of the drawer, Sadie held the mirror out to get a better look at herself. Maybe Fern was right. Even though it had only been a week, Sadie's tummy didn't seem to stick out so far, maybe because she didn't have so much time to eat. Fern was forever sending her on errands, and she made Sadie walk, not take the buggy. And every time she wandered into the kitchen for a snack, Fern found something important for her to do right away—take notes from some books about healing herbs, help Menno harvest fruit in the orchard, dig out a new section of Julia's garden to add another section to the herb garden. And this was all on top of her daily chores! There was hardly a moment to rest. To eat.

Fern refolded everything in the drawer and closed it with a satisfied sound. She turned to Sadie and frowned. "Grab that book over there, put it on your head, and walk."

Sadie didn't want to, but she crossed the room toward the table and put the book she found there on top of her head. It slid off right away. She picked it up and tried again with a little more success. Three steps, before it fell and crashed to the floor.

Fern folded her arms across her front. "That was better. I want you to walk like this from now on, got it? Back straight, shoulders straight. The way I do." Fern carried herself as if she had a fire poker strapped to her spine, but there was a poise about her that Sadie longed to emulate. All starch.

Sadie walked across the room with the book carefully perched on her head. She felt taller, more grown-up. And less like a person who was scared of her own shadow.

───────

Rome finished packing up a few things he would need for a trip to the other side of the county. Jacob Glick had made him promise to bring a beehive over right as his pecans started to blossom. Last year, even with the drought, Jacob's pecan crop doubled in production. "The time is now!" Jacob's phone message had said. Rome would move the hive onto the wagon tonight, after sunset, so the bees wouldn't be stressed by the move.

He glanced around the cottage. Had he forgotten anything? His eyes locked on the hand-sewn quilt lying on his bed. His mother called it a memory quilt and that it was. It was one of the few things he brought with him from the farm. His mother wasn't a fine quilter; she used old scraps

154

of fabric to make quilts. A piece of the quilt held his baby clothes. His sisters' dresses. Every time he looked at it, the warm times he and his family had shared before their deaths came flooding back.

Once or twice, he had even thought about giving the quilt away, but he couldn't do it. Instead, he would flip it over to the backside, banishing those images. Usually, it worked, but lately he had trouble keeping memories from popping back up again.

He traced the outline of a lavender patch. His mother's best dress. It reminded him of the day he had deceived his mother for the first and last time. It was a hot August day and Rome was twelve years old. His mother had changed into her lavender dress to go to a quilting frolic. She put Rome in charge of his sisters, but a few friends dropped by with a more interesting plan: swimming in Black Bottom Pond. He paid the next-in-line sister two dollars to take over his baby-sitting duties, another dollar to each sister to keep quiet, and took off with his friends. One boy brought a rope to loop on a sturdy tree branch that hung over Black Bottom Pond—it was a vine and they were jungle boys. Rome was having the time of his life.

Two things Rome forgot to factor in: the end time for the quilting frolic, and that his mother had to pass right by Black Bottom Pond. He was swinging out over the pond, naked as a jaybird, hollering out ape calls, when he caught sight of his mother standing on the shore, arms akimbo. One thing about his mother: you could always count on her to give you her opinion. And she wasn't shy about implementing that opinion with a willow switch. What he would give to have that August afternoon back again, switch and all.

Rome rubbed his face with the palms of his hands. His mind had traveled so far back in the past, he didn't even realize where he'd gone. He had to stop letting himself wander down those paths. He wanted to leave the past a few hundred miles down the road, shake it off like dust. But that was the problem with the past. It kept finding him.

———❖———

Sadie went out to the garden to pick strawberries for breakfast. Lulu and her puppy tagged along, doubling the work for Sadie because the puppy kept beating her to the ripe berries. Annie had taken home the one puppy, but Menno still hadn't found the right owner for the remaining pup. When Sadie's bowl was finally full, she walked back to the house and practically bumped into Rome as he came around the corner.

"Mornin', Sadie! I was coming by to let someone at the house know I'm heading out tonight."

Hearing Rome's voice, Lulu and her puppy abandoned Sadie and bounded over to him. Rome reached down to stroke Lulu's fur.

Rome was leaving? Just like that? He wouldn't be here for her fifteenth birthday? When she realized she was staring, she stumbled over nothing and practically spilled the bowl of berries. "Don't leave. I mean, won't you at least come in for breakfast? I'm paking mancakes. Pancakes. I'll make pancakes!" Mortified, she rushed past him and into the kitchen, straight into the pantry, and closed the door behind her.

Sadie heard Julia open the squeaky door for Rome. "What in heaven's name did you say to her?"

"Nothing!" Sadie heard Rome say. "I said good morning.

And that I wanted someone to know I'll be gone for a few days."

Just a few days? Hallelujah! Sadie breathed a deep sigh of relief and grabbed the flour bag. She sneaked another glance at him as she came out of the pantry with the flour bag. "Found it! I'll just get to work on those mancakes. Pancakes!" She flushed bright red and whirled around. She hoped Fern wouldn't shoo her out of the kitchen like she usually did.

M.K. burst into the kitchen from the upstairs, Menno trailing behind her.

"Sadie! M.K. wants to throw us a surprise party for our birthday!" Menno called out.

M.K. stopped and looked at him. "Well, *now* it can't be a surprise." She shrugged. "But we'll still have a party!"

"Julia, can Annie come to the party?" Menno asked.

Sadie saw Julia frown. Lately, all Menno talked about was Annie, Annie, Annie.

Rome accepted a mug of coffee from Fern and poured cream into it. "Why, Sadie and Menno, is this your birthday week? So you're both going to be fifteen?" He took a sip, hiding his smile.

"No, Rome," Menno answered seriously. "Sadie and I happen to be born on the same day, but we're not twins. I know it's confusing, but I'm two years older than Sadie. I'm going to be seventeen. We're birthday twins, but we're not really twins."

"You aren't supposed to tease Menno," M.K. whispered loudly. "He doesn't understand teasing. We have to mean what we say when we say it."

"An example to us all," Rome said good-naturedly.

Sadie was grateful that all of the noise in the kitchen

diverted attention away from her acute self-consciousness whenever she was within shooting distance of Roman Troyer.

"Well, I can't miss your birthday, Menno. Or Sadie's. I'll just have to be sure I'll be back in time."

M.K. slipped onto a chair next to him. "Friday, Rome. Suppertime. This is one party you don't want to miss."

Fern sighed. "That girl takes everything to extremes."

Sadie poured the batter onto four circles on the hot griddle, waited until they bubbled up, flipped them, and put them on a plate. Then she added pats of butter and ladled them with sticky syrup. She was going to deliver Rome's pancakes without a glitch. Cool as a cucumber. She carefully avoided looking at him so she wouldn't blush, and in doing so, somehow managed to slide the pancakes into his lap. She dropped the plate on the table and ran into the downstairs bathroom.

Sadie stalled as long as she could in the bathroom, brushing her teeth and washing her face, feeling thoroughly foolish. Her feelings for Rome felt like a herd of wild horses, galloping out of control. This had to stop. Finally she managed to creep outside without being detected. When Rome returned from his trip, this idiocy was coming to an end, and she'd behave like a mature woman.

As Fern mopped up Sadie's pancakes from the floor, Julia noticed someone walking up the drive to the farmhouse. She went outside to see who it was.

Rome followed her out. "Julia, I actually stopped by to talk to you for a moment. Privately."

She saw M.K. tip her head in their direction, eavesdropping, so she closed the kitchen door.

"Don't you get nervous wearing those during hunting season?" Rome's dark eyes were dancing as he pointed to Julia's feet.

She had forgotten that she had on a pair of bunny slippers that Menno had given her for Christmas. She knew they were a little fanciful, but she loved them because they were from Menno. She drew herself to her full height, trying to look dignified while wearing bunny slippers. Ignoring him, she waved at the approaching figure. "It's Annie."

"Who's Annie?"

Julia frowned. "A girl Menno seems to be quite taken with."

"No kidding. Little Menno is growing up, Julia."

Julia slowly shut her eyes and pulled in a breath. "Do you think I don't know that?" The irritation in her voice sounded a bit strident even to her ears. She couldn't think about Menno and Annie right now. So much to worry about! "What did you want to talk to me about?"

He shook his head. "I'm heading over near Lancaster tonight. Switching hives from one farm to another. Tomorrow, I want to talk to someone at the hospital about getting Amos on the transplant list."

"At the hospital? You want to march in and put him on the transplant list?"

Rome took his hat off and raked a hand through his hair. "I don't know how I'll do it. I just want to know what needs to happen and how much it will cost and what we could do to persuade him to consider it."

"Dad won't even consider a transplant."

"I know," Rome said with a sigh.

"So you've tried talking to him?"

"A couple of times. He shuts down the conversation."

Rome looked so earnest that Julia found herself softening, just a little. But then she reminded herself that this was the Bee Man, the source of great aggravation. "It really is Dad's decision. No one else's."

"Julia . . . it's just that . . . there aren't many things in life that we can do anything about. Here you have a chance to save him, to keep him around for another couple of decades. You've got to make him see . . . that you all need him to stick around."

She found herself baffled by this man, mildly fascinated by his contradictions. It bothered her when people refused to fit into pigeonholes. It made life murky. The longer he was with them this summer, the more her curiosity about him grew. "You know, Rome, you're starting to break your own rule."

"What rule is that?"

"Not getting involved in people's lives. Isn't it easier just to dole out advice and move on your way?"

For once, Rome had no answer for her.

This was no way to start a day. M.K. gave some serious consideration to canceling the birthday party for Sadie and Menno. If this morning was an indication of how much cleaning Fern thought needed to happen to prepare for the gathering, then the week ahead looked grim. Fern had given her enough extra work to rub the skin off a person's knees.

"I just washed the floor. Now look at it. Just look at the dirt those shoes have left. Do you think I have nothing better to do than to clean up after the likes of you?" Fern must have carried on about those shoes for nearly an hour before diverting her attention to M.K.'s rumpled bed. M.K. had sat on it to tie her shoes. The way Fern set to caterwauling, you would have thought she had committed a murder. It seemed the tiniest mishap could set Fern off.

Personally, M.K. thought Fern's irritable behavior was directly attributable to consuming too much roughage. Fern took everything seriously, especially food, and since Amos and Sadie were on a low-to-no-sodium diet, the entire family was put on it. It was steamed rice and vegetables, broth or tofu, and enough bean sprouts to keep a small barnyard well fed.

At the end of the school day, M.K. burst out of the door to find Fern scowling at her, waiting by the door with arms crossed against her thin chest. M.K.'s mind flipped through the week, trying to narrow down which particular misstep had traveled straight from the schoolhouse to Fern's ears.

Fern pointed to Menno, waiting in the buggy, and told M.K. to wait while she talked to the teacher.

"What did you do now?" Menno asked as she climbed into the backseat.

"Never mind," M.K. grumbled.

Ten minutes later, Fern joined them and told Menno to head home.

From the backseat of the buggy M.K.'s voice welled up. "It was Jimmy Fisher's fault! He said something I took exception to—"

"I got that part of it," Fern said. "You always have your knickers in a twist over something that boy said or did. But I can't be running to that school every whipstitch. And school's just about out for the summer. There's limits on what I can do." She swiveled her head to the backseat and gave M.K. a long look.

"I'll keep a closer eye on her," Menno said.

M.K. glared at him.

At the turnoff to Windmill Farm, Fern pointed to the side of the road. "Menno, you go up to the house and find Sadie. She's got a list of chores for you. I want them finished by suppertime. I want to see that list checked off."

Menno hopped off. "Where are you two going?"

"M.K. and I have an errand," Fern said.

"What kind of an errand?" M.K. waved a sad goodbye to Menno.

Fern slid over to the driver's side and flicked the horse's reins. "Mind telling me why you had a pile of *Seventeen* magazines under your bed?"

M.K. rolled her eyes and rested her chin on her hand, caught red-handed. Of course, she thought. In this house, Fern knew everything. "I got 'em when Julia and I went to town last week to sell cherries and peaches at the farmer's market."

"And just why did you buy them?"

"Someone was selling the whole pile for one dollar."

"So you bought them because they were cheap?"

M.K. shrugged. "I just like to read. And we keep running out of things to read at the house. I've read the *Martyrs' Mirror* a dozen times. I've read *Young Companions* so often I have them memorized."

Fern gave up a rare smile. "And *that* is why we are going to the public library."

They spent time getting a library card set up for M.K. Then Fern walked around the bookshelves like she owned the place, piling up books in her arms. Every time M.K. pointed to a book that looked interesting, Fern gave off a clucking sound. She had titles in mind.

On the way home, Fern pulled the top book off the pile and handed it to M.K. "There's no time like the present. Start with this one."

M.K. picked up the book: *Keeping Bees* by John Vivian. "Rome said you've been pestering him to harvest honey."

"He won't let me. Nobody takes me seriously!"

"Well, maybe you need to learn something first. Maybe then he might be inclined to take you seriously." Fern tapped the cover of the book. "And I want a one-page summary of the book when you're done with it. Mind your penmanship too."

Fern! So bossy! M.K. silently fumed, but then she opened the book and her eyes caught on this paragraph:

A hostile colony will warn you in unmistakable terms. The hum becomes loud, shrill and strident, a high-pitched beeeeeeeeeeeee sound—possibly where they got their name in the old days; our word is Old English *beo*, or *bia* in Old (High) German. The vibration rate is unpleasant bordering on fearsome to humans, high enough to cause inner ear discomfort in many animals. It is an adrenalin-generating alarm signal that strikes a primordial chord in humans, the same as a rattlesnake's burrrrr or a dog's grrrrr or an infant's high keening wail. Bees usually will give you enough time to think better, to close up and return another day. But they may not.

Danger! She was hooked.

Rome had just finished checking on his hives. He moved some brood frames in the center—combs nearly filled with honey—to the back so the bees would start filling the empty frames. He closed the lid, picked up the smoker, and turned to leave, startled to see M.K. running toward him, spewing news like a popcorn popper. Menno trailed behind her, like he always did, and caught up with them in his own slow pace.

"Rome! Am I glad to see you! You'll never guess what's happened. I'm going to be a beekeeper!"

"Slow down, M.K. Start from the beginning," he said, pulling her away from the hives before she got too close to them. As they walked back to the cottage, he yanked his beekeeper helmet off and slipped it under his arm.

"Fern got me a book about beekeeping. So I can help you!" She was ecstatic.

Oh no. Rome wished Fern would have asked him first. If it were Menno who were interested in beekeeping, Rome would have been happy to start training him. Menno had the temperament for beekeeping—calm, unflappable. Menno was never in a hurry. But M.K.? She was overly blessed with enthusiasm and energy. Never still, never quiet. Yet how could he refuse her? She was waiting for him to respond, an earnest look on her small face. "So, you want to be an apiarist."

"No," she said. "I want to be a beekeeper."

Rome sighed. "M.K., bees are wild creatures. You're going to have to first develop a respect for them."

"I have a great respect for bees. I love honey!"

He shook his head. "That's not what I mean. There's much more to bees than honey."

"Well, they can sting. I know that for sure."

"Honeybees are engineers. Brilliant ones. They build homes for themselves that are identical in measurements."

"That's like me," Menno said. "I'm an engineer."

"Huh?" M.K. said.

"I build homes for birds. Each one is identical." Menno looked pleased with himself.

"That's true, Menno," Rome said. "You know how important it is to be precise so the birds will return to nest their young. That's what bees do, M.K. They are constantly working to help the next generation." He glanced at her. "M.K., do you know why bees produce honey?"

"For people to eat."

"Not really. Honey is bee's food. A honeycomb is a bee's pantry. They store up food for the winter. Good beekeepers always leave enough honey for the bees. The bees come first." By the look on her face, Rome could tell M.K. hadn't given any thought to bees other than eating honey.

What had Fern gotten him into?

M.K. jumped up to leave and suddenly reached her hand into her apron pocket. "I forgot! Fern said the mailman delivered this to you." She handed him a letter addressed to The Bee Man at Windmill Farm and dashed up the hill.

Dear Roman,

I have no evil intentions in buying the farm; I am only trying to right the wrongs I've done in my life.

          Sincerely,
          R.W.

As soon as it was dusk, Rome moved four of his hives onto the bee wagon. It would take him most of the night to get to those pecan orchards, so he wanted to get going while there was still some light left. He had one foot hitched up on the wagon when he heard a familiar voice calling to him.

Fern.

Rome stepped back off of the wagon and walked out to meet her. He had only met Fern a handful of times when his uncle Tom had courted her. He didn't know much about her, other than she was a spinster who worked as a housekeeper for families. As he saw the determined look on her face, he knew the moment he had dreaded had arrived.

"Have you made any decision about the farm?" she asked, when they met on the path that led to the farmhouse.

One thing he had to hand to her, Fern Graber didn't beat around the bush. "No, Fern, I haven't." He tried to sound neutral, unaffected.

"You knew this, Rome. You knew the farm couldn't be ignored forever. I told you to do some thinking."

"You did," Rome said. "You surely did."

"But you haven't done the thinking."

"No. Not really."

Fern crossed her arms against her thin chest. "It's time, Roman. It's past time."

"You mean, put it up for sale?"

"Yes."

"I don't think I can do that," Rome said.

"If you're not going to sell it, then you ought to go home and work the farm. You've been gone a long time. Long enough."

"Six years."

"Six years." Fern shook her head in disbelief. For the briefest of moments, sadness flitted through her eyes. Then it was gone. It happened so fast that Rome thought he might have imagined it. "This isn't what your father would have wanted you to do with his land. I think he'd rather see you sell it than let it fall to pieces."

How dare she assume she would know what his father would think, would feel. How audacious! But he kept his face unreadable.

"Give it some serious thought, Roman," Fern said, before spinning around and marching back to the house.

He wanted to shout out: Did she think he hadn't given the farm serious thought over the last six years? Did she think he didn't care about his family? But he stayed silent. Instead, he went to the bee wagon, hopped up on the seat, and slapped the mule's reins to get it moving.

Sell his family's farm?

Rome couldn't imagine selling it. The farm was the last place he'd kissed his mother's cheek, worked side by side with his father, played with his sisters. He was born and raised there. Sell the farm? Or return to it and leave his migratory life? An impossible decision.

12

Julia found it amusing that Fern took M.K.'s grand idea of a birthday for Menno and Sadie and turned it into a way to keep her little sister busy and out of trouble. Fern and M.K. cleaned the house together, made a grocery list together, shopped together, cooked together. Well, Fern did the cooking and M.K. did the dishwashing.

M.K. invited very specific people to come to the party and wouldn't say who. Julia hoped Paul was on the list but didn't want to ask. M.K. didn't know when to say things and when not to, and the last thing Julia wanted was for Paul to hear from his brother Jimmy that Julia was pining for him. She was *not* pining. Well, maybe she was, but Paul didn't need to know.

On the evening of the party, Gideon Smucker volunteered to arrive early to help barbecue chicken on the grill. Sadie looked annoyed with M.K. for inviting Gideon. Julia couldn't understand why Sadie didn't see how wonderful Gideon was. He clearly was sweet on Sadie, yet she was smitten with Roman Troyer . . . who hadn't shown up yet. On the other hand, M.K. seemed to glow like a lightning bug around Gideon. Maybe that's the way things always were. Maybe love was always mixed up.

When Paul arrived, Julia's heart skipped a beat, then two beats. Paul had come! There was still hope.

From the window up above, Amos sat by the windowsill, a look of longing on his face as he watched Gideon at the grill, slathering tangy barbecue sauce on the chickens. "A fellow could starve to death waiting on his meal up here!"

"Then come down and join the party," Fern called up to him. But Julia knew he wouldn't leave his room tonight. He said he would get pecked to death by well-meaning neighbors, asking questions he couldn't answer.

Uncle Hank emerged from the house, eating a cupcake. "Uncle Hank, be on your best behavior," Julia warned, but she knew he was pretty much on the same kind of behavior regardless of the company he was in.

"Men are all alike. Grown-up children," Fern muttered as she went past Julia with a bowl of strawberries. "There's more in the kitchen to bring out."

Julia went back inside and grabbed a bowl of potato salad from the kitchen. She crossed the yard to put the bowl on the picnic table with the rest of the food. Paul was standing by Gideon at the smoky grill. When he saw her, he made his way over to her.

"Is that German potato salad?" he asked her pleasantly, peering into the bowl. "Sure do love potato salad." He scratched his neck and shyly added, "Jules, I was hoping we could have a talk—"

"I'm sure hoping we can get dinner started." Roman Troyer appeared out of nowhere. "It looks like it's going to rain soon." He put a hand on Julia's elbow and steered her over to the picnic table.

"What are you doing?" Julia hissed. "I thought you'd left town."

His mouth curved faintly. "What, and miss all the fun?"

Julia searched in her mind for a snappy retort, but she was never good at those. Out of the corner of her eye, she saw Menno and Annie slip into the barn. "Oh no. That isn't good."

Rome saw it too. "Who's to say whether it's good or not? Menno isn't like us."

"Exactly."

"I don't mean that the way you're thinking. He doesn't worry about the future like you do, he doesn't trouble himself about endless responsibilities like you do. He views the world as a place of wonder."

"He can barely take care of himself."

Rome took the bowl of potato salad from Julia and placed it on the table. "He's seventeen and he's got a crush on a girl. Why do you have to spoil this for him? Maybe you should try to be more like Menno. Maybe we all should."

She stared at him, astounded. What did Roman Troyer know about her brother, her family? She planted her fists on her hips. "Why did you pull me away from Paul? He wanted to talk to me!"

"Not looking like that." He pointed to his mouth. "You have something in your teeth."

She bolted for the house and hurried into the bathroom. Sure enough, a parsley leaf was wedged between her two front teeth.

--- ❖ ---

Over on the side yard, Sadie was watching M.K. play volleyball with her school friends when she noticed one of the girls, Alice Esh, look like she was about to cry. When the ball rolled toward Sadie, she tossed it to M.K. to continue playing and went over to Alice, steering her to a bench to sit down. Alice's face was red and blotchy. "What's wrong?"

"I don't know," Alice said, taking deep breaths.

Sadie noticed that Alice's skin was starting to look strange—like giant hives were forming, making her skin look pebbly and rough. "Were you stung by anything? Or bitten?"

Alice shook her head. "I don't know what's the matter with me!" She was turning redder and redder but not perspiring, though it was a warm evening.

"M.K.!" Sadie yelled. "Go get some rags from the barn and drench them in cool water. Dummel!" *Hurry!*

M.K. ran off on her toothpick legs and returned with wet rags. Sadie draped them over Alice's hot neck and arms and legs.

"Go get more," she ordered M.K.

A crowd started to gather, but Sadie was so focused on cooling Alice down that she didn't notice. Sadie knew she had to remain calm, for Alice's sake, and tried to let that calmness flow out of her hands. Little by little, with numerous trips to the water pump by M.K., Alice started to breathe normally. Her skin lost that fire-engine-red color and returned to a healthy pink.

"What was wrong with her?" M.K. said.

"Heat rash, I think," Sadie said. "She was getting overheated."

"You saved my life," Alice whispered solemnly to Sadie.

"I don't think so," Sadie said, helping Alice stand up.

"You did, Sadie," said Gideon, who had been watching

the entire episode. Someone shouted to him that the chickens were on fire, so he ran back to the grill.

Fern had been watching too. As the crowd dispersed, Fern walked up to Sadie and took hold of her hands. She looked at the palms. "Sadie girl, we have finally found what you were born for. I don't know how I missed it before. You are a healer."

Sadie peered at her hands. "I am?" she asked, amazed.

"You are," Fern said confidently.

When the time came for birthday cake, Julia noticed Menno carry over a piece of cake to Annie. It bothered her, seeing her brother act so smitten with a girl. But everything bothered her tonight. The wistful look on her dad's face as he watched the festivities from his window. Rome and his assumptions that he knew what was best for everyone was particularly annoying tonight, but that was nothing new. Rome always annoyed her.

But what topped the list of annoyances tonight was seeing Paul hover near Lizzie. Lizzie was her friend. How could things have gone so terribly wrong? Why couldn't life remain simple? She wanted to be where people stayed in place, where only good things happened, where fathers didn't have heart problems, where boyfriends didn't cancel weddings, and where she would feel as if her future was safe.

Suddenly, Rome appeared at the bottom porch step. He extended his hand to draw Julia to her feet. "Let's go someplace where we can talk."

"We already talked. I don't want to talk anymore."

"Too late. Let's go." He pulled her to a standing position. "I want to tell you what I learned at the hospital."

The bumpy path they were walking along abruptly ended at a rusted barbed wire fence bordering an overgrown pasture. Rome stopped and turned to her. "There was a doctor who overheard me trying to get some information out of the hospital administrator. Later, that doctor found me walking in the lobby and said he would help me. He's a Mennonite and seemed to understand the situation. He got me on the phone with the transplant coordinator over at Hershey Medical. That's where the heart transplants are done. The coordinator said that if Amos is willing, his doctor has already qualified him to be placed on the national transplant list. There's no guarantee as to when a heart will turn up—the priority list is based on need, not how long a person has been on the list. They said the list turns over quickly because patients die. But he also said that hearts come in a lot—mostly from motorcycle accidents, and mostly right after holidays like the fourth of July. They call them donorcycles."

The gist of Rome's message was positive, but the word "transplant" hung in the air between them. There was an awful finality about it; a transplant might be treatment, but it had a ring of desperation to it, a sense of last resort.

"But if a heart is a match for Amos—the right blood type and size, and he said that the donor has to be within twenty pounds of Amos's weight—then the transplant could save his life. Amos is the right age for a transplant—he's young and fit and doesn't have any other health problems." Rome stopped. "Julia—you *have* to talk your father into getting on that list. He'll listen to you."

Julia looked up and was surprised she hadn't noticed how the sky had become clotted with clouds that were gray as pewter. When had that happened? One moment, the sky was clear. The next, it was filled with clouds. So like life. She thought she felt a raindrop, then another. More raindrops. Rome didn't seem to notice.

"If money's the problem, well, maybe I could find a way to help with that. I'm not saying it isn't expensive, but even the coordinator said that money shouldn't be the reason a person doesn't go on the list."

She was touched by Rome's concern for her father. Truly touched. "I appreciate what you did, Rome. And that you're trying to help. I really do."

"Just tell me that you'll talk to him. Soon."

"All right. I'll give it another try. Tomorrow. I promise."

He looked so pleased that she couldn't help but smile. And then he smiled, and their eyes held for a beat too long. His eyes traveled down to her mouth, as if he might kiss her. She could see him thinking about it, then he shifted his glance away.

Suddenly, he looped an arm around her shoulders as if drawing her in for a hug. She was so surprised she was speechless.

"That," he whispered in her ear, "is going to drive Paul Fisher right over the edge." He kept his arm tightly around her so she couldn't pull away. "Don't look now but he's standing about one hundred yards away from us. I can't be positive, but I think there's a scowl on his face."

She looked. Paul stood silhouetted against a tree, his legs braced, arms tensed at his side. He dropped his head, turned, and walked away.

Julia felt a shock run through her. Even though she knew Rome was teasing, she felt a funny quiver down her spine. She was oddly disappointed—for a brief moment, she had wanted him to kiss her. The realization was startlingly powerful. Her attraction to him irritated her, and she pulled herself out of Rome's grasp. "What do you think you're doing?"

"I'm trying to help you get Paul back."

How had so much arrogance gotten packaged in one man? Julia jabbed her finger at his shirt. "I don't need your help. I can take care of myself."

He wrapped his hand around her finger. "Aw, now, that's not fair. You said yourself that you know I only have eyes for you."

She calmly extracted her finger from his hand. "And I told you that I wasn't interested."

As she walked back to the house, she repeated to herself, "I am *not* attracted to Roman Troyer. I am not interested. No, no, no, no, no."

```
Dear R.W.,

You said you are trying to right your wrongs.
Well, there are many farms for sale in Ohio,
especially after this drought. Why my farm?
What could it possibly mean to you?

            Cordially,
            Rome Troyer
```

Rome finished writing the letter and went outside to sit on the porch steps and watch the sunset. The last time he was in town, he had done everything he could to get the Stoney Ridge postmistress to reveal who had rented P.O. Box 22. He flirted, he cajoled, he complimented. She acted as if she was guarding gold at Fort Knox and refused to reveal anything. He must be losing his touch.

175

The light sprinkling of rain had quickly passed through, just a tease. The sky was clear again for the sunset. The sun reminded him of a shimmering copper globe hanging low over the hills. He saw an owl swoop out for an evening hunt, accompanied by the sawing sound of crickets. As he leaned his back against the porch post—which felt warm against his back—he thought about Julia, something he'd been doing with increasing frequency. So many women believed they had to flirt with him to get him to notice them. But Julia didn't act like that. She was always herself—amusing, bold, gentle and patient with her father's illness, fiercely protective of her family.

If the timing were different . . . if he had a steady job, a place to live . . . if she weren't in love with Paul Fisher . . . if he were the type of fellow who wanted to settle down in one place . . . but none of that was true. With autumn only a few months away, who'd know if he would still be around?

Rome was a realist. He could have started a respectable business in any of the towns where he visited. He never did, though. Sooner or later, he started feeling panicky, itchy, and he knew the time had come to move.

He stood and stretched. Then he poked around in the shed for a shovel and hoe to start attacking the weeds growing near the cottage's foundation. As he breathed in the smell of honeysuckle, he thought about how he loved this land, the way the hills sheltered the farm. What made Windmill Farm feel different to him, like he was part of it? It wasn't really unusual, not by Amish standards. Those orchards—planted long ago by Amos's grandfather—were keeping the family going through Amos's heart trouble, as well as this drought. Rome knew that his bees were a significant help to the Lapps' yearly income. The cherries were redder, the peaches and apricots were plumper. It felt good to be needed. Was that it? Was that why he found himself drawn to this family?

He wondered how Julia was able to stand Amos's illness, how she had stood it all these months, watching her father dying, breath by breath. She must know how sick Amos was. There was no denying that the disease had taken its toll. A year ago, Amos weighed nearly 180 pounds. Now he weighed 150. The man Rome had once seen effortlessly pick up a hundred-pound bale of hay and toss it in the back of a cart could barely lift a hayfork. Even in the weeks Rome had been there, he'd seen Amos decline—gasping for breath after six stair steps, now only four. Always coughing. Thin and weak from lack of physical activity, despite Fern's steady pressure to make him get up and get moving. Julia must see it too, yet she seemed accepting of what was to come.

She was a curiosity to him—why was she fighting so hard to get Paul back, yet not fighting at all about her father's future?

Normally so strong and determined, tonight Julia had appeared almost fragile. He wasn't used to being confused about a woman. Watching her stomp away, indignant and adorable, whole parts of him were suddenly alive with possibility. A well of tenderness had grown inside him, and something had shifted. He wanted her. No—that couldn't be right. He wanted her to want him.

M.K. had read *Keeping Bees* twice and felt she had a firm grasp on the subject. Rome thought otherwise.

Late on a balmy afternoon, M.K. talked Menno into paying a visit to Rome. It wasn't uphill work to talk Menno into going; if he wasn't off visiting Annie, he could be found hanging around Rome. "Why can't I go out with you to gather honey?" she asked Rome when they arrived at the cottage. "I know plenty about bees."

"Oh? Then why are you wearing those?" Rome pointed to her outfit. She was wearing Menno's favorite fishing shirt, his big leather gloves, and his knee-high rubber boots.

"You said to cover up, head to toe."

"You smell like a fish. That smell will make my bees angry."

"But I figured the fish smell covered up the human smell."

"Honey-loving bears have been robbing bees for a lot longer than you and I have. Bees react to any dark, moving object with a strong animal scent." He raised an eyebrow. "Beekeeping lesson number one: Dress to make friends with your bees. Light-colored clothing, freshly laundered, sun-dried."

"If I go change, will you let me go out with you?"

"Not today."

"Why?!" She was indignant.

Rome frowned. "Mary Kate, you move too fast for bees."

"I'm always telling her that," Menno added.

M.K. scowled at him.

"Lesson number two: bees like things slow, gentle, deliberate. Fast movement makes them feel threatened. They know that predators move quickly—darting bee-eating birds, batting bear claws, lapping raccoon tongues. Move slowly and the bees will know you're a friend."

"I can move slow! I'm just usually in a hurry."

"You came crashing down to the cottage just now like your hair was on fire. Until you learn to enter a room quietly and calmly, I will not consider taking you out to gather honey."

M.K. turned and started to run out the door, then stopped

herself. She quietly exited, and as soon as she was out of Rome's viewing range, she bolted to the farmhouse, ran upstairs, changed her clothing into a pale pink dress Fern had just ironed, dashed back, then stopped at the crest of the hill to walk slowly to the cottage. Quietly, she entered, sat on a chair in the kitchen, and primly crossed her ankles. Rome looked up from writing labels on honey jars and shook his head.

"Now?" she asked.

Rome looked at her for a long while.

"She did come in quiet," Menno said.

Rome sighed and put down his pen. "The first thing to do is to observe the door to the hives. That's all. Nothing else."

M.K. was thrilled. "Can I go now?"

"We will go together. You don't go near the hives without my permission. Ever." He glanced out the window. "It's about dusk. Their instinct is to head for shelter, so you should see a lot of bees returning to the hive." He handed her a pad of paper and a pencil. "Take notes and write down what you notice. Even the sounds—are the bees hissing? Or humming? They sing, you know. A sweet and low tone is the sound of a contented hive. Music to a beekeeper's ears. Listen well. That's lesson number three. Remember, you are to do everything slow and smooth. You keep your distance. And lesson number four: do nothing until you feel safe."

This was starting to sound like school to M.K.

Rome walked to the door and held it open. "You two coming?"

Observing the bees was a little disappointing to M.K. Or maybe it was the vigilant way Rome watched over her. He wouldn't let her get closer than twenty feet to the hives. Have patience, he kept telling her. Lesson number 542. He was getting to be like Fern! Even Menno got bored and wandered back to the farmhouse.

On the way back to the cottage, Rome asked M.K., "Well, what did you observe?"

Not much, she wanted to say, but instead she looked at her notes. "Bees fly up high and dive down to the hive entrance."

He nodded. "They nest naturally in hollow trees or someplace well above ground. What else?"

"The lower the sun was setting, the more bees returned to the hive."

"Those were forager bees. Their job was to be out gathering nectar and pollen, to bring it back to the hive. Anything else?"

"A couple of bees just stuck around the outside, like they didn't know what to do."

"Every bee has a job to do. Those were guards to the hive."

She snorted. "Guarding from what?"

"From mice. From hornets. From moths. From birds. From skunks and raccoons. From little girls who get too close to the hive—"

"I get it." She blew air out of her mouth. Maybe beekeeping was harder than she thought.

"Did you notice what kinds of bees they were?"

She knew this one, hands down. "Honeybees."

"There are all different strains of bees. My bees are brown bees. Most beekeepers don't like the brown bee. They're a little more work than other bees, but there's no better bee to collect thick, wild honey. My great-great-grandparents brought them from Germany. They've been in my family for five or six generations. I'm the Keeper of the Bees."

Maybe that's why Rome was so fussy about his bees, M.K. thought. It's his tie to his family.

"A good beekeeper learns to gauge much about the bees' condition from outside the hive, and that time is spent quietly observing."

New subject! Enough talk about being quiet. As they reached the fork in the path that led either to the cottage or the farmhouse, M.K. turned to Rome. "There's something I've been meaning to tell you."

"Go ahead."

"You're fired."

"From teaching you to be a beekeeper?" He whistled, one note up, one down. "That was fast."

"No! I still want to be a beekeeper. You're fired from trying to make Paul Fisher jealous. The birthday party provided ample opportunity for you. Ample opportunity! And all you managed to do was to make Julia as mad as a wet hen. Paul took Lizzie home in his courting buggy!"

"I see," he said, stroking his jaw. "The thing is, M.K., that I don't like to leave a job half finished. And we had a bargain. A deal is a deal."

"Well, you can keep the down payment. Besides, I can't pay you the rest anyway. Fern found out—" She clamped her lips shut.

Rome narrowed his eyes. "Found out what?"

"Never mind. Let's just say, my income has been temporarily cut off."

"Seeing as how I'm living rent-free on your father's land, I'm willing to forgive your debt."

"Rome, did you hear me? You have done a terrible job of making Paul jealous."

"I hear just fine. But I disagree. I'm pretty certain that he's coming around. I think I just need to turn up the heat a little."

How much clearer could she be? "Julia is impervious to your charms. I know this must be embarrassing to you."

"Not as much as it should be."

M.K. shook her head. "I'm sorry, Rome. You're good at beekeeping, but you're just no good at making a fellow jealous. I'm moving on to my second inspiration."

"Mary Kate, are you sure you know what you're doing?"

"I'm sure." She wasn't sure at all.

"Give me another chance. I'll do better."

She blew out a puff of air. "Fine. You keep working at it, but I'm going to give my inspiration a try too." She started to run up the path to the farmhouse, then remembered bee etiquette and slowed to a fast walk. It nearly undid her to move so cautiously.

13

The skies had turned an angry steel gray, but Julia ignored the ominous warnings. She wanted to get out to the southeast corner of the cornfields before the rain broke. They counted on that corn to feed the animals through the winter, when there was no grass left to graze. If they didn't get some more soaking rain soon, the corn crop would be even smaller than last year.

The distant rumble of thunder surprised her. She'd almost forgotten what a summer storm system could be like as it blew through. It had been such a long time without any significant rain to saturate the fields. She looked up at the sky. Maybe today.

As she walked along the dirt path that led to the north field, she pondered an idea for a quilt top that was brewing in the back of her mind. She wanted to get home and draw it in her journal before she forgot it. That's what she did with the quilt tops that popped into her mind, unbidden. She filled up her journal with sketches drawn with colored pencils. She wasn't sure what she would ever do with the sketches—she still hadn't recovered from the sting of criticism from last year.

I wasn't being proud, she thought, as she walked through

the knee-high corn rows. She had just done the very best she could. She had used an old Lancaster pattern but gave it a fresh twist with explosions of color and design—was that being prideful? If so, she just couldn't help it. It was the way she gave glory to God. To have Edith Fisher accuse her of pride stung her to her core. She'd lost the joy she felt when she created a new quilt top.

As she stood looking out across the land she knew so well, she felt a flutter of panic. It was no surprise to see the furrows Menno had dug weren't straight and narrow the way they were before her father took sick, but it worried her to see brown on the edges of the cornstalks.

The first drops of rain began to fall. With them came that smell of rain, that dusty smell that was like no other. It was synonymous with joy, with renewal, with life itself. After two years of drought, Julia would never again take a drop of rain for granted.

And rain it was, warm and welcome, with fat drops that splashed on the parched ground. A bolt of lightning split the skies, followed by a clap of thunder that made her ears ring. The rain started falling in curtains, fast and furious. She hurried out of the cornfield and back onto the path. She blinked her eyes, wiped her nose on her sleeve. She was so soaked that her dress stuck to her skin, and her woven bandanna felt like a sodden pancake around her head. Another blast of lightning struck. She jumped as something brushed her legs. Lulu stared up at her, her head cocked to the side. Julia sank to her knees and buried her face in Lulu's wet, musty fur. Her arms trembled as she drew Lulu close. The dog scraped Julia's wet cheek with her rough tongue. Another blast of lightning struck. Lulu howled, and Julia jumped to her feet.

She needed to find shelter. The cottage where Rome was staying was much closer than the farmhouse. She ran, her bare
feet making her sure-footed in the gritty mud.

When she arrived at the cottage, she knocked on the door.
"Rome?" She waited, then knocked again, and gave the string
latch a gentle pull. She took a step inside and waited until
her eyes adjusted to the dark. "Rome, are you here?" No
answer. She hadn't been in the cottage since Fern fixed it up.
She used to play hide-and-seek here with Sadie and Menno
when they were children, but studiously avoided going inside
since the day a bat flew down from its rafters and scared her
to the other side of Sunday. Today, it looked quite charming.
Clearly, Fern's doings. Just like the produce table transforma-
tion. The cottage looked warm and inviting, swept clean and
left tidy. The kitchen had been turned into a well-organized
honey extracting room: clean jars lined the shelves. Labels
for the jars were stacked in a neat pile. The extractor and
buckets were spotless.

She closed her eyes, taking in the smell of beeswax infused
in the cottage walls. She realized now why it seemed familiar.
It was a scent she associated with Rome—a fragrance that felt
strangely reassuring, that all would soon be right with life.

A crackle of lightning sounded in the distance. Shuddering,
Lulu chose that moment to shake herself off. Julia grabbed a
towel from a hook near the sink and began rubbing the dog's
chest. As she put the towel back, she was startled by what she
saw on the kitchen table. Medical books were spread out all
over the table. She looked closer and saw they were opened to
heart disease. She saw a yellow tablet filled with notes Rome
had taken about idiopathic cardiomyopathy. And next to the
books was an open Bible, with another yellow tablet half-filled

with Scriptures he had found that referred to a man's heart. His handwriting, Julia noticed, was strong and legible, as if he had been well schooled.

Rome must have bought these books when he went into Lancaster last week.

She doubted he would want to know she had seen what he was researching—otherwise he would have mentioned it. Maybe not. Rome didn't volunteer much.

Something caught at her throat, something that hurt and made a curious melting feeling deep in her chest. A mixture of sadness and happiness, and a strange, sweet ache that after a moment she realized was hope.

Yesterday's storm had washed the air, leaving it sweet and fresh. The first solid rain of the summer, Amos thought, and he thanked God for it. At Fern's urging—some might call it steady nagging—he sat in the rocker on the front porch and tilted back his head, letting the warmth of the morning sun pour over him. Lately, he couldn't get warm, even on hot, humid days. The problem was his circulation, the doctor said at his last appointment. His heart had to work harder and harder to get oxygen-rich blood circulating through his body. He rubbed his hands. They felt stiff and clumsy, like he was trying to play a wooden whistle with mittens on a winter day.

Suddenly Menno came flying up the driveway and blew past him into the house, not even acknowledging Amos was there. He heard Menno's heavy footsteps pound up the stairs, then silence. A moment later, a loud "I FOUND IT!" floated out the upstairs windows. Amos leaned forward on his rocking chair, waiting to see *what* had been found.

Menno came thundering down the stairs again, two at a time, out the back door, and thrust his dog-eared *Birds, Birds, Birds!* book into Amos's hands. It was opened to the American pipit, a small sparrow-sized bird. "Look. I found my bird."

"The American pipit?" Amos read its description. *Pipits nest in the Arctic and migrate in spring and fall. Birders sometimes hope (but never expect) to find American pipits. Occasional stragglers appear south of Canada out of season during storms.* He looked up at Menno. "You think you spotted a lone American pipit? At the feeder?"

"No. Not at the feeder, Dad. It eats bugs." He gave Amos a look as if he couldn't believe he didn't know such things. "I found it on the woodpile." He pulled on Amos's sleeve. "Come see!"

He dragged Amos out to the woodpile, with Amos puffing for air, which triggered a coughing fit by the time they got there.

About ten feet from the pile, Menno stopped abruptly and pointed. "There!"

Sure enough, there was a small brown bird, perched on top of the woodpile, staring back at them. It was completely unafraid of humans—probably wasn't accustomed to seeing them, Amos surmised. The bird bobbed and fanned its tail, hopping from one stacked log to another. Its beak disappeared between wood pieces as it nabbed an ant or cricket or spider.

Amos held up the book and compared the markings of the bird to the picture in Menno's book. "Well, I'll be," he whispered. "I wonder if it missed its north-going bus in the spring? Or maybe it's early for going south. Probably got blown off its course in yesterday's storm." He and Menno stood there, in awe at the sight. "Menno, this little bird travels all the way

187

from the Arctic to Mexico, every year. Across thousands of miles. And yet, it stopped on our farm to pay us a visit." He patted Menno on the back. "And you alone had the vision to notice it. That was no small coincidence, son."

Menno shook his head. "There's no such thing, Dad. You always said that what man calls a coincidence, God calls a miracle." Then his eyes opened wide. "I should call the Rare Bird Alert. They need to know about our miracle." He backed away slowly so he wouldn't startle the bird. When he reached the driveway, he bolted to the phone shanty by the schoolhouse.

Amos stayed awhile longer, watching this little brown bird enjoy lunch on the woodpile. "Thank you, God," he prayed. "For blessings large and small. For a little lonely bird that reminds us that not a sparrow can fall from the sky without your notice." Finally, he turned to leave. He felt lighter, happier, than he had in a long while. *Maybe today*, he thought, *my heart is starting to heal. Maybe God is bringing me a miracle too.*

June turned out to be M.K.'s busiest month, thanks largely to the American pipit, which seemed to enjoy its stay at Windmill Farm. It was in no hurry to leave. When word got out about such a rare bird sighting, visitors came from all over southeastern Pennsylvania. M.K. had never seen so many people at Windmill Farm in all her life. Many Amish bird lovers, but mostly English ones. Sadie ran to the house whenever a car pulled up the long drive. She peeked out the kitchen window as they emerged from their cars—she was curious about English folk but far too shy to speak to them. Menno, on the other hand, greeted each guest like a long-lost friend.

M.K. had the crackerjack idea of charging folks for seeing the bird, but when Fern caught wind of it, she made M.K. give the money back.

Fern. So meddlesome!

Fern bought Menno a guest book so that the visitors could sign their names. Each evening, Menno counted up the names. Last night, the number had topped three hundred! Menno was thrilled. Sadie said she was hoping that little bird would soon be on its way and life at Windmill Farm could return to normal. It hadn't occurred to Menno that the bird wasn't staying. His face grew red and blotchy as he tried not to cry, so Sadie took it back.

This afternoon, M.K. was directing cars to park alongside the barn so they didn't clog the driveway. To her delight, the man in the panama hat drove up in a truck and waved to her. His truck was pulling a big silver recreation vehicle that reminded M.K. of a giant can of soda pop. M.K. ran up to the truck and waited until the man hopped out of the cab.

"Hello!" she said. "Are you here to see the bird?"

"I am!" he said, looking pleased. "It's the talk of the town that there's a rare bird on an Amish farm. Wasn't hard to find which farm." He pointed to the long line of cars.

"I'll take you out to see it," she said, abandoning her duties as parking director.

As they walked out to the woodpile, the man said, "Let's see. The last time I saw you, you were in the library, looking for ways to make a quick buck. Did you have any luck with the shell game?"

She frowned. "I wouldn't exactly call it luck."

"Were you able to earn enough money to help your family?"

"*That* would take a mountain of money."

"Why is that?" He seemed genuinely interested.

"My father needs surgery and I don't think I could ever make enough nickels off of the shell game to pay for a new heart."

The man stopped in his tracks. "What's wrong with his heart?"

M.K. scratched her head. "His heart is wearing out. But we're praying for a miracle."

The man rubbed his chin, deep in thought. "I don't believe in miracles."

How sad! M.K. counted on miracles. Every day. She watched the man in the panama hat observe the bird until Fern shouted at her to get back to the driveway and direct cars. A traffic jam had formed at the top of the rise.

Later that afternoon, Uncle Hank stormed into the kitchen. "WHEN IS THAT BIRD GONNA HIT THE ROAD?"

Fern was giving a serious beating to egg whites in a metal bowl. Without looking up, she asked, "What's eating you?"

"MENNO SAYS HE'S TOO BUSY TO GO TURKEY HUNTING WITH ME! And I spotted a flock just this morning. RIPE FOR THE PICKING!" Uncle Hank pulled off his straw hat and tossed it on a bench, then pulled out a chair at the kitchen table and plopped into it. "I need his keen vision."

"Maybe Fern would like to go with you," M.K. added, trying to sound helpful. She looked at Uncle Hank with wide and innocent eyes. The truth was, she was still mad at Fern for making her return money to paying bird visitors. It was a substantial amount of money. And folks didn't bat an eye when she pointed out the cardboard sign listing admission prices: $5 per adult, $2 for children under 12. "She's always telling me she's got eyes on the back of her head."

Uncle Hank eyed Fern with his good eye.

"That's not a bad idea," Amos said, sitting in a chair in the far corner of the room with his feet raised. "She doesn't miss a thing."

Fern continued to beat the egg whites.

Uncle Hank gave that some serious thought. Then he slammed his palms on the tabletop. "Fine! We'll leave at dawn." He jumped up from the table and grabbed his hat. He pointed a finger at Fern. "AND DON'T BE LATE!"

Fern examined the egg whites, now stiff and in peaks, and set down the bowl. "Well, then, Mary Kate, I hope you don't mind getting up extra early to fix breakfast, seeing as how I'll be out chasing turkeys in the morning." She arched an eyebrow in M.K.'s direction. "And I'll expect this kitchen to be spotless when I return."

M.K. exchanged a look with her father.

He shrugged his shoulders in a "Don't-look-at-me. You-started-it" way. "Maybe next time you have a brainstorm, you could run it by me first," he said.

Amos was paying bills at his desk when he heard a commotion on the back porch, then the kitchen door squeak open and shut with a bang. He really should oil that hinge. He leaned back in his chair and saw Fern scolding Uncle Hank.

"Hank Lapp, you're mucking up my perfectly good clean floors with those rubber boots of yours! Look at the tracks you're leaving! Now I'll have to get down on my hands and knees with a Brillo pad to get them off the linoleum."

Something seemed odd to Amos. Getting chewed out by Fern was nothing new to any of them, but he could tell her heart wasn't in the scolding today.

Uncle Hank saw Amos and stomped straight into the living room, hands perched on his hips, rubber boots still on. "You and your big ideas! I will never take that woman shooting with me ever again!"

"That bad, eh?" Amos said, smiling.

"Fern did everything wrong, got nothing right! She chattered too much, disturbed the undergrowth, loaded the wrong gauge shot in the gun, used the wrong luring whistles."

Fern came into the room with a glass of water and a handful of pills for Amos. "Tell him," she said primly. "Tell him what happened."

Uncle Hank glared at her. "Worst of all," he bellowed, "SHE SHOT MORE TURKEYS THAN ME!"

A broad grin spread over Fern's face. "The truth is too much for some people and too little for others." Though she didn't gloat, she did look satisfied as she swiveled on her heels and returned to the kitchen.

⟡

Friday began as a mild, sunny day. Julia was pleased to see her father downstairs at the kitchen table, reading the newspaper. She knew this was Fern's doing. Every day, Fern insisted that Amos get out of bed, get dressed, join his family, and do something physical to stay active. No excuses.

This morning, she needed to talk to her father privately and waited until the house was empty. As Julia sat in the chair across from him, he patted her hand with his. He had such big hands. Now they looked frail. When had his skin taken on such a grayish tint? Had she grown accustomed to his frailty? "Menno thinks he's fallen in love with Annie. He wants to marry her."

Last evening, as Julia was turning off the lamp in the kitchen, Menno had come downstairs and announced to her, "Me and Annie are getting married."

"Oh, Menno, for heaven's sake," Julia had said, pushed to the limit of her patience. "How can you get married? You don't know the first thing about marriage, either one of you."

"We know," Menno had said. "We know about marriage."

Julia had hardly slept last night, she was so bothered by Menno's news.

Amos studied the coffee mug in his hand as if it could portend the future. "I always had a feeling," he said, thoughtful and far-off. "Like this was bound to happen, one day or another. And now it has."

"That's it? That's all you have to say about the matter?"

He leaned back in the chair. "They're young, Julia. It'll fizzle out."

Julia was not sure, though. She had a funny feeling from the start about Menno's relationship with Annie. "What if it doesn't?" Julia said. "What if it's a huge mistake?"

Amos lifted one bushy eyebrow. "Folks make mistakes all of the time, Julia. And God has a way of bringing good out of those mistakes." He dropped his chin to his chest. "We need to leave our Menno in God's hands."

Julia rubbed her face with her hands. "I know you're right. I wish I could talk to Rome about this. He might have an idea."

"You can."

"I can't. He hasn't come around in weeks."

Amos pointed a thumb toward the window. "He's right outside."

"Paul?" She hurried to the window, peered out, and turned back to her father. "That's Rome."

"That's who you said. You wanted to talk to Rome about Menno."

"No. I said Paul."

"My heart may be giving me trouble, but my hearing is just fine. You said Rome."

"I *meant* Paul."

"You said Rome and I think you *meant* Rome."

Julia shook her head and left the room, exasperated.

On Sunday evening, Paul went to a singing at Rose Hill Farm, Lizzie's home. He had been looking forward to it all week, until the moment when Rome Troyer pulled up in a buggy with Julia. When Paul saw Rome help Julia down from the buggy, he set his jaw and looked away. But a moment later his gaze had gone back to studying Rome and Julia. He felt something like fear roil up sour in his belly. Why? Paul was the one who kept holding Julia at arm's length. He should be relieved that someone else was courting Julia. And in a way, he was. But what bothered him was that person happened to be Roman Troyer.

It was the way Rome had looked at Julia. Not that snagging a look at Julia—at most of the girls—was unusual for the young men. It was part of every singing. As the girls arrived, the boys gathered in small clumps and watched them. Tonight, as Julia walked from the buggy to the stone farmhouse, every fellow present had stopped talking, stopped moving. Why, even the buggy horses stilled. Paul had heard the fellow next to him, Isaac Yoder, ease his breath out in a slow, slow whistle.

"She's mine," Paul shot back, surprising even himself with the force of his protest, so that of course he flushed.

Isaac turned his head slowly away from watching Julia gracefully climb the steps of the farmhouse. "Oh? Does Rome Troyer know she's yours?"

Paul looked at Isaac sharply, and Isaac nudged him in the ribs to make him smile. Then, as if of one accord, their gazes had been pulled back to Julia, standing on the porch, laughing at something Rome had said.

Paul felt a surge of jealousy. Julia was his.

This evening wasn't going at all the way Julia had planned. She agreed to go to the singing with Rome with hopes that Paul might notice. She had lingered a little extra long out on the porch, laughed a little extra loud at something funny Rome had said. She hoped to be heading home tonight in Paul's courting buggy, but her plans went awry. Paul seemed to have vanished, and just as Julia started to look for him, suddenly she was being ushered to the buggy by Rome.

"Paul Fisher is a fool," Rome whispered to her as he helped her into the buggy. A lump rose in Julia's throat and emotion welled behind her eyes. He couldn't have imagined how much she needed to hear that right now.

"Thanks." She swallowed hard, trying to get herself under control. An emotional moment with Roman Troyer wasn't anywhere in her plans for this evening.

As the horse jerked forward, Julia decided to steer the conversation away from anything too personal and on to something safer. She spilled out her worries about Menno and Annie to Rome. "Menno simply cannot live by himself, not even for a day. If a fire broke out, he would be frightened and wouldn't know what to do."

Rome was quiet for a moment. "He wouldn't be alone. He would be with Annie."

"He could never be responsible for another human being."

"Who are you to say?"

Embarrassment warmed Julia's neck and cheeks. She was the one who usually had the answers, not the one needing advice. Maybe Rome and her father were right. Maybe Menno and Annie would be okay, more or less, together. Menno seemed not to worry very much about things, but rather to accept the world as a fascinating place where anything might happen. Why did she have to spoil his dream, his life, with troubles about the future?

Julia wasn't entirely persuaded, but she felt calmer now. Talking to Rome had that effect, she noticed; his presence felt so normal, so reassuring and right. Such kind thoughts about Rome surprised her. An image in her mind shifted, like a reflection in a pond turning wavy after she tossed in a stone. As the ripples slowed and stilled, a new picture emerged: Rome Troyer—sincere, steady, even wise. Not at all the arrogant oaf she had made him out to be. He turned to her suddenly, as if he could read her thoughts. His gaze met hers and held it. A soft breeze tickled loose hairs on the back of Julia's neck. For just a moment, she imagined herself as Rome's Julia.

Rome leaned closer to her, surprisingly close, and she thought he might be thinking about kissing her. But at the last moment, he nudged her softly with his shoulder, the way a friend might after a joke. "Listen, Julia," he said, his voice kind and empathetic. "You need to take your mind off all these 'what-ifs.' Things like this have a way of working out for the best." Then he turned his attention to the horse, prodding him to hurry along.

The moon slid behind a cloud. In a passing field, a screech-ing barn owl swooped in and pounced on a squealing mouse. As the buggy turned into Windmill Farm, Julia wished Rome had taken the longer way home, past Blue Lake Pond. The conversation between them felt unfinished, and for reasons she couldn't explain, she felt a little disappointed that the ride was over. She suddenly realized it had completely slipped her mind to notice whether Paul's buggy was still at Rose Hill Farm.

14

Sadie was luxuriating in an hour of uninterrupted time, a rarity at Windmill Farm on any given day. She was sitting on the porch steps, reading through a book about home remedies that Fern had checked out of the library for her. Fern and Julia had taken Amos into town for a doctor's appointment, Uncle Hank was delivering a long overdue and finally repaired buggy, and Menno had slipped off with Lulu and her pup to visit Annie. M.K. had gone to the orchard to observe the beehives. Rome was . . . who knew where? It was one of those perfect July days when temperatures dipped into the low eighties and an occasional puffy cloud sailed across a flawless sky. The air was filled with birdsong and the subtle scents of dianthus and wild violets. How easy it was to lose herself in the beauty of the day.

Suddenly, an ear splitting scream sliced through the quiet. M.K. ran toward the house from the path that led to the peach orchard. "SAAAADIEEEEE! There's a bear! BEAR!" She flew past Sadie and into the house, galloped up the stairs, and slammed her bedroom door.

Sadie blew out a puff of air. M.K.'s vivid imagination could wear a person out. It was high time for school to start. She went back to reading her book.

A few minutes later, Sadie glanced up and saw a yearling bear lumbering down the dirt path toward the house, as calm and relaxed as if he had been invited to Sunday supper. Sadie threw down her book and ran into the house and locked the door behind her.

"I *told* you so!" M.K. said as she peeked her head around the stairwell. "No one ever believes me!"

"Hush!" Sadie had to think. What to do?

The bear climbed up onto the porch and pressed its nose against the kitchen window. It was looking right at them!

"Don't move a muscle, M.K."

The bear sniffed around the porch, knocked Sadie's book around, then lumbered down the steps and into Julia's garden. Sadie got Amos's double-barreled shotgun off its wall hinges and found some steel shot shells in a drawer. She had never shot anything before, but she had watched her dad load a gun many times. She knew enough to choose light shells. She didn't want to kill the bear, just hurry it on its way. She went into Fern's bedroom, opened the window a few inches, aimed the gun at the bear—which was helping itself to Julia's ripe raspberries—and pulled the trigger. She peppered the bear in the rear. It howled and ran off to the nearest tree.

The bear sat up in the tree, staring down at the house for the longest while. Finally, it climbed down and lumbered off into the woods. No sooner had Sadie put away the gun but M.K. spotted the mamma bear lumbering along, sniffing after the scent of her cub. Eventually it too disappeared into the woods behind their house.

Sadie and M.K. stayed inside the house for the rest of the afternoon, rifle loaded.

⁕

Summer had deepened. The days were hot and humid, the nights cooler, the air drifting with evening mist.

M.K. spent half of an afternoon trying to find Paul Fisher. She knew he was in town because she saw his buggy and sorrel mare parked at a hitching post. She had tried the hardware store first, then the bakery, but no luck so far. Her next stop was the Hay & Grain, so she slipped inside and looked around. Bingo! Paul was chatting with the store clerk. M.K. grabbed a bag of birdseed, hoisted it over her shoulder, and went up to the cash register. She slapped the birdseed onto the countertop and tried to look surprised when she saw Paul.

"M.K., what are you doing here?" Paul glanced around to see if she was alone.

"Ran out of birdseed at Windmill Farm." She tried to pretend she was out of breath. "Needed some. An emergency."

Paul smiled. "Why would birdseed be an emergency?"

M.K. busied herself with getting her money out of her shoes. "Oh . . . because it brings such happiness to my sister."

Paul watched her count out five one-dollar bills. "I thought Menno was the bird lover at your farm. Since when has Sadie been such a bird-watcher?"

M.K. shook her head. "Not Sadie. *Julia*. We're trying to make Julia's last few days on earth happy ones."

Paul cocked his head as if he hadn't heard her right.

"Oh, didn't you hear? Julia's dying. She has—" She searched around the store for something. Her eyes landed on a flyer posting a warning about chickens. "Salmonella poisoning."

"What? I passed your farm just this morning and saw her setting up her stand."

M.K. regarded him sadly. "So brave." She handed over the dollars to the clerk and picked up the birdseed. "I'd better get back." She raised her eyebrows. "Not a minute to spare, you know. Salmonella acts like this." She snapped her fingers in the air.

She was down the street when Paul's buggy came up beside her. "Hop in," he said, eyeing her suspiciously.

This was playing out just as she had planned! Paul opened up the buggy door and grabbed the birdseed from her. In the backseat of the buggy was Jimmy, who looked at M.K. as if she were a rattlesnake.

She froze midair. "Maybe I'll just walk home."

"I told you she was lying!" Jimmy jeered.

M.K. scowled.

Paul pulled her in. "Knock it off, Jimmy. M.K., let's go see how bad off Julia is." He yanked the buggy door closed. "She sure didn't look too poorly when she was nuzzling Rome Troyer the other night."

M.K. drew herself up straight. "Lapp women do not nuzzle."

"I'll say!" Jimmy piped up. "They're as mean as black racer snakes."

She turned around and caught the smug look on his face. "Jimmy Fisher! You know you were the one who put that black racer in the girls' bathroom."

Jimmy shrugged. "Prove it."

M.K. stared at him, astounded. How could one boy be so thoroughly obnoxious?

Jimmy stared back and rested his folded arms on the backing of the front seat.

Paul elbowed him back. "Jimmy, you stop bothering Mary Kate."

M.K. looked at Paul appreciatively. He was a mild fellow, inoffensive, a little awkward, but if M.K. worked hard and squinted her eyes, she could see his appeal. Jimmy, though, was another story. She was making a mental list of Jimmy's faults when they arrived at Windmill Farm. There was Julia, at the stand, the very picture of health. Uh-oh! She thought Julia said she was going to a comfort quilt knotting this afternoon. She doubted Julia would understand why she had fibbed to Paul. On the other hand, Julia might be pleased to see that Paul was worried about her dying. This created a wrinkle, but nothing M.K. couldn't handle.

Paul hopped out of the buggy and started toward Julia. M.K. had one leg out the door, hoping to get to Julia before Paul did, but Jimmy grabbed her arm.

"Since Julia's dying and all, we should give her and Paul a moment alone to say their sorrowful goodbyes."

M.K. tried to uncurl Jimmy's hand and ended up biting it as hard as she could.

He yelped. "You little brat! The only one who's dying at Windmill Farm is your father!"

M.K. gasped. "You are going straight to the devil for telling such a lie, Jimmy Fisher!"

He examined his hand. "You broke the skin with your fangs. I'm probably gonna get rabies."

"Serves you right, you big liar."

Jimmy glared at her. "I ain't lying! Your father is dying. His heart's giving out on him. Everybody knows. It's plain as day." He looked closely at his hand, glanced up at her, then took a second look. "M.K., you must know that." He looked down again and added, softer this time, "Don't tell me you didn't know . . ."

M.K. got out of the buggy and started running toward the house. About halfway up the hill, Julia caught up with her and made her stop running. "Why would you tell Paul such a ridiculous lie?" Then she took in M.K.'s face. "What's happened? What's wrong?"

"Is Dad dying?"

Julia's head shot up like a mother lion sniffing the air for danger to her cub. "What? Who told you that?"

"Jimmy. Is it true?"

Julia bit her lower lip. "He's not getting better like the doctors had hoped he would."

Both of M.K.'s hands flew up to cover her ears. She tried, tried, tried to block out Jimmy's words, but they kept bouncing into her head. She blinked a couple of times, and Julia reached out and wrapped her arms around her and hugged her as tight as she could.

When she let go, she gave M.K. a smile that didn't quite make it to her eyes. "Let's go to the house. Fern baked a peach pie."

A breeze filtered in through a partly open window, leaving in its wake the soft scents of late summer. Amos breathed in as deeply as he could without triggering a coughing fit, allowing the scents to uncap forgotten memories of happy moments. Days spent on his farm with his Maggie, when the children were just babes. The warmth of the sun on his cheeks as he lay on a hay wagon during a lunchtime break; the down of his grandmother's cheeks as she kissed him goodnight; the feel of his father's big hand covering his as they hammered nails at a barn raising. How easy it would be for Amos to just close his eyes and explore the trails of memory, twisting and turning, winding their way toward this moment.

All things considered, Amos felt blessed. He had been steward of a fine piece of land that had been in his family for four generations. He was given a happy, albeit far too brief marriage to Maggie Zook. He had good friends and neighbors. But of all his blessings, he especially gave thanks for his four children.

Aside from the current condition of his heart, he had lived a wonderful life.

After Amos heard about the blowup between M.K. and Jimmy, he told Fern to send the children upstairs to his room. Who was he kidding? He knew he wasn't improving. Julia knew. Uncle Hank knew. Fern knew. The doctors knew. The time had come to prepare the children for what was coming. Was it so bad for a man to know how God was calling him home? His dear Maggie had no such foreknowledge. He had no fear of death; his great hope was to live in the fullness of joy in God's presence. He would be reunited with his wife, his parents, a brother, and two sisters who had gone before him. It was only when he thought of his children that he felt a great despair, a longing to remain with them for a while longer. It was so hard seeing them, all of them, every day and knowing . . . it might be coming to an end.

They filed into his bedroom and stood around his bed like little soldiers, solemn and serious. M.K.'s red, swollen, staring eyes. Julia, stoic. Sadie, head bowed. Menno, his silent self. Amos looked at each one, his children. He loved each one so dearly. What wouldn't he do for his children?

Rome joined Fern at the doorjamb of Amos's room, and he waved them in. "Where's Uncle Hank?" Amos asked.

"He's off trying to track that bear," Fern said. "It was spotted near the Glicks' sheep last night."

"We need to have a talk," Amos started, his voice shaky. He coughed softly, ending with a dry-airy sound like wind blowing through a whistle. That blasted cough! "I had hoped that the new treatment the doctors were trying would help my heart get stronger." He took a deep breath. "But it doesn't seem to be the case. It seems as if the Lord might be calling me home a little sooner than I would have liked. But it's not for us to question God's timing."

M.K. let out a sob and threw herself on top of Amos. He wrapped his arms around her and stroked her back. Tears started blurring his vision, but he fought them back. He needed to be strong for his family. He knew this was a moment that would affect how they perceived God for the rest of their lives. Isn't that what Rome struggled with? Some tragedy, some kind of loss, that altered him forever? He didn't want that for his own children. Loss was part of life, dying part of living. There was a time for all things, King Solomon said. Amos believed those words with all his heart. And he wanted his children to believe them too. To hold tight to the Lord through these seasons. What else did we have, when all was said and done, but the Lord God?

He glanced at Rome, whose eyes were fixed on Julia. She stood at the foot of Amos's bed, hugging her elbows tightly, holding herself in one piece. Her face was tight. This wasn't new information for her. She had spoken to the doctors last week about what the future looked like. That was his

Julia—she looked delicate, like the faintest gust of wind might blow her over, but she was strong where it counted most. Inside.

He remembered when he had first noticed her inner strength. It was the day she had seen her mother buried, and she knew she had three little siblings who looked up to her. He knew he could always count on Julia.

His gaze shifted to Sadie. She looked so sad. *Oh Sadie, don't be sad.* Of all of his children, Sadie worried him the most. She always had, even as a little girl. You'd think he would fret over Menno, but his son was blessed with an abundance of simple faith in God. His mind may not run as quickly as others, but his faith never wavered. God was good, and God loved Menno. That was all the information that Menno seemed to need.

But Sadie—she was so gentle, so timid, so fearful, so un-sure of herself. Always in the background, trying hard to be invisible.

Mary Kate lifted her tearstained face. She, of all the chil-dren, was the most like his Maggie. She would be fine, even if she didn't know it yet. "What does it feel like to die?"

He put his hand on her small head. "Do you remember how we would wake up before Menno and Julia and Sadie? And we'd sit together—you and me and Mom—and Mom would make hot chocolate for you, and I'd have my coffee, and Mom would have her tea, and we'd sit quietly, listening for the rooster to crow? Then Mom would take the lamp that sat on the kitchen table, and she'd blow out the wick. Because she knew morning had come." He lifted her chin. "That's what it's like, M.K. It's like blowing out the wick of a lamp because morning is coming."

Menno crouched down by Amos's bed. "Dad, does a person have two hearts? Like he has two kidneys?"

He put his hand on Menno's soft hair. "No, Menno. Just one heart per person."

"If I had two, I could give you one."

With that comment, Amos's tears flowed freely. Rome dropped his head, and Sadie sniffed loudly. Finally, Fern had enough of this emotion. "That's enough. Everybody out. He's not going anywhere today." She waved everyone downstairs. As they filed out past her, she said, "We don't put a question mark where God has put a period."

Rome waited at Amos's door until they all left. He had one boot against the doorjamb, with his arms crossed. "What Fern just said—those words are true. But Amos, what if God has just put a comma? Not a period?" He reached a hand for the door and quietly closed it as he left.

A comma? Amos knew what Rome was getting at—a heart transplant. He'd been hammering that home the last few weeks. Amos leaned his head against the pillow. He had been against the idea since he first heard the word mentioned at the doctor's office, months ago. It didn't seem right to him. The Bible said a man was appointed to live once and to die once. He closed his eyes. How could he dare hope for a new heart? That would mean a person's life had been taken. How could he even pray such a prayer?

There were seasons in a person's life. A time when one knew heaven couldn't be far away, when a man's life was ebbing away. This was Amos's last season. He needed to search his soul, to confess all sin—what he had done and what he had failed to do—and to seek God's forgiveness.

A comma, Rome had said. *Lord*, Amos prayed, *you will*

have to tell me clearly if that's what you want me to pursue.
I just don't think I could accept such a thing. It's asking too
much.

A few days later, M.K. was playing a game of checkers with her father when Julia and Sadie came into the room, interrupting. They plopped down in the chairs that had been put in Amos's room for visitors.

"Fern said you wanted to see us," Julia said.

Not *now!* M.K. thought. She was winning!

"Where's Menno?" Amos said.

"He and Uncle Hank are out bear hunting," Sadie said. "Uncle Hank thinks he's got the bear's whereabouts figured out. Between the Smuckers' and the Stoltzfuses' farm." She sat back in the chair. "Of course, Uncle Hank has thought that for days now."

"And he's always wrong," M.K. added, jumping two of Amos's checkers.

Amos frowned at her. "He's doing his best." He picked up his checker and jumped one of hers.

Surprised, M.K. studied the board. "It's no secret that Uncle Hank is a terrible hunter. Even Stern Fern has a better shot."

Just as Amos opened his mouth to defend Uncle Hank, Julia interceded. "Speaking of Fern, she said you had something important to talk to us about."

Amos leaned his back against the headboard. "I'm going to sell off the orchards. I can get big money for that acreage. Enough to put a dent in these hospital bills."

Julia slapped her forehead, gave it a real crack. "So that's it. Well, you can just forget it. We'll find a way to pay down that debt, Dad. The church will help us—you know they will."

"Everyone's suffering after this drought. I can't expect them to pay what they don't have. They've already helped us—above and beyond."

"We can get along without selling off the orchards." Julia's chin lifted a notch. "We always have."

"I'll keep the house for all of you, so you'll always have a home, free and clear. I don't want to leave behind any doubts or debts. And I'll keep a few acres surrounding it, for a garden and pastureland for Menno's livestock."

"Just who do you think you'll sell it to?" Julia asked, firing up. "What if one of our neighbors can't afford to buy it and you end up selling to a developer? Why, they'll bulldoze everything right up to the house. And they'll stick in as many houses as they can fit in. You've seen what it looks like. No yards. Just house after house after house."

"I've made up my mind," Amos said, very dignified. "And you know what my mind is like when I've made it up."

Boy, that upset Julia.

It got quiet then, very quick, while M.K. and Sadie waited to see what Julia had to say to that. It was like watching a Ping-Pong game.

Fern walked in with a stack of fresh laundry. She set the stack down on the bureau top before she turned to Amos. "Just because the boat rocks doesn't mean it's time to jump overboard." Then she left.

15

After supper, Julia and Menno went out to check on the animals and lock the barn. She sent Menno back to the house, and tousled his hair when he gave her a puzzled look. "You go in. M.K. is waiting for you to help her with a puzzle. I'll be in soon."

"But . . . the bear," Menno said. "Dad said not to go out at night by ourselves. He won't even let Lulu out."

She smiled. "I won't be out that long. I promise."

She walked down the drive to the roadside stand. The last few hours had been so emotionally churning, she had forgotten to close up the stand for the day. The honor jar was still there, plus the day's produce that hadn't sold. As she walked, she mulled over the conversation her father had with them. She knew that he was settling his accounts, preparing all of them for his passing. He was trying to solve all of the tangible problems his absence would create—but what about those intangible problems? What about M.K. needing a parent in a role that a sister couldn't fulfill? And how would Sadie cope? She was so tenderhearted and sensitive. If her father sold most of the land surrounding the house—and maybe that was the right thing to do, maybe not—what would Menno do without a farm? What would he do without a father to guide him each day? What would any of them do without their father? He was their anchor.

No, that wasn't right. God alone was their anchor, she reminded herself. God's ways were good and just. If he took their father home now, he must have a good reason.

But what?

She had prayed so often for God to heal her father. She believed in prayer. Prayer worked. Lately, she had prayed and prayed and prayed as she had never prayed before. She prayed one large circular prayer beginning with "Lord, thy will be done" and ending with "Please, God, please, please, please, don't let my dad die."

But God seemed to be saying no.

She reached the stand and saw the honor jar was gone. The produce was gone. She had *thought* she had heard a car door slam during dinner. Someone had driven by and taken it all. It wasn't the amount—maybe twenty or thirty dollars—but it was the last straw on a bad day. Self-pity, which had been buzzing around her all afternoon, settled in. She looked up at the sky. "It's not fair!" she said to herself, eyes filling with tears. "It's just not fair!"

"What isn't fair?"

She whirled around to find Rome watching her, a curious look on his face. "What do you mean, sneaking up on me like that?"

"I wasn't sneaking." He took a step closer to her. "So what's not fair?"

"Everything!"

"Like what, exactly?"

"Like . . . my father wants to sell the land to pay off his

hospital bills because he's sure his heart is wearing out on him. And he's probably right!"

"That's why I keep encouraging him to get on the heart transplant list."

"He won't do it. I've tried."

"We have to try harder."

"This is between my father and God. A heart transplant is no simple thing. I don't know how I would feel if I were in his shoes." She crossed her arms against her chest. "Do you?"

"I would fight to live, that's what I'd do. I can't understand why Amos won't fight for all of you. He has a chance—but without that transplant, he's going to die."

"Stop it!" Julia lifted her hands and held them over her ears to shut out the words. She stood frozen, her spine rigid, her hands clamped to her ears. Tears coursed down her cheeks.

Rome wrapped her stiff body in his arms and began stroking her back and shushing her. "There, now, it's all right. I'm sorry I made you cry. Last thing I want is to hurt you. There, now, everything's going to be all right."

Gradually the tension ebbed from her body, and for a moment she sagged against him. He was so solid. So safe.

Safe? The thought made her jerk away. She drew back her shoulders and stood back, despite the tears she couldn't quite stop shedding. "I have to go." She turned her back to him and began to walk toward the house.

"Julia, wait!"

She turned back. Rome reached down and picked up a basket. In it was the honor jar, filled with money, and the day's unsold produce. "I saw you hadn't closed up for the night. I was bringing it up to the house when I noticed a fence board had fallen over there, so I stopped to nail it."

He handed her the basket. "Everything's going to turn out all right, Julia."

It was a nice thought, but Amos wasn't Rome's father, and Windmill Farm wasn't his home. Still, he was trying to be reassuring and Julia did appreciate the sentiment. Something caught her eye and she looked in the basket to see a handful of fives, tens, and twenties stuffed in the honor jar. So much money for one day! The most she had ever made. And here she thought it had been stolen.

Impulsively, she leaned over and pecked a kiss on Rome's cheek. Her action surprised them both. She felt her breath catch as Rome turned to look at her more fully. In the fading evening light, his dark eyes seemed black and serious and compelling.

"Hi, guys!" M.K. pranced up. "What are you two doing all alone out here?"

M.K. ran ahead of Rome and Julia to the house. It was close to lightning-bug time, and Uncle Hank said he might have a yarn or two to spin. When Uncle Hank was in a storytelling mood, you didn't want to miss a minute of it. She told Rome and Julia to hurry, but they didn't seem as eager to get to the house as she thought they'd be. Uncle Hank and her father were sitting on the front porch, in rockers that Menno had brought out, like two dotty old men. She'd never thought they resembled each other, but the thinner her father became, the more he looked like Uncle Hank. The thought made her sad.

"THERE YOU ARE, MARY KATE!" Uncle Hank thundered. "I can't start my story without you!"

She sat on the steps with her back against the railing. Sadie sat next to her, and Menno jumped up to sit on the porch rail. Rome sprawled out on the grass, below the steps, where Lulu found him and covered his face with licks. Julia found a place next to Sadie, who had Lulu's pup in her lap. Tonight, even Fern was joining them. She brought an upright chair from the kitchen out on the porch and sat in it like she was at church. "Shoulders," she tossed in Sadie's and M.K.'s direction, and Sadie immediately straightened her back.

Uncle Hank leaned back in the chair, feet spread apart, his head tilted up toward the ceiling, an indication that he was ready to begin. "It was the winter of '58," he started. "I was just a lad, not much bigger than our Mary Kate." He looked down at her when he said that and she smiled. He always began his stories in the same way.

"There had been sightings of a large white buck that winter. Ten points on his antlers! It had become something of a legend. Folks weren't entirely sure if that buck had been made up or if it was a real thing. Lots of speculation was going on about the big white buck that winter.

"Sure enough, one day, that buck passed the schoolhouse, and a farmer was on his tail. The farmer opened the schoolhouse door and called out for all hands to join in a grand hunt. We had a man teacher and, knowing his boys and what would happen, he put his back to the door to keep us boys from fleeing. No sooner had he done it than up went three windows and out poured a live stream of boys. There wasn't a boy left to chew gum. Finally, the teacher followed." He winked at M.K. "He was too timid a fellow to stay alone with the girls."

Menno rolled that over in his mind for a moment and let out a loud "Haw!"

Uncle Hank leaned back in his chair and crossed one big boot over the other. "The deer took off across a field and onto the lake, covered with ice. The deer slipped and one of the big boys—Mose Weaver—came very near to overtaking it. But just as he reached out to touch it . . ." Uncle Hank reached a hand out in the air as if he was trying to touch the buck ". . . the deer found its footing and set off again. Quick as a wink, the deer was on the north shore of the lake. We boys kept our sight on the deer and lit out after it.

"After a long hunt I found the deer in some brush, and gave vent to my gentle voice," to which M.K. snorted and Uncle Hank nudged her with his boot, "and out it ran, well rested and as good as ever. By this time two of the boys had run home and returned with guns. As the deer passed within a few feet of them, they just stood in awe of this magnificent beast. Neither took a shot at it until it was well hidden in the thick bushes. Each blamed the other for not shooting the deer."

"Did anyone ever get that deer?" Menno asked.

"Alas, Menno, none of us tasted venison from that hunt."

"What ever happened to the buck?" M.K. asked.

"What became of the deer I never knew, but that winter, we were all seriously afflicted with buck fever, something only time and experience will cure."

Fern gave a guffaw. "Hasn't done much to cure you. You've got yourself a serious case of bear fever. You spend half your time trying to track that bear and cub!"

Uncle Hank looked offended. "That bear is going to hurt somebody soon. She's getting bolder and bolder. Came right up to old Fannie King's kitchen door last week. Scared Fannie so bad she dropped her choppers!"

Sadie gasped. It didn't take much to scare Sadie, but even M.K. felt a tingle down her spine.

"Uncle Hank!" Amos said. A warning passed between the two. They all noticed. Well, maybe not Menno.

That bear and cub were starting to get everyone edgy. It was the top news of every gathering—who had seen them last, what damage they had caused, how crafty that mama bear was, if it was time to call the game warden in. Sadie shivered, though the night was hot.

Uncle Hank eased up out of his chair, stretched, and yawned. "It is a well-known fact that a buck's tail is not very long, but this one will be an exception unless I come to a close."

It had sprinkled a little in the morning, but now the clouds had broken up and the August sun was bearing down. Julia found Rome out in the pasture where Menno kept his small flock of ewes. She called to him and he waited for her at the top of the meadow. Before she reached him, he wiped the perspiration from his cheeks with his sleeve. He was pushing a small cart filled with clover hay. Menno's ewes had crowded around the cart, trying to snatch hay, and made it difficult for him to move. As she walked toward him, the ewes looked up, regarded her with their sweet, blank faces, and then went back to the serious business of eating. She shaded her eyes from the late-afternoon sun.

When she reached him, she held out a napkin with fresh hot doughnuts on it. "Fern made these for you. She thought Dad and Sadie's diet might be wearing thin on you." They had all lost weight this summer, all but M.K. and Menno, for whom Fern relaxed kitchen rules.

He pulled off his gloves and threw them on top of the hay. He took the napkin from her, lifted it, and breathed deeply. "I could smell those doughnuts frying way out here." He took a bite and closed his eyes. "Takes me right back to my boyhood."

"You haven't mentioned your family. Where did you grow up?" She found herself often wondering about Rome and wasn't about to let this opportunity pass.

He broke off a section of his doughnut. "Here and there." He popped the last bite of doughnut in his mouth and reached for his gloves. He broke open a dense clump of hay, releasing a sudden scent of white clover. He scattered the hay over the ground, so the ewes would leave the cart alone.

"Rome, what would you think about staying a few extra months this fall to help us get through the harvest? Menno does well when he has someone working with him. If you could stay through October—work with Menno on the hay cuttings, supervise the threshing frolics, help us get the corn into the silo." She paused. "The truth is, having you here has brought a peace of mind to my father."

"It's about time for a change of scene soon." He grinned at her. "There's roaming in my blood."

Julia couldn't imagine such a thought. She looked out over the fenced fields, the cows clumped together under a shade tree, a creek that wound its way through the pastures to nourish the land. In the sky, high overhead, she could see the arrows of a flock of geese heading toward the lake. "A home like this—it seems to me that you couldn't find a better place to be than right here. The earth here is generous and outgoing, like the people in Stoney Ridge. It's a place that keeps you anchored to life." She turned and found him staring at her. "But maybe you don't want to be anchored." She hadn't posed it as a question, but she waited for an answer all the same. The emotions that played over his face ranged from sadness to coldness, then settled into something that looked like discomfort.

"Would you at least consider staying through October for my father's sake?"

The rascal returned to his eyes. "What about for your sake, Julia?"

"What about me?"

He gave her a sly grin. "Do you want me to stay?"

"I wouldn't be asking if I didn't think you provided a benefit to my family."

He threw the last of the hay onto the ground. Then he pulled off his gloves and turned to her. "So you want me to stay. Just admit it."

She could feel bright red patches burning in her cheeks. "I'm only admitting that your presence provides peace of mind to my father. That's all."

His gaze slipped from her eyes to her lips. "So you don't really care if I stay or leave?"

"No. I'm only asking for my father's sake."

He stepped closer to her and brushed her cheek with his knuckles. "So this doesn't make you feel anything?" His voice was deep and teasing.

She drew up her chin and met his gaze. She thought about stepping back but decided she should hold her ground. Even the smallest retreat would show weakness, and she wouldn't reveal any vulnerability. At the same time, his nearness made her head swim.

"And this?"

Slowly, Rome lifted his thumb and slid it upward along the curve of her jaw. His touch was surprisingly gentle. She knew she should pull back, she wanted to break away, but her legs wouldn't obey.

As she gazed up into that chiseled face, she tried to remember every grievance she held against the Bee Man. But as he lowered his head and his lips found hers, her reasoning was blotted out. One of Rome's arms slipped around her back, then another around her head. She found herself falling into the kiss. Seconds, minutes, hours later, Rome pulled away. His forehead rested on hers.

"Still nothing?" he whispered.

His kiss was gentle and persuading, sweet and tender, nothing at all like Paul's pleasant kisses.

Paul. PAUL. She sprang back. "Not a thing," she said coolly, trying to not appear as shaken as she felt. She pushed past him to leave.

"Julia, where are you going?"

"Back to the house," she called out without turning around.

"Then you're headed in the wrong direction."

Rome chuckled softly. Julia's small figure was strangely dignified as she walked away from him.

Until that moment, Rome had never seen a woman blush on top of a blush, but Julia managed it when he pointed out she was starting out to the house in the wrong direction. He had to bite on his bottom lip to keep from laughing out loud.

It was mean, he supposed, what he had done to her. Kissing her like that, in broad daylight. It's just that she looked so adorable, standing there with confectioner's sugar on her cheek. She was warm in his arms, and she smelled like a doughnut.

What he couldn't get out of his mind was that she kissed him back! Never in his wildest imagination would he have thought that prim and proper Julia Lapp would have kissed him back, with that much passion. And when she couldn't meet his gaze, he knew she was embarrassed.

Just look at me, he thought, *like some moonstruck teenager.* Roman Troyer, the Bee Man, Roamin' Roman, acting like an adolescent. He felt as if he were eighteen again, young and hopeful and naive, believing that anything was possible.

Julia had done him a favor, asking him to stay, making it seem like it was her idea. He'd already decided he was going to stick around a few more months. He felt a burden to help Amos get through this heart business. To help the whole family get through it. But how long would he stay? Would he still be here through Thanksgiving? Through Christmas? He hoped he might, and it was a strange feeling.

He shook his head and let out a long sigh. Where were those thoughts coming from? He hadn't felt this way last year, had he? Or the year before that?

Before Julia interrupted him, his thoughts had been traveling to another Thanksgiving, years ago, when his mother burned the turkey. And then he remembered the year when his youngest sister had tripped over a dog bone as she was bringing the turkey to the table and sent it flying into his father's lap. Oh, the surprised look on his father's face! The memory made him laugh out loud. But, as always, a sharp tug of pain swept in right behind it. He swallowed hard, banishing the images of the past as he tried to concentrate on feeding the sheep.

When memories of those days popped up in his mind, the images were still as crisp as a new dollar bill. Why were those thoughts hitting him so squarely in the jaw this year? Was it part of turning twenty-five? Feeling older?

He drew in a long breath, inhaling the woodsy scent laced with a clover hay fragrance. He leaned against the wagon and pulled out of his pocket an envelope. He reread the letter that he had picked up this morning at the post office.

Dear Roman,

Suffice it to say, I am someone who has made mistakes, and in buying the property, I am trying to remedy them. You may think I intend to raze the farm and build homes, or condominiums, or a strip center of shops, or an industrial park. Although that would be most lucrative, that's not what I will do. You have my promise. I want to keep the farm as it is.

Don't be a fool, Rome. Take the money.

R.W.

16

Julia awoke in the morning thinking of that kiss with Rome. The question she'd been trying to avoid asking felt like a fist in her stomach. How could she have let him kiss her like that? Then she remembered the way it felt—natural and wonderful. Yet what had she been thinking? Maybe there was something wrong with her.

Julia had no illusions about why Rome had kissed her. By acting immune to his charms, she'd turned herself into a challenge—a challenge he'd forget about the instant one of the local beauties caught his eye.

Yes, the kiss was quite . . . memorable. The only other man she had kissed was Paul, and his kisses were rather staid and formal. Avuncular, almost.

Rome's kiss wasn't like a relative's kiss, not at all. That kiss with Rome . . . she couldn't bear to think of it, of what he made her feel.

She could never deny that Rome was an attractive man, because he was. She also could not deny that he could be a caring, giving man—if he ever truly learned to love someone other than his bees.

Besides, her heart belonged to Paul. Was it wrong to let

Rome kiss her? A twinge of guilt washed over her, but she decided to dismiss it. And she didn't kiss Rome—he kissed her! She was only indulging him. Just a whim. Flushing it out of her system. She had to forget what had happened and keep her wits about her. It would never happen again. Never. It was a terrific mistake. Never again!

Determined not to spend any more time analyzing that kiss, she jumped out of bed. Today was a new day. No ruthless man with dark eyes, no kiss she couldn't explain.

<hr />

Amos smelled something delicious waft up the stairs and into his room. Fern's rich coffee, fried eggs, home fries seasoned only as she could do. Amos savored the savory smells. They were downright intoxicating. When had he last felt like he had an appetite? He couldn't remember.

Was that bacon? Better still, could it be scrapple? Menno must have asked her to cook for him. Fern indulged him. Just the thought of a bite of fried scrapple, slathered in ketchup, filled him with a spurt of energy to go downstairs. He slipped his feet onto the floor and pulled himself to a standing position. There. Step one.

Slowly, he tiptoed to the top of the stairs and waited until he heard Fern go out the kitchen door to hang a load of laundry. He was glad he hadn't gotten around to oiling that rusty hinge, after all. He went down the stairs, into the kitchen, and looked for the crispiest piece of scrapple there was, cooling on a paper towel. He slathered it with ketchup and was just about to take a bite when he saw Fern heading in from the yard. He scurried to the stairs and tried to get to his room as fast as he could, which wasn't too swift.

Back in his room, he sat on the bed trying to catch his breath and suddenly felt an enormous pressure on his chest, like it did when he and Menno used to wrestle and Menno would sit on him. He was faintly aware that the muscles in his left arm were beginning to constrict. His hand couldn't hold on to the scrapple and it fell to the floor, ketchup side down. Blast! He had worked hard for that scrapple.

Amos bent down to pick it up. That's when the room started to spin.

⬩⬩⬩

Julia laid the table with silverware. Fern was frying scrapple and two eggs apiece for all of them, like it was Christmas morning.

Uncle Hank burst into the kitchen and sat down at the table. "I came for your coffee, Fern!"

Fern raised an eyebrow and brought him a cup.

He took a long sip and smacked his lips. "That coffee is so rich and sturdy it could float a nail!"

Julia sized up Uncle Hank. His hair and beard were trimmed and his clothes looked clean. He was transformed! Menno stood by the kitchen stove with a mug of tea in his hand, giving Fern suggestions about how to make bread toasted just the way he liked it—nearly burnt but not quite. That was the longest speech that Julia ever heard come out of her brother's mouth. What was happening to him? To Uncle Hank? Even M.K. was chirpier than usual this morning. They all seemed changed, overnight. It was Fern's doings.

Fern sent M.K. upstairs to tell her father to stop ringing that bell incessantly because breakfast was on its way. M.K. was no sooner there than she was back again. She shot into the kitchen like a pack of hounds was on her tail. Her mouth was stretched in a wordless scream, and she was gray-faced.

She grabbed the edge of the table, then fetched up a breath and howled out, "Come quick! It's Dad! He's dead!"

On the way to the hospital in the ambulance, Amos heard the medic declare, in a voice that sounded distant, that he could not find a pulse. Why was he saying that? Amos wondered.

In the emergency room he heard a nurse say, "No pulse, no pressure." Twice, she said it. He also remembered being told, by a calm, soothing, yet authoritative voice, that it wasn't time yet for him to die.

Later, when he woke up in the intensive care room, Amos was told what had happened. He had collapsed, right on the bedroom floor, a bell in one hand, a piece of scrapple in the other. Caught red-handed!

All that Amos remembered was feeling pressure in his chest, a squeezing, as though his heart were a balloon about to burst. The E.R. doctor was able to revive him, but just barely, he was sternly told. "Next time, you won't be so lucky," the doctor warned. "Your heart is at war with itself. Your final defense is a transplant . . . or it is a war you will lose, Amos Lapp."

The doctor looked like a boy himself.

Amos asked the doctor if he had been the one who told him in the emergency room that he was not going to die. The doctor looked baffled. He replied that he hadn't, nor did he recall anyone else in the room saying such a thing.

Then the doctor gave a broad grin. "Aren't you Amish the God-fearing type? Maybe it was an angel with a message from God." He leaned in close to Amos. "Maybe God is trying to tell you: AMOS LAPP! Get. Your. Name. On. The. Transplant. List."

Amos scowled. He knew the doctor was being facetious— but, he decided, strangely enough, he might be on to something. It wasn't a human-sounding voice. It was too deep, too melodious, too beautiful. Suddenly, Amos had no reservations or doubts about its claim. He believed that voice was from God. Maybe an angel, a messenger, but definitely sent from God.

Julia had told Rome once that he had a smile for every occasion, and he reluctantly realized . . . she was right. He was giving the nurse at the Intensive Care Unit his "Aw, shucks. You-don't-mind-doing-a-little-favor-for-me, do-you?" treatment.

"Ordinarily, only family members are allowed in," the nurse said. She batted her eyes at him with such alarming speed that Rome was afraid she'd blind herself. "But seeing as how all of you Amish folk seem to be related to each other, I'll just say you're a cousin if anyone asks." She gave him a wink.

"Well, thank you, Miss . . . ," Rome cast a quick glance at her nameplate, "Miss Chelsea."

The nurse led him to Amos's room. "Just fifteen minutes, though. Okay, honey?"

He smiled again and the nurse smiled back at him, touching the curls on the back of her neck. The smile slipped off his face as the nurse disappeared around the corner, her white rubber shoes making a squeaky sound as she walked down the hall. He felt a twinge of remorse—the first time he could ever remember such a feeling. Julia had him pegged. He was a flirt. A shameless flirt.

Rome pushed the door to Amos's room and gasped when he saw him, lying in the hospital bed with tubes attached to his nose, one to his arm, blinking machines that let out beeps every few seconds. He saw Amos's beloved Bible grasped in his hands and forced a smile. "Have time for a visit?"

Amos looked over at him. "Well, well, the Bee Man. I can't think of anybody I'd rather see right now." His voice was weak and raspy, but he managed a thin smile.

Rome sat down on a chair across from Amos and stretched out his long legs. "Amos, I only have fifteen minutes and there's something I need to tell you."

"Shoot."

"I spoke to the heart transplant coordinator over at Hershey Medical about what needs to happen to get a person on the list."

Amos stilled and looked away.

"Not that I would interfere in any way—"

"What would you call it then?" Amos asked gruffly.

Rome put up a hand. He wished he weren't sitting below Amos on the chair, like a child. "Hear me out. Julia has told me why you won't consider a transplant."

Amos's gaze shifted to the window.

Rome drew in a long breath. "You've always been willing to give someone a chance. Would you at least listen to what I have to say on the subject?"

Amos turned back to Rome. "Speak your piece."

"Julia said you didn't feel you could accept the heart of another person, knowing he had sacrificed his life for you. But Amos, I think you've got it all wrong. There are parallels between the gift of a donor and that of Christ's gift of eternal life. Your new heart will be given unconditionally, with no strings attached, and without compensation. Free, but it comes at a high price. It requires a great loss be inflicted on the donor. Like Christ's sacrifice for us."

Rome reached over and took Amos's Bible out of his hands. He turned it to Ezekiel 36:26 and read aloud: "'A new heart also will I give you, and a new spirit will I put within you: and I will take away the stony heart out of your flesh, and I will give you a heart of flesh.' That verse is for you, Amos. God is in the business of giving out new hearts. New life." He paused to see how Amos was responding, but Amos had closed his eyes. He waited a moment and then, discouraged, decided Amos had fallen asleep. He left the Bible open to Ezekiel and placed it next to Amos on the bed.

Amos opened his eyes. "Rome, you can tell that boy doctor to put me on the list." Then he closed his eyes again.

Rome heard a sniffling sound and looked up. At the door was Julia. He walked over to her, and for an instant they were looking straight at each other, everything between them falling away. He reached up and touched one large hand lightly against her cheek. She pressed it with her own hand, tears in her eyes.

"Thank you," she whispered.

--------◦◦◦◦--------

Amos was discharged by the end of that week, sent home with a beeper that had to be with him at all times. "When a compatible heart is harvested, the transplant coordinator will beep you. You get to Hershey Medical immediately!" the doctor had told him. "Whatever you need to do—taxi, racehorse, or call 911. You just get yourself in there, Amos Lapp."

Harvested. The very word made Amos shudder. It wasn't a crop; it was a human being. A heart.

Still, he felt a confidence that proceeding forward to have a heart transplant was the right thing to do, a conviction that God was guiding him in this direction.

For now, though, he would have to wait. For someone to die so that he could live.

"We need to get prepared," Rome told Julia on the evening after Amos was discharged from the hospital. "To think of some ways to raise money for the heart transplant. Maybe get some folks to help us have a fundraising auction."

It amazed Julia to hear Rome use the pronoun "we." She didn't think it was a part of his vocabulary. I, me, myself, mine. But never "we." Was it possible Roman Troyer was starting to grow attached to people? To care about them? "Do you really think it will happen soon?"

"When the multitudes needed to be fed, Jesus gave them food. When the disciples needed to pay their taxes, he provided a coin. When the time is right for Amos to get a heart, God will provide." Rome pulled out a pen and started jotting things down on a sheet of scrap paper. "So let's do our part and get ready, so we're prepared when God brings your father that heart."

"Julia can quilt," Fern said quietly.

Julia stared at Fern.

"You could make another quilt like that one you made last year that went for such a big pile of cash," Fern said.

"Dad loved that quilt best," M.K. volunteered after slipping into the room.

"How did you know about that quilt?" Julia asked Fern.

"Hank wrote about it in the *Budget*," Fern said. "Fetched big bucks, he said. People called it a Julia Lapp original."

Uncle Hank! Julia's mouth set in a firm line. He hadn't mentioned to them that he wrote about the quilt in his weekly letter. Talk about stoking Edith Fisher's fire.

"You can make another one," Fern said. "Just like that one."

Julia shook her head. "I can't."

"Why not?" Rome asked. "I haven't seen you design a quilt all summer. What's made you stop?"

M.K. sidled up next to Rome. "On account of Edith Fisher," she whispered.

"Mary Kate!" Julia said. "That's family business!"

"Rome's practically family," M.K. said. "So is Fern." She turned to Rome. "Edith Fisher told folks that Julia was becoming prideful after her quilt brought in so much money. And then just after that, Paul postponed the engagement for the first time. So Julia stopped making quilt tops."

Fern huffed. "Edith Fisher has an opinion about every subject and gives it unsolicited."

The conversation about raising money started M.K. brainstorming dozens of ways to raise cash—most of them had to do with other people: Fern could whip up doughnuts and sell them at the fork in the road where construction workers gathered to be picked up by their crew each morning. Menno could double his birdhouse output and sell them door-to-door. M.K. even offered to stay home with Amos during church in the morning to think up more ideas, but Fern waved her off like she would a pesky fly.

"You need church more than most," Fern told M.K.

Julia moved toward the open door that led from the kitchen to the side porch. It was dark and quiet outside, and she could smell jasmine in the night breeze. She loved it all so much. The trees and brooks, the sights and smells. Best of all, she loved watching the moon cast its shadow over the farm.

Rome joined her. They stood silently for a long while, listening to the rustle of the wind as it made the dried corn tassles dance in the fields. Even under her father's efficient management, Windmill Farm hadn't looked this good. The fences that stretched around the paddocks had been repaired and whitewashed. The broken arm of the windmill had been fixed. Everything about the farm looked well tended and prosperous. It was because of Rome. There wasn't anything he couldn't do. He had taken Menno alongside him and worked steadily through Julia's expansive to-do list.

"Fern's right," he said. "You shouldn't let someone else steal your joy in making something you're good at."

"Edith Fisher had a point," Julia said. "I was proud, after winning that ribbon and raising so much money. I love quilt making, but it can become an idol to me. It was best to put it aside for a season."

Rome looked at her in surprise. "But the quilt was auctioned away for a good purpose."

She gave a half shrug. "Even something we love to do can become an idol. I was neglecting my friends and family just so I could create a quilt. I was always preoccupied, thinking about designing my next quilt top. When Dad took sick and needed so much of my attention, it made me realize how selfish I had become."

"You could never be selfish," he said softly.

Julia saw in Rome's eyes something new, something of joy, even hope. Just a flicker. And then it was gone.

After Rome left to go to his cottage, Julia turned off the gas lamps in the living room to get ready to go upstairs to bed. She turned in a slow circle, taking in every inch of this oh-so-familiar room until she faced the trunk that butted against the wall, holding her mother's quilts.

She set the lamp on the bookshelf and knelt on the floor to open the trunk. The soothing smell of cedar chips drifted up as she pushed the lid against the wall. The tissue paper that wrapped the quilts crackled as Julia lifted one, then another. There was a small blue-and-white Nine-Patch crib quilt that had covered each of Maggie Lapp's babies. Below it was a Log Cabin pattern, made of cobalt and yellow, one her mother had made for Menno when he turned ten. Her hand brushed the vibrant colors, neatly stitched with the three-strand thread that her mother had insisted on. She had said the thread reminded her of the Holy Trinity, holding the world together, just the way thread held a quilt together. It was the last quilt her mother had made. Would Menno remember?

Almost every afternoon of Julia's childhood was spent sitting on the floor next to her mother while she sat sewing at her quilt frame or tracing around templates for quilt blocks. When it came to quilt-making, Maggie Lapp's quilts stood out. She said her quilts were designed to wrap a person with the warmth of loving arms, as healing as homemade chicken soup. She had more orders than she could handle and was often weeks behind in her work, but she always had time for her family—to listen to them natter away about school, teachers, friends, animals, crops, anything that might be weighing on their minds. And the thing was, she didn't just pretend to listen while slipping her needle through the fabric, making tiny, even stitches. She truly listened. She made everyone feel important.

Why, that's where Sadie got that quality, Julia realized.

She wrapped Menno's quilt up carefully, wondering when it might be used. Was he serious about Annie? Was she serious about him? What would her mother say about Menno having a girlfriend? Julia used to try to cobble together conversations she would have with her mother, but the older she became, the less she felt she knew her mother. She had known her as a child, but not as a woman. What would Maggie have said about Edith Fisher—accusing Julia of being prideful over her quilts? What would she say about Rome's idea to raise money to help her husband with a heart transplant? Julia really had no idea.

She startled when she heard a sound behind her. There was Fern, standing against the doorjamb in her usual way, arms crossed against her chest. "My father had a saying: 'Burying your talents is a grave mistake.'"

Julia looked down at Menno's quilt in her lap.

Fern walked up to Julia. "In the Bible, Jesus tells a story about a king who gave his servants some talents and told them to use them in his absence. He gave five talents to one servant, three to another, one to the last servant. When he returned, he wanted to know how they had used their talents. The five talent fellow had doubled his talents. So did the three talent fellow. But one servant—he buried it." Fern put a hand on Julia's head. "God has given you a good gift and you have an opportunity to give God back a gift. But not if you bury it."

"But . . . Edith Fisher—"

"Edith Fisher is not the king returning to ask the servants

about their talents." She bent at the waist and cupped Julia's face in her hands. "You are to answer to God for your life." She turned and left Julia alone.

As Julia sat in the dimly lit room, a frightening—almost exhilarating—sense of purpose came over her. She placed Menno's quilt back into the trunk and gently closed it. She opened the bottom drawer of the corner hutch and plunged her hand beneath a pile of seldom-used linens to pluck out her hidden journal. In it were pages and pages of quilt top ideas, waiting. Just waiting. Waiting for the right design, the right fabrics, the right moment. She slipped the journal into her apron pocket, picked up the lamp, and hurried up the stairs to her room. Maybe the right moment was now.

17

Contrary to popular belief, Julia did very few things in her life with extreme self-confidence, but designing a quilt top had always been one of them. Her mother used to tell her she had a gift for design and construction, the ability to create the most beautiful and intricate quilts imaginable. And now that she'd started designing again, she felt ideas pouring out of her. They were flooding her brain so fast she didn't have time to get them down on paper. Something special happened as she put swatches of fabric against each other, something instinctive. She tackled the quilt top with a surety of purpose, led by an inner prompting.

Everyone honored Julia's request to stay out of the dining room and let her work without interruption or well-meaning suggestions. She started a few patches as trial pieces, just to see how the colors interacted. She laid them out on the dining room table. She stood back to observe her work and ended up throwing them away. She had to start over. They were good, but not good enough.

It was hard. Time was growing short. The fundraising auction Rome had organized was only two weeks away. He was working so hard on it. She wiped a bead of sweat from her forehead. She felt hot, nauseated, and more than a little panicked. What if she couldn't create something special? What if she created the quilt top but couldn't get it quilted in time? What if it didn't raise as much money as last year's quilt? So much to worry about! But she wouldn't think about all that now. She had to stay focused.

This quilt was for her father's new heart—it had to be her best work.

———— ❖ ————

Sadie kept nudging Menno to finish up his breakfast. Julia had scheduled the grand unveiling of the quilt top this morning, and Sadie couldn't wait to see what this quilt looked like. She felt more nervous than a long-tailed cat in a room full of rocking chairs. Finally, Menno swallowed his last spoonful of oatmeal and Sadie jumped up from the table.

"Now, Jules?"

Julia took a deep breath. "Now."

Julia had been working on this quilt fourteen hours a day for the last ten days. She'd barely been seen. She had put up sheets to block off the living room so no one could even peek at the work in progress. Now and then she would emerge to send someone off to the fabric store in town for more thread or a certain color of fabric.

Finally, the moment had come. M.K. ran to the room, with Sadie right on her heels, then Fern and Rome and Menno. M.K., barely able to contain herself, grabbed the sheet and looked for a nod from Julia, then pulled the sheet off.

It was the most exquisite thing Sadie had ever seen: the Lone Star—a common Lancaster pattern—set into bright turquoise blue. Julia had sewn such tiny points together that they almost blurred together like a child's kaleidoscope. Bold colors, ones that normally would never be thought to lie next to each other, came together to provide incredible depth. A two-inch border of simple but tiny nine-patch pieces rimmed the star. The tiny squares—made up from the very fabrics that she had sent M.K. and Menno off to the store with crayons and orders to match that specific color—blended into each other. Dark green faded softly into light green, reds into pinks. Only the corner patches—made up of boldly contrasting colors—jolted one's eyes back into focus. The quilt top was fastened into a large quilting frame, ready for quilting.

Sadie wasn't the only one who was speechless. She, Fern, Rome, Menno, even M.K. who was rarely without words, walked silently around the table, absorbing the sight.

Julia stood by the living room door. "Someone, please say something."

Rome looked up at her. "Words fail me, Julia. It's . . . overwhelmingly beautiful."

"It's awesome," Menno said, using a word he had picked up from Annie.

M.K. threw her arms around Julia's middle for a hug.

Fern was eyeing the quilt with a critical squint. Finally, she gave Julia a satisfied nod. From Fern, that was high praise.

Julia's eyes filled with tears. She tried to blink them back, but Sadie could see relief flood her face.

"Now, you all need to leave so I can get busy with the quilting."

"That's one thing we can help with," Fern said. "The ladies are coming to quilt today." She pointed out the window to two buggies, jammed full of women, rolling up the driveway to Windmill Farm.

Julia joined her at the window. "How did they . . . how did you know?"

Fern shrugged. "Figured it was about time." She turned to Sadie and M.K. "They're expecting lunch, so you two . . . hop to it."

Sadie was stunned.

M.K. read her mind. "She's letting us in the kitchen!"

Fern whirled around and pointed to M.K. "Only because I've seen your quilt stitches." She frowned. "You might as well use knitting needles. All you're doing today is preparing the food that I've already made. And cleanup." She wagged a finger at the two. "That's all. Nothing more."

Even Sadie couldn't hold back a grin when she saw a slightly worried look dance through Fern's eyes.

* * *

Two days later, on Thursday afternoon, Sadie was self-conscious beyond belief as she sat in the buggy next to Rome. He happened to be driving by as she was walking home from town after helping M.K. and Menno canvas Stoney Ridge with flyers in storefronts that said "Have a Heart for a Heart." She tried to think of something wise, something witty to say to Rome, but her mind was a blank canvas.

Rome pointed to the flyers in her hands. "Did M.K. talk you into working for her?"

"She came up with the idea of talking the *Stoney Ridge Times* into running a story about the fundraiser, so she and Menno went to go find a reporter," Sadie said. "M.K. can talk anybody into just about anything." They'd all been working hard on getting the fundraising auction organized, especially Rome.

He laughed. "You've got a good heart, Sadie. I knew it the moment I set eyes on you when you were just knee high to a grasshopper."

Her capstrings dipped as she shook her head.

"Can I let you in on a secret?"

A little thrill went through her. "What's that?" She realized her heart was racing, even as her mind spun with new possibilities.

He pointed his thumb toward the backseat. Sadie turned to look and saw a number of stacked boxes of Kerr jars. "Not those. The jars are for my honey. The other box." Then she saw what he meant: a large box, covered with a saddle blanket. "It's a new treadle sewing machine."

"You're learning to sew?"

He smiled. "Not hardly. It's for Julia. I've fixed that one she has for the last time. It's so old that belts are snapping and screws are rusting out. If it weren't for the fact that your dad kept a box of old parts, I wouldn't have been able to patch it together as long as I have." He lifted a shoulder in a careless half shrug, but a slightly embarrassed look flickered through his eyes. "This one was on sale at the hardware store. The paint chipped when it shipped, so they gave it to me for a song. I can touch up the paint and it'll be as good as new."

Sadie was stunned. Did Rome have feelings for Julia? The truth burst over her. Had she been so blinded with love for Rome that she hadn't even noticed? She fussed with the apron in her lap as if it were a chick she was trying to calm.

"It's not a big deal," Rome said hurriedly. "I just got tired of trying to keep that thing running." A flush stained his cheeks.

She looked up, then immediately looked down again.

"She'll be thrilled, Rome." She tried to smile, but it came out feeling fake. "Really. It's a wonderful surprise for her."

At supper that evening, Sadie carefully watched Julia and Rome, sitting side by side. They stole little glances at each other, laughed at each other's comments. It was revelatory. It was a moment of clarity, like the sun breaking through the clouds.

Something had passed between them and Sadie had not even seen when it had happened. She felt a sharp, clean slice through her gut. She had held out hope that, some day, Rome would fall in love with her. She knew it was juvenile, but that was how she felt.

Her life was over.

Rome liked his cottage. It was comfortable, with enough furniture to be functional but not enough to crowd him. The bed was large enough to accommodate his tall frame. Next to it was a washstand and across the room were a chest and a bookcase. Once he was at the cottage, his heart started to settle, like a dog by the hearth, like a baby in its crib.

It was strange. He caught a whiff of something—lavender? —that brought Julia to his mind. That woman had gotten under his skin, and it bothered him. It was more than her beauty, there was something sweet and vulnerable about her that unearthed feelings inside him that he hadn't known he possessed. Feelings that made him think differently about his life.

This summer, an unacceptable longing kept piercing his heart. It was for home, an end point. Everyone kept telling him he was not supposed to be constantly in transit. He was supposed to stop somewhere and feel a sense of belonging. Until now, he kept dismissing such unasked-for advice. But pangs of homesickness kept needling him these last few months despite his efforts to push them away.

He leaned his head back. Rome was sometimes struck by images of his Ohio home: opening up the farmhouse, filling it again with family—a wife, four or five or six children, a dog like Lulu. He could practically see this imaginary family of his playing in the yard, bees humming in their hives near the garden just where his mother had kept them.

What if he returned to the farm in Ohio instead of traveling this winter? Was he ready? Was it time?

These were foolish thoughts. What was wrong with him? He pulled off his straw hat and slammed it on the table. Lulu looked up in surprise.

"Don't pay me any never mind, Lulu. I think I'm getting a little touched by too much sun."

The dog stared at him with soulful brown eyes. Idly, he fingered one of her long, silky ears. He trailed his fingers over the dog's back. Rome didn't like admitting it, but he was going to miss Lulu when he left. He was going to miss all of the Lapps.

What was the matter with him lately? Everything in his life had gone off balance, and he didn't know how to straighten it out. He wished he could talk to Julia about his mixed-up feelings, but that would be counterproductive, considering she was the major cause of his confusion. These last few months, Julia had become much more to him than Amos's daughter. She was his friend. She was more than his friend. There was something about Julia that made him feel at home, at rest. She understood him better than anyone else. Also, he didn't want to kiss his friends. And he definitely wanted to kiss her again.

Was it possible? One thought kept hammering at his thick head like a woodpecker, filling him with an odd mixture of excitement and dread. Could it be? Had he let himself get blindsided? *Me? Roamin' Roman? The Bee Man? The solitary bee?* A queer ache settled deep inside and he felt himself start to sweat.

He was falling in love with Julia Lapp.

At first, the realization stunned him, but as he rolled it around in his mind, he found he liked the sound, the thought of it. He liked it very much.

After the auction, he'd tell her. Would she even believe him? He could hardly believe it himself.

He was going to do his best to start over. A new beginning. For the first time in six years, he was going to set aside his refusal to be attached to anyone. He was going to reach out to someone. To a woman. To Julia.

The very idea of it made him feel foolishly happy. For the first time in a long time, Rome felt an excitement about the future.

One by one, Julia sliced the stems of the massive heads of sunflowers that lined the back row of her garden and carefully laid them on a sheet. She would store the flower heads in the greenhouse. Those sunflower seeds would fill Menno's bird feeders this winter.

Julia saw someone out of the corner of her eye, silhouetted by the setting sun. Paul stood there, waiting for her to notice him. "Jules, I need to talk to you."

"Now?"

"Yes," he said.

She studied his face. He was earnest, supplicant, hurting. He was all there, concentrated on her. Tears welled in his beautiful blue eyes.

"This is just awful. This is just, well, it's confusing." He sounded hurt and lost and miserable. "You and me. This wall that's gone up between us."

She closed the pocketknife. "Paul, this is what you wanted. You said you wanted us to take a break."

"I was a fool. I don't want a break any longer." He reached out for her hands and gazed down into her face.

She risked a look at him. His eyes were the clear blue of a cloudless summer day, his hair the pale bronze of sun-steeped tea. He was considered a handsome man by all who knew him. She had known him most of her life, yet she suddenly felt awkward and uncomfortable around him.

"Marry me, Jules. This time for real."

Julia's heart plummeted and skipped at the same time, like a stone skimming the surface of a pond. She had been waiting for months for this moment. This was what she wanted to hear, wasn't it? Why, then, did she feel so stiff, so detached? "What about Lizzie?"

With a gentle tug, Paul pulled Julia closer to him. His gaze swept her face and lingered on her lips. "I've never gotten over you. You know that, don't you? I don't want anybody but you."

But Julia wasn't quite ready. "How do I know you won't want to have another postponement? That you won't find yourself attracted to another girl?"

Paul's voice was urgent. "Because I won't. I promise."

She was surprised at how hope broke open inside her like a radiance, softening her sorrow and anger. She wanted to believe him. She wanted to trust him.

And then she heard him draw in a deep breath, and when he spoke again, his voice was clear and strong. "Jules," he said again, impatient now. "Say yes. Say you'll marry me. It's not too late for things to be made right between us. Remember? How easy it used to be?" He slipped his arms around her waist. "Remember how we would meet up at Blue Lake Pond when our folks sent us on errands into town?"

Julia hadn't been to Blue Lake Pond in a long while. The place had been special to them, it was their spot. It was the place they had always met when they wanted to be alone. The pond lay like a small, glimmering jewel in the center of the world, where it was safely tucked away from the bustle of town life. It had always been her favorite place. Even on the hottest August days, its spring-fed water was clear and cold, and the thick barrier of trees and underbrush acted like a fence around it. The spot was quiet and private, perfect for secret thoughts.

It was where he had first kissed her on her sixteenth birthday. They had first talked about getting married there, and then he had called off the wedding there, claiming he needed more time.

Julia thought back to that day. They met at dusk, like they always did, after their chores on their family farms for that autumn day were done. It was mid-October, just four weeks before the wedding. Paul was waiting for her, leaning against the tree with his hat brim hiding his face. She called to him and he slowly lifted his head, then dropped it again. Julia knew something was wrong the moment she reached him and looked into his eyes. A person's eyes, they could tell you everything. An awful shudder ripped through her. She never imagined anything could hurt that badly.

Six months later, they talked about getting married again, right on that very spot. And then, this April, he called it off again.

Paul's eyes were partially shadowed by the brim of his straw hat, but she could see him looking at her mouth.

She reached up and gently lifted off his hat, noticing as she laid it aside that there was a small red line across the upper part of his forehead from the band. He leaned forward and pressed his mouth to hers. She was glad—she wanted him to kiss her. She needed to prove to herself that Paul could spark those same fires as Rome.

Julia's first thought was that Paul's lips were dry, stiffer than Rome's. This was a pleasant kiss. It was adequate. Her mind got to wandering, and she tried to bring her attention back to what she was doing by raising her arms around Paul's neck. Were his shoulders a little more narrow than she remembered? Were Rome's shoulders a little wider?

Paul pulled back from her, as if he sensed her disappointment. The kiss hadn't proved anything. No sooner had she thought this than she admonished herself: What kind of thinking is that, Julia Lapp? Are you really so shallow as to decide about love based on a kiss? She lifted her eyes to look into his. "So . . . the first of November, then? Just like we had planned?"

There was a speck of silence, a silence so short, so small, so infinitesimal. So profound.

Paul blinked and focused on the fence, his hat brim hiding his face as he slowly shook his head, then squinted up at her again, clearly struggling to say something. A person's eyes—they told you everything.

Paul had finally given her the truth and she recognized it for what it was. Deep down, she had known it all along. Julia knew he would end up calling the wedding off again. Paul didn't want to marry anybody. Not Julia. Not Lizzie. Not anybody.

"I guess I was thinking next year." He licked his lips. "On account of your father and all. I assumed you'd want to wait."

Julia bent her chin to her chest, and Paul—misunderstanding—kissed her forehead. She lifted her head and gave him a long, steady gaze. "I'm sorry," she said softly. "I can't do it. I can't marry you, Paul."

Blinking wide-eyed, Paul looked like an owl caught in a wash of light. "You can't mean that, Jules. I need you."

"Maybe you need someone, but that someone isn't me."

"It is you. You're telling me you don't feel it?"

She felt something. What was it? Delight at seeing him, at hearing him tell her he wanted her. She had a lot of feelings, but she did not mistake any of them for love.

"You're just upset."

She shook her head. "Strangely enough, I'm not upset. For the longest time, I thought the problem between us was me. I thought I just wasn't enough for you, wasn't good enough or pretty enough. Or my family wasn't respectable enough. But the problem wasn't with me, Paul. It's with you. You don't want to grow up. And I do. I deserve something better." She hadn't wanted to humiliate him, but the words were spoken and she wouldn't take them back because they were true.

"I'm sorry," she whispered, backing away. "I'm really sorry."

246

She was filled up with an emotion that was as thick as syrup, an emotion she could only describe as bittersweet. She was so sure she had loved him, so sure he was the only one for her. She had felt such a bright intensity for Paul that it had blinded her. But now, finally, it had burned itself out.

◇

M.K. could hardly believe her eyes! She was running from the barn to the house when something large caught her eye over at the far end of the garden. She stopped in her tracks.

Bear!

Oh, wait! Scratch that. It wasn't a bear. It was two people. She tiptoed behind the greenhouse and squinted her eyes to see who they were. One figure was Julia and the other was a man. Paul! It was Paul. And now . . . Paul was kissing Julia!

M.K. galloped into the house, up the stairs, grabbed her bag of nickels from under her pillow, and ran like the wind down the path that led to Rome's cottage. In record time, she arrived and banged on his front door. When he opened it, she thrust the bag of nickels at him. "Here! You did it, Bee Man! You did what no one else could do. You got Paul and Julia back together!"

Rome looked skeptical. "What are you talking about?"

"I just saw Paul give Julia a serious kissin' in the garden. And she was not objecting!"

The color drained from Rome's face. "What? Are you . . . sure?"

Boys! So dense about matters of the heart! "I saw it with my own two eyes." M.K. was so excited she felt like she might burst apart. "I'm sorry I doubted you!"

He just stood there, a blank look on his face, and she knew

Fern would be wondering where she went to, so she grabbed his hand and slapped the nickel bag in it.

"You earned it, Bee Man. Good work!" She turned and skipped away, so pleased with the turn of events. Suddenly, she stopped and spun around. "Best if we don't say anything about this, though. Let's wait until Julia tells us herself."

And then she was off to the house, the strings on her prayer cap dancing in the dark.

Some days, you would've been better off staying in bed. Rome had opened his eyes that morning to a beautiful autumn day, and spent the day working on an elaborate plan of how to reveal his feelings to Julia. After the family returned from the auction tomorrow, he was going to get Julia in the buggy on some ruse—something forgotten back in town—and whisk her off to Blue Lake Pond in time for the sunset. He had spent most of this afternoon at the Pond, putting clues in place for a treasure hunt. A balloon tied on the hitching tree with instructions to look for two oars. The note on the oars said to find an upturned gray rowboat. The note on the rowboat said to take the oars and row out to the floating dock in the center of the lake. Once there, Julia would find a chocolate fudge cake—her favorite—from the Sweet Tooth bakery that he would have already hidden in a basket on the dock. Earlier today he'd gone into town to pick up the cake and practically choked with embarrassment when he told Nora Stroot, the bakery owner's granddaughter, that he wanted piped icing on the cake to read: Bee Mine.

"Really?" Nora Stroot sniffed, disappointment dripping in her voice. "That's the best you can do?"

Yes, it was. He wasn't good at this expressing-your-feelings stuff.

He had spent hours trying to think of something clever, something heartfelt, something with a hint of romance without going over the top. Then he remembered an anniversary card his father had given to his mother with the Bee Mine tagline. She had loved it. But the disgusted look on Nora Stroot's face fizzled Rome's confidence like a sparkler under a firehose. A portent of things to come. Just a few hours later, M.K. came along with eyewitness information that changed the picture entirely.

That night, Rome lay motionless in the dark, one arm crooked behind his head, staring at the ceiling. So Julia would most likely be marrying Paul Fisher in a few short months. What if Rome had told her he loved her? Would it have made any difference? But he'd never chased after a woman in his life, and not even Julia Lapp could make him start.

Maybe this was a blessing in disguise. The lesson Rome had learned from his family's accident had been a hard one, and he'd never forgotten it. He'd learned that to love meant to open yourself up to excruciating pain. Hard-earned lessons were the best remembered. He gave away books when he finished them, traded mules before he could grow too fond of them, kept on the move before anyone grew dependent on him.

Things could go wrong. So many things could go wrong.

He couldn't sleep, so he got out of bed, grabbed a slice of chocolate fudge cake, and wandered out on the porch. He tried to enjoy the stars, but his heart wasn't in it. This cottage had been a refuge, the place where he could relax. Tonight, it felt too quiet. He gazed out into the darkness with unseeing eyes.

He wasn't used to feeling unsure of himself, so he swallowed the last bite of cake, brushed the crumbs from his hands, went back inside, and headed to bed. As he passed the kitchen table, he noticed the letters Fern had given to him. He picked them up and read through them again. Then he grabbed a sheet of paper and sat down at the table to write.

```
        Dear R.W.,

        I accept your offer.

                Cordially,
                Roman Troyer
```

He stuck the letter into the envelope and licked it shut. Tomorrow, he would mail it. A pending matter, decided.

Now, maybe, he would feel an inner release of all that had been troubling him this summer. He would be free. Of memories, of obligations.

Gradually, the nighttime rasp of crickets and the soft, wheezy cry of a distant barn owl lulled him into a dreamless sleep.

18

The day of the fundraising auction had arrived. Julia could hardly sleep. When she heard the first rooster crow, she got out of bed and dressed, then went downstairs and into the living room. The Lone Star quilt was folded neatly on the sofa. Word had spread about the auction, especially after M.K. had posted flyers up all over town, with the slogan "Have a Heart for a Heart." Every single family in their church district had donated goods or services for the fundraiser. Rome had talked a professional auctioneer into providing his services for free. Julia overheard Rome tell Fern they hoped to raise $10,000 today. Imagine! That could take a dent out of her father's heart transplant bill . . . whenever it might occur.

The Lapp family had their hopes raised last week when Hershey Medical called and told them to get Amos in, that they might have a heart available. But no sooner had they arrived than they were told to go on home. The heart wasn't a match for Amos. Julia didn't understand all of the necessary requirements for a heart transplant, but she did believe in prayer. Prayer worked. She prayed daily that a heart would arrive for her father. Then she prayed for the person whose heart would be given, because she knew that meant his or her time on earth had come to an end.

It felt like an odd prayer.

Main Street was bustling. Julia never expected to see such a turnout for her father's fundraiser. Folks from neighboring towns poured into Stoney Ridge after the newspaper article ran a story on the fundraiser—with a special emphasis on the Amishness of the event. M.K. said the reporter was eager to run the story once he heard that there would be Amish foods and handicrafts. "He said that folks would flock to buy anything if they thought it all came from the Amish," M.K. explained as she read the article aloud last night. "He called it the Amish brand." She looked up at her father. "What's a brand?"

"Today," Amos had said, "we will call it God's goodness."

The auction was held on a closed-off section of downtown Stoney Ridge, right in front of the Sweet Tooth bakery, on a Saturday morning in late September. There were people everywhere: Nora Stroot agreed to let them set up the produce wagon in the parking lot in exchange for a caseload of Rome's honey. A swarm of people surrounded the wagon, buying the last of Windmill Farm's vine-ripened tomatoes, sweet corn, pumpkins, and early apples.

Rome was polite enough to Julia as he helped Menno load the wagon with produce early today to sell at the auction, but she could sense he had raised a wall around him. He was just about to climb in the buggy when he saw she was in the driver's seat. He paused for a moment, mid-climb, then said he'd keep Menno company pulling up the wagon in the rear. As soon as they reached town, Rome vanished.

They had come so far in their friendship. What had

happened? Why was he acting . . . well, to be fair, like he usually did? Detached, pleasantly amused. Had she done something wrong? Had she said something? She reviewed in her mind the last time they were together. Was it only yesterday morning? They had laughed over something M.K. had said—laughed so hard they both had tears running down their faces.

She slumped down in a seat at the wooden picnic table. Only after she was settled did she realize that her position gave her a clear view of Rome standing in the middle of a herd of women. He looked as if he were having the time of his life, laughing and carrying on, obviously enjoying himself. Almost as if he could feel Julia watching, he lifted his head and turned, letting his gaze sweep over her. Their eyes locked, and for a moment neither of them moved. Then he turned his attention back to one of the girls standing at his side.

If Rome wanted to send a message to Julia, loud and clear, he couldn't have found a better way.

Fern joined Julia on the picnic bench and handed her an apple, cut up into slices. Julia took a slice. "You're awful quiet today. Sadie too." Fern took a bite of an apple slice. "Only one who's never quiet is that Mary Kate." It was true that there weren't many quiet moments with M.K. in the vicinity. Julia could hear her voice now, over by the bakery, calling out to Menno to toss her more corn, lickety-split.

They sat in companionable silence until Fern said, "You're not sorry about Paul."

Julia looked at her sharply. How had she known?

"I saw the happy look on his face when he came to the house last night. And I saw how dejected he looked when he left."

So it looked like Fern knew everything anyway, without any need to tell her. Julia gave a nod. "I'm not sorry."

"Because of Rome?" Fern peered at her, sniffing out the truth.

She read Julia's heart situation right. It was one of her talents. "Honestly, I don't know how I feel about Rome," Julia said. "One minute, he acts as if he's in charge of Dad's future. The next minute, he's as skittish as a sheep if you even ask if he's planning to be home for dinner."

Fern's gaze followed Rome as he walked across the lawn. "That's because he doesn't know what he wants out of life."

"He wants what he wants when he wants it. That's what I think about Roman Troyer."

Fern shook her head. "He's struggling. He doesn't know if he should stay or leave."

Julia turned to face Fern. "How do you know so much about Rome?"

Fern's gaze shifted out to Rome as he joined Menno and M.K. and helped lift some bushels of corn to the front of the wagon. Her forehead knitted. "Six years ago, Rome's family was headed to a wedding. Rome's uncle, Tom Troyer, was getting married. They hired a van to take them since the bride lived quite a distance away. Rome stayed home to take care of the farm. Along the way, there was a collision and the entire family was killed."

Julia closed her eyes.

Fern kept talking. "Rome packed up the house, locked it, sold off the livestock—only thing he kept was his mother's bees—and never looked back. No one knew where he went."

Julia looked over at Rome. No wonder he didn't talk about his family, his past. "I'm surprised he told you all that, Fern. He's never said a word about that to me. Not to Dad, either."

Fern closed up the bag that held the apple slices. Then after one of her long silent spells, she said, "He didn't have to tell me. It was my wedding that Rome's family was headed to. I was going to be Tom Troyer's bride."

Fern? A bride? A brokenhearted bride. "So that's why you're here? You came to Windmill Farm to get Rome back to Ohio?"

She shook her head. "That's not up to me or anybody else but Rome. I take care of people. That's what I do." She put the apple slices into her apron pocket. "But Rome does have a decision to make. Last year, the Troyers' neighbor contacted me. Someone wants to buy the Troyer farm since it's just sitting there abandoned, getting run down. They wondered if I knew how to find him. A few months later, I happened to read your Uncle Hank's *Budget* letters where he talked about the Bee Man, a fellow who wandered from place to place. When he mentioned that they were brown bees, I knew those bees belonged to a Troyer. Nobody has that strain of bees anymore. It was Rome's mother who kept that strain going, and it wasn't hard to figure the Bee Man was Rome. I wrote to your uncle and he wrote back. He added something about he was running himself ragged, holding Windmill Farm together because his poor nephew had a bum heart."

Julia rolled her eyes at that.

"So I asked if he'd be in need of a caretaker for his nephew. Seemed like the right time. Thought I'd come and check up on Rome."

M.K. gave a shout out to her, waving her arm like a windmill to come over to the corn wagon, and Fern released a martyred sigh.

"And I ended up with a batch of troublesome children to keep on the straight and narrow way." She didn't seem too bothered.

Julia grew pensive. How strange and interwoven lives could be.

Fern rose to leave. "You know, Julia, boys get their hearts broken too."

At the Sweet Tooth bakery, Sadie stood in front of the counter trying to decide what to get. It all looked so good! Cinnamon rolls drizzled with thick white icing, cupcakes of every flavor topped with a swirl of frosting, gigantic crackled gingersnap cookies (her favorite), small fruit pies. Nora Stroot stood behind the counter, arms crossed tightly against her chest, losing patience with Sadie's indecisiveness. She let out a long-suffering sigh.

Sadie looked up at Nora. "Everything looks so delicious, it's hard to choose just one!" She bit her lip. "So maybe I'll try one cinnamon roll, one red velvet cupcake, and one gingersnap. Oh, and a gooseberry tart."

"Cancel that order," Fern said as she swept into the bakery. "We'll have two cups of tea."

Another grievous sigh escaped from Nora Stroot before she turned to get their tea.

Fern pointed to a table with two chairs. "Sit," she told Sadie.

Sadie looked longingly at the bakery goods as she sipped on her tea.

"So what's got you looking as sad as a gopher hitting hard ground?"

"Nothing. I'm just starving. I wanted a snack, that's all."

Fern snorted. "You had ordered enough for a week's worth." She added a dollop of cream to her tea and stirred it. "So? What's making you so down in the mouth?"

Sadie's eyes filled up with tears. "Rome loves Julia. And I think she loves him too."

"Keeping Rome Troyer in one place is like . . . well, you may as well chase smoke rising from a fire." She sipped her tea. "So you're disappointed that he doesn't love you?"

Sadie nodded. "Why couldn't Rome have chosen me? What's so wrong with me?"

"You mean, except for the fact that you're eleven years younger than him?"

"Age shouldn't matter!" In many important ways she was practically twenty. Maybe thirty.

"Age matters plenty when a girl is barely fifteen and the fellow is on the sunny side of thirty." She frowned and set down her tea. "Sadie, did you ever wonder why you're filling your mind with thoughts of Rome and ignoring all the boys your own age?"

Sadie was confused. "Because . . . he's Rome!"

Fern shook her head. "Because he's safe. He's a dream. A hope. The real thing is much harder work, but at least it's real. As long as you keep feeding that fantasy about Rome, you hold all these fellows at arm's length." She pointed out the window. Gideon Smucker was talking to Menno at the wagon and kept casting sidelong glances in Sadie's direction. "Fellows like that boy. He hangs around like a summer cold."

With her chin propped on her fist, Sadie pondered that remark. Was Fern right? Was she hiding behind her fears?

She looked over at the bakery counter. Was spending most of her time in the kitchen just another way to hide?

Fern reached out and covered Sadie's hand with hers, a rare display of affection. "Sadie girl, don't waste these years. Time is like the Mississippi River. It only flows in one direction. You can never go back." She glanced at the wall clock, swallowed the last sip of tea, and set the cup down. "Let's go. Julia's quilt will be getting auctioned off soon."

The formal auction had started at two and began with the auctioneer selling off farm tools, some livestock, a handful of quarter horses, flowers and plants, other quilts and wall hangings. The crowd was small at first, but the gathering grew as the time came for Julia's quilt to be auctioned off at 4:00 p.m. The last item of the day. Julia wasn't sure if she should stay for it. What if it didn't bring in the money she had hoped? What if no one bid on it? She should leave.

As she spun around, she caught sight of Paul, standing on the fringe. He had been waiting for her to notice him. She walked over to him. For a moment they simply stared at each other, saying nothing. He looked utterly dejected. She wanted to reach out and take his hand, but she could not do that. She wanted to cry for him, but she could not do that either. So she simply said, "I am very sorry, Paul. Truly sorry."

He tried to smile at her, but he couldn't quite manage it. "I hope your quilt brings in more than last year."

"Thank you." She heard the auctioneer sing out something about her quilt, and she thought she should slip through the crowd, fast, make a quick exit. But suddenly Fern, Sadie,

Menno, M.K., and Uncle Hank surrounded her. Sadie clasped her hands around Julia's and squeezed.

"NERVOUS?" Uncle Hank bellowed.

She gave a shaky laugh as she watched the auctioneer. "Extremely."

"DON'T BE," he said, with typical Uncle Hank–like assurance.

She glanced in Paul's direction, but he was gone.

The auctioneer motioned to two men to bring the quilt out. It was hung on a rack, but folded up so no one could see the pattern. The auctioneer started talking in that rushed, frenetic way of his: "And here we have an original Julia Lapp quilt!"

Why did he have to say that?! Edith Fisher turned slightly and caught Julia with the corner of her eye, and Julia cringed.

A hush fell over the crowd as the auctioneer unclipped Julia's quilt so that it draped to the floor. It was so quiet you could have heard a barn owl hoot in the next county. *Everybody hates it,* Julia thought. *It's a disaster. The worst quilt ever created.* Her cheeks felt flushed and she thought about bolting. No, she couldn't do that. She was a grown-up. But she felt like an embarrassed five-year-old.

"Let's start the bidding at one thousand dollars. Do I hear one thousand?" A hand bounced up. "I hear one thousand. Do I have one thousand five hundred?" Another hand. "One thousand five hundred. Do I hear two thousand?" Another hand in the crowd popped up. The auctioneer looked pleased. "Do I hear three thousand?" Another hand. "Do I hear four thousand?"

This went on for another moment—an eternity—until the bidding slowed at ten thousand dollars. Ten thousand dollars! Julia was stunned. The auctioneer picked up his gavel.

"Ten thousand dollars going once. Going twice!" He held his gavel suspended in the air. The crowd caught its breath.

"Twenty-five thousand dollars!" shouted a voice.

After a moment of stunned silence the crowd started clapping like summer thunder.

"Sold!" the auctioneer said, slamming the gavel with enthusiasm. "Sold to the man in the panama hat!"

* * *

On orders from Julia, M.K. darted through the crowd to find the man in the panama hat at the checkout table and escort him to the family. Julia wanted to thank him, but she also wanted to find out why in the world he had bid so much for her quilt. M.K. wove her way through clumps of people who were buzzing in wonder over the amount of the bid. She was having fun! On a mission of top importance. She stopped now and then to jump up and see if she could still locate the top of his hat. And stopped another time to take note of a woman's teetery red high-heeled shoes. How could anyone walk in those? They were practically stilts. Her eyes caught sight of the man, bending over the checkout table as he wrote a check, so she ducked down one more time and zigzagged through the crowd to reach him. When she made it to the table, she looked around triumphantly.

NO! She was too late! The man in the panama hat had paid for the quilt and left.

* * *

A week after the auction, Rome was out among the pippin apples in the orchards, the last variety to be harvested, checking on a row of trees that were twisted and bent, heavy with fruit. When these apples made it safely into the baskets and to the farmer's market to sell, he wouldn't be needed at Windmill Farm any longer. Autumn had come.

He climbed a ladder to reach the crown of one tree, and nearly fell off when he was startled by a voice. He moved a branch out of the way to find Julia peering up at him.

"You're planning to leave, aren't you?"

"These are the last of the crops to harvest. Menno and I finished up three cuttings of hay. It's stacked and in the barn. The corn is in the silo. Your father is on the waiting list for a new heart. And with the money from the fundraiser, you're in good shape to pay for the transplant, at least enough to persuade Amos to go through with it." He gentled the branch back into place. "Seems like the right time to move on."

"Paul wants to marry me."

Rome stilled. "Well, congratulations."

When she didn't answer, he moved the branch again. "Isn't it?"

"What do you think I should tell him?"

He looked through the branches at her, then climbed slowly down the ladder, protecting the apples he had stored in the canvas pouch secured about his neck and lying against his chest. "You should tell him yes. That's always what you've wanted. For as long as I've known you, that's what you've wanted."

When he had both feet on solid ground, she asked him, "Why are you leaving?"

Rome removed the white cotton gloves he wore while harvesting. "This was our deal. You asked me to stay through harvest."

"Fern told me about your family and the car accident."

Rome felt his chest tighten. There it was again—that feeling that his shirt collar was too tight. Like he couldn't breathe. He took a step back. The memories surfaced, one by one, until he shoved them to the back of his mind again.

"I'm so sorry," she whispered, meeting his gaze when he finally looked at her. "I had no idea how difficult the last six years must have been for you."

He wanted to shout out that he didn't need anybody's sympathy. He brushed past her to empty the bag of apples into the basket. "Fern had no business telling you."

"I wish you could have told me yourself." She took a step closer to him. "I thought we were friends. I thought we had something . . . special. Was I wrong?"

He kept his head down, gently letting the apples pour into the basket. "You're mistaken. I've told you over and over that I'm not that kind of man."

"What kind? Are you trying to tell me you're not a good man? Or a caring man?"

He tossed the empty canvas bag on top of the apples in the basket. He faced her, hands on his hips. "I meant . . . the settling-down kind. The marrying kind. The kind of man a girl can count on, for keeps. I'm a drifter. No ties, not to anyone or anything." He was sure that hearing this hurt worse than anything else he could have said, but what could he do? It was the truth.

"Maybe you're the one who's got it wrong, Rome. I think you're the kind of man a girl can count on. You just can't let go of losing your family. You can't let yourself love because you think your heart can't handle it . . . that something bad will happen. But you're wrong. It's true . . . grief is the price for love. But hearts are made to mend. Christ can do wonders with a broken heart, if given all the pieces."

She didn't expect an answer, and she didn't get one. She squared her shoulders, tilted up her chin, but held silent. He thought he saw tears welling in her eyes, but she blinked them away before he could be sure. "So go. Take your bees and head off down the country roads." She took a few steps away, then turned back. "You know what's so sad? Your heart is every bit as damaged as my father's. The difference is that yours is a choice. You think you can avoid pain if you don't let yourself care about anybody. Maybe that's true. But you'll also never feel any love, or any joy."

She walked away, down the dirt path of apple trees. He couldn't let her leave like this. She didn't understand.

"Julia—wait!" He caught up with her. "This summer—it was just a game between us. A game to get Paul back. That's what you said you wanted. That's what you've got." He looked down into her hazel eyes.

For a moment their eyes met with all the hurt and pride and pretense stripped away.

"You, Roman Troyer, are a coward." She turned and left the apple orchard.

Rome stared at Julia's retreating back. How dare she! No one had ever had the audacity to talk to him like this. No other woman had ever challenged him the way she had over the past few months. No other woman had ever been as confident of herself, either.

Was it true? Was he a coward? Things were backward. Things should have been the other way around: he should be wanting to go, she should be begging him to stay. Maybe he had a warped sense of what love should be, but he thought that in love everything would be clear—instead of the muddy, confused, back-and-forths he'd had with Julia.

He threw the gloves on the ground. It didn't matter! He was leaving soon.

19

The door of the cottage squeaked open one afternoon as Rome was packing up his equipment.

Fern.

"I'll be sure to scrub the floor," he told her. "I don't want ants taking over the place." He went back to dismantling the extractor. "Just so you know, I sold the family property. Sent off a letter accepting the offer a few weeks ago. I should be getting the paperwork any day. As soon as the cashier's check arrives, I'm going to give it to you. I want the money from the property to be available for Amos's heart transplant. I'm hoping you'll use it when Amos gets his new heart. But no one, and I mean no one, should know where the money came from."

She walked around the kitchen with her arms folded against her. "So, I guess that means you're not planning to return to Ohio."

He shook his head. "No, I'm not." He took the extractor out to the wagon and placed it carefully in a wooden box. She followed him out. "Fern, if there's something you want to say to me, why don't you just come right out and say it?"

She lifted her chin a notch. "God doesn't make mistakes."

He recoiled at the words. In a way, he'd been expecting a conversation like this with Fern since the day he arrived and found her at Windmill Farm. *Well, fine, let's get this out in the open.* He glanced up at her. "I assume you're talking about the car accident."

"That accident passed through the hand of God."

If Fern had blamed the devil or the fallen world, Rome would agree. He could accept an explanation that involved imperfection, mankind's fallen state, or even his own lack of faith. What he couldn't accept was that God might have allowed the death of Rome's family when he could have prevented it. "Fern, I'm sorry you lost my uncle Tom that day. You lost a man who was going to be your husband. But you didn't lose your entire family in one fell swoop. You lost a new life, I suppose. I lost my old life. My whole life."

"The problem isn't in God—" she glanced toward the sky— "but in us. We can't see things from an eternal perspective."

"I know that." He threw the words like stones. "But why them? Four little girls, each one as precious to me as Sadie and M.K. Two parents—fine, loving people. My uncle, who was like another father to me. Why *every* single one? And why did I survive it?" He frowned. "It's hard to accept the idea that God didn't make a mistake on that day."

Fern stopped him with an uplifted finger. "None of us know the mind of God. The minute we think God needs to answer to us, we are teetering toward pride. God's ways are perfect and ours are not." Her voice softened. "Rome, you're going to have to let go, so your life can move on. Over time, new memories, new people, fill up that emptiness and your life will be complete again. If you don't let go of your grieving, you'll just stay in one spot, suspended in time."

Rome kept his head down and focused entirely on packing empty honey jars into a cardboard box. He didn't know how to respond to Fern. What could he say? That she didn't understand? But she did.

Fern turned to leave but stopped after a few steps. "I'll be sure the money goes to Amos's new heart. And I won't tell anyone where it came from."

"Fern."

She turned back to face him.

"Thank you, for everything. You uprooted your life for me this summer."

She tilted her head. "You were the reason I came. But you're not the reason I'm staying. God never takes without giving. He gave me a new family to look after. I needed them as much as they needed me. Maybe more."

Floating down on the wind from the house came a loud whooping sound. Fern and Rome looked up and saw M.K. running down the path toward the cottage with an empty pail in her hand. Menno was closing in on her, an outraged look on his face. His clothes and his hair were drenched with water.

Fern sighed. "And heaven only knows this family needs some serious looking after."

That night, after the sunset, the Lapp family gathered outside to say goodbye to Rome. The mules were harnessed to the bee wagon, the bees were safely settled into their hives, Rome had packed his few belongings.

He went first to M.K. "You keep studying bees, M.K. Next lesson is to observe how bees wind their way back to their hive. Beekeepers call it a beeline."

"Easy," she said.

"It's not a straight line."

Her little face squinted in confusion. She was about to object, then she burst into tears.

Rome wrapped M.K. in his arms.

"We're all going to miss you, Rome," Sadie said.

That nearly undid him. Somewhere in the passing week, Sadie had lost her shyness in Rome's presence. He pulled her into the hug.

He released the two girls and moved down the line to Menno. With a lightning-quick motion, Rome hit the tip of the hat and flipped it off the boy's head. Menno flinched and stepped back; his hair was matted as though he hadn't even run a comb through it that morning. "Keep your eye on Uncle Hank, Menno. Since he won't act his age, you'll have to be grown-up enough for two."

Menno thought that over for a long moment, then let out a honk of laughter. He shook Rome's hand solemnly.

"Slander!" Uncle Hank roared as he walked over to them from the Grossdaadi Haus. "If I leave for a second, my good name gets slandered!" He grabbed Rome for a handshake, pumping his hand up and down.

Rome moved to Amos, who held out a fistful of long fire matches to him. "Hold these sticks together," Amos said. "See if you can break them." Rome looked puzzled but did as Amos asked. The sticks wouldn't snap. Amos reached out and took one long match. He snapped it in half like it was a dried leaf. "By itself, one can be broken. Each one of us can be broken. But together, we're strong." He put his hand on Rome's head, a prayer, a blessing. "Never forget you have a place in our family circle, Bee Man."

And now Rome felt a well of emotion. He should be the one offering the blessing to Amos, but he found that words failed him. Would he see Amos again on this side of eternity? All he could do was to grip Amos's hand with both of his and hope that it conveyed all the gratitude he felt toward this kind man. He moved to Fern and found the emotional relief he needed.

"Would you at least send a card now and then?" she said. "Just let us know you're still among the living?"

He smiled and gave her a stiff hug.

Then he reached Julia. She looked at him and he looked at her and he felt himself waffling. What could he say? He had dreaded this moment, even more than saying goodbye to Amos. "Take care of yourself," he told her awkwardly.

Lulu jumped up on Rome's cart and sat down, facing forward. Rome reached up to get her down, but Menno stopped him. "No, Rome. Lulu has picked you. She wants to go with you."

For a split second, Rome thought he might crack. He looked at Lulu's dark brown eyes and could feel her pleading with him. *Take me! Let me go with you!* He inhaled sharply. "I can't, Menno. She belongs here, at Windmill Farm." He ordered Lulu down and she hopped off, tail between her legs, and sat down next to her puppy—the one Menno had still to find the right master for.

Rome turned away and jumped onto the wagon without looking back. He picked up the reins and the mule started to move along, slowly and steadily, into the darkness.

The old patterns of Rome's life were repeating themselves. He was drifting.

A silvery mist hugged the ground like a blanket, and the slanting rays of the sun brushed the leaves still lingering on the trees, painting them yellow, red, and brown. Fall had always been Julia's favorite time of the year. As she walked along the apple trees, trying to decide if there was enough fruit to justify another picking before a deep frost hit, she wondered if she would forevermore associate autumn with saying goodbye. First to Paul, then to Rome. Maybe, soon, to her father. Amos was weaker with every passing day.

Julia tried not to wonder where Rome was. Where did he go? What had he been doing? It didn't matter, it was none of her business, he owed her nothing, they had taken no vows and made no promises.

The odd thing was that after Fern had told her about Rome's family, she began to understand his strange inner workings. The accident had made him fiercely, desperately independent. No wonder he couldn't tolerate growing attached to her. She knew Rome cared for her, she saw it in his eyes and his actions. But she also knew he wasn't capable of anything more. He wouldn't even take Lulu with him, and that dog had meant something to him.

As she walked among the apple trees, she prayed. She prayed about the mixed-up feelings, the uncertainty she felt about Rome. Prayer worked. She believed in prayer. The word *trust* kept circling through her mind. Trust. She turned the word over and over in her mind. Trust went hand in hand with faith. *That's what I need*, Julia thought. *To trust God's ways.*

Maybe that was her problem with Paul. She was so busy telling God how to fix things between her and Paul that she hadn't given God a chance to chime in. Maybe she could have saved everybody a lot of trouble had she ever asked God if

Paul was the right person for her. *No!* God would have said. *I've got something better in mind for you, if you'd just have a little patience.* She could practically hear God's voice. Not out loud, but in her mind. In her heart.

So, Lord, this time, I am asking you to take over. Rome is yours, and you know his heart. You know what's best for him. And you know what's best for me. Please watch over him now, wherever he is. Help him find what he's looking for. Give him joy, Lord. Give him peace.

Overhead, a fluff of a cloud was framed with pure golden light from the sun that was hidden behind it. Awed by the sight, she studied the outline of the cloud within the frame, light splaying around its edges.

As she gazed at the cloud, she was filled with feelings she couldn't explain. Peace, joy, reassurance—all swirling together. It seemed as if the heavens parted and she caught a glimpse of God's connectedness to this earthly existence. She'd never had such an awareness of the presence of God.

The sun was starting to set now, and it was getting cold, but in her heart there was radiant light. She remained where she was until M.K. called to her to come in. She wanted to savor this new peace. She knew she would never, ever forget this moment in the apple orchards. It was meant to stay with her.

The air was bright and pure; the leaves on the trees glistened and the Blue Lake Pond flowed softly, lapping against the shore with a gentle rhythm. Rome closed his eyes as though to contain the landscape and the deep sense of peace it evoked. He had been camping by the lake with his bees the last few days, waiting for a certified letter to arrive from

Ohio, bearing a cashier's check for his family's farm. Waiting, waiting, waiting. What was taking it so long? He wanted to get that check to Fern for safekeeping. To leave Stoney Ridge with clean accounts. No regrets. No second thoughts.

And yet, he did have second thoughts. He leaned his head against a tree and closed his eyes. Suddenly he was overcome with a sense of homesickness, a dull ache that had settled around his heart. He missed Windmill Farm. He missed the cottage. He missed the Lapps. He missed Julia. He hated knowing he'd hurt Julia. "Take care of yourself," he had said, as if he were talking to a pal. How inadequate. How childish!

The only reason he'd acted so cool and detached was so he didn't leave her with any mixed messages, any confusion.

This was better for her, for him. She would marry Paul. He would have an unencumbered life. It was better for both of them.

So why did he feel as if he had lost something precious? As if he was losing his home all over again?

What was home, really? Just a place to lay your head.

No. It was so much more than that. It was the place where a person belonged. Where a fellow would be missed. It was a part of a man. Something that couldn't be sold or taken for granted.

He was seized by a moment of panic. Why had he sold the Ohio farm? It was like giving away his right arm. How could he have done such a thing? His father would be ashamed of him. Was it too late? Could he stop the process?

He hurried to town to get to the post office before it closed at five. He would send a letter—a telegram. He would stop the sale.

When the postmaster saw him come into the post office,

she reached below the counter and pulled out a large manila envelope. "It just arrived, Bee Man. Those papers you wanted from Ohio. Now you can be on your way."

It was too late.

The transaction had been completed. He ripped open the envelope and read the enclosed letter. Then reread it, again and again. He had to sit down. He went outside of the post office and found a bench. Was someone playing a joke on him?

The cashier's check was included for the full amount of the property. But also included was the deed to the farm. Paid in full. Returned to Roman Troyer. A gift.

At dusk, Fern sent M.K. and Menno over to the Fishers' with two bushels of apples to make cider. "Edith said her apple tree wasn't delivering the goods this year because we hogged Rome's bees."

"It's cuz those bees have good sense to stay away from Jimmy Fisher," M.K. muttered.

"Go," Fern said. "And don't dawdle. It'll be dark soon."

They got about halfway to the Fishers' when M.K. was struck with inspiration. "Menno, let's cut through the cornfields. It'll save us going way down on the road."

"I don't think so. It's getting dark."

"Come on!" She started into the fields. "I do it all the time. Just watch for snakes." She was deep in the middle of the field when she stopped abruptly. Staring intently through the dried cornstalks, she thought she heard a strange sound. Maybe she heard a snake behind her, maybe not.

Menno caught up with her. "Let me go ahead of you. I'm taller than the corn."

M.K. grinned. Menno was proud of his height, nearly as tall as their father. He worked it into conversations all summer long. "Fine, but just keep going in a line, along that row. Can you see the lights from the house straight ahead?"

A dog began barking and Menno stopped. "That's Jimmy's dog, Menno. He won't hurt you."

"I don't know about this, Mary Kate."

"It's fine!"

"Do you hear that dog yapping?"

"He's always yapping." That dog was crazy, as crazy as Jimmy. It was barking its head off like it had seen a ghost. She gave Menno a gentle push to move forward. "Hey, I heard a good joke we need to remember to tell Uncle Hank. What's got a head and a tail, but doesn't have a body?"

Menno worked on that for a long moment before giving up. "I don't know."

"A coin! Like a dime or a quarter. Get it?" She then explained the joke to Menno until he understood it and gave out a big haw. By the time he stopped laughing, they were nearly through the cornfield to the woven-wire fence that ran alongside the yard to the Fishers' large henhouse.

"Let's cut through the chicken yard to get to the house."

Menno started to object, but before he could get the words out, M.K. found the gate into the chicken yard and led the way across hen grit and worse. "Pinch your nose, Menno, so you don't have to smell the stink. And be careful where you step or Fern will have a fit." Nothing smelled worse than a henhouse on a windless night.

M.K. could hear the chickens flapping their wings in the henhouse. Chickens weren't the brightest of birds, and easily flustered, but something felt eerie to her. It didn't help that

Jimmy's dog was having fits. She was glad to see it was on a tie-down.

She heard a strange ripping metal sound, as if the henhouse door was getting wrenched from its hinges, then every hen in the place rose up and screamed. The bucket of apples dropped from Menno's fingers, spilling everywhere. M.K. stopped to help him, when suddenly, something or someone burst out of the henhouse and stood, scanning the yard. The air behind it was white with feathers. M.K.'s breath was cut off, and her heart hollered.

"Bear! Run, Menno!" M.K. screamed. "It's the bear! Run! Get to the farmhouse!"

She flew toward the house and landed on the top step of the porch, banging on the front door. Rapid explosions went off from an upstairs window in the house, followed by a burned-powder haze that hung in the air. And an eerie silence. Even the dog went still. Everything was waiting.

"Menno?" M.K. shouted into the night. "Menno? Where are you? Menno?"

As M.K. realized he wasn't answering, she screamed.

20

At seven o'clock that night, Sadie came downstairs and asked Julia where M.K. and Menno were. When Fern told her they hadn't gotten back yet, a strange look came over Sadie's face. She went outside on the back porch to wait for them, restless and anxious. "Something's wrong."

Within minutes, a strange wailing sound drifted up the hill. Julia ran to the kitchen door and saw a small figure running toward the house. "Juuu-Leee-Aaaa!"

Julia flew out the door and ran down the hill to reach M.K. Her little sister flung her arms around her waist. It took awhile to calm M.K. down and get the facts straightened out, but Julia pieced together that Menno had been accidentally shot and was taken to the hospital in Lancaster by ambulance. As they came back up the hill, they found the family—Fern, their father, Uncle Hank, Sadie—waiting on the porch.

"We'll all go," Amos said gravely.

"Dad, are you sure you should go?" Julia asked. "I'll go, find out the extent of Menno's injuries, and call you. Sadie or M.K. could stay in the shanty until I call."

Sadie stood next to her father and held on to his arm. "He needs to be there, Jules. We all do."

It would take forever to get her father dressed and ready to go. He struggled to get enough air for the simplest of acts, how could he hurry for this?

The same thought must have run through Fern's mind. "You and Sadie go on ahead. The rest of us will follow as quickly as we can."

Julia nodded. Fern's voice was calm, reassuring.

"I have to come too," M.K. said. "Please let me come. Please, please, please." Her little face was white and pinched.

Julia and Sadie went down to the phone shanty, called for a taxi driven by a Mennonite fellow who lived nearby, and waited. And waited.

Finally, two headlights appeared on the road. The ride to the hospital felt like an eternity. When they reached the Emergency Room, they tumbled out of the car. Julia told the driver to go back to Windmill Farm to get her father. The hospital door slid open and Sadie, M.K., and Julia stepped into a crowded waiting room. Julia asked a man at the counter about Menno. He looked up Menno's name on the computer, asked if they were family, then pointed toward a hall and said to go talk to a nurse at the station through the doors. They walked down another hall to a door that said NO ADMITTANCE. Julia had to push the button and talk into a speaker box to tell the nurse why they were there and whom they wanted to see.

A nurse was waiting for them as the door opened. "Come with me."

"Where's Menno?" M.K. asked, starting to cry again.

Julia held her close against her. She wanted to cry too. This all felt like a bad dream that she couldn't wake from. How could Menno have been fine, just a few hours ago, and now he was in a hospital? How could life be so fragile?

The nurse handed M.K. a box of tissues. "I need to talk to your older sister about a couple of things first. Then I'll take you to your brother. I promise." She motioned to a quiet space by the nurse's station so Julia followed her. "Were you told what happened?"

"I know there was an accident. Someone was trying to shoot a bear and they ended up shooting Menno."

"Your brother received a bullet wound to his head. He's on a ventilator and IV, oxygen and a catheter."

"Is he in pain?"

"No."

"Good." Oh good! Oh, thank God. A wave of relief washed over Julia. "We'd like to see him."

"Soon. You need to know, he's in a coma. He's unresponsive."

Julia felt as if she might faint. She held on to the counter with both hands.

"Do you need to sit down?" the nurse whispered.

Julia breathed deeply for a moment. Was she going to be sick? She closed her eyes and tried to recite a psalm. Finally, she said, "All that matters is that he is alive."

"Yes, but—" The nurse stopped abruptly. "Let me take you to see him."

Julia followed her through another door and into the room where Menno lay, but the boy who lay on the bed did not look like her brother. Julia glanced around at the monitors. She recognized the jagging line for the heart, the numbers for the blood pressure and oxygen levels—it was the same kind of monitor her father had been hooked up to. Menno's chest rose and fell, his left hand was taped to a board with the IV line in the back of his hand. His head was bandaged down to his eyebrows with a turban of white gauze. It was a horrible dream. Like someone was pummeling her with hard blows. One more and she might crumble.

It was so hard to see Menno like this. She wanted to protect him. She was *supposed* to be able to protect him. She was his older sister! She had always watched out for him. Julia curled her fingers around his right hand on top of the sheet. His hand was so cold. She had heard once that even in a coma, the patient could hear.

"Menno, it's me. It's Jules. Your sister. Can you hear me?" No response, not even a flicker.

Julia sat down in the chair by the bed, still clinging to Menno's hand. She remembered a time he'd fallen from a horse and his sweet face had been so battered and bruised she hardly recognized him. She stroked his hair that was sticking out under the gauze.

She shot a look through the window at Sadie, who had tears running down her cheeks. M.K. had her face buried in her hands. Julia glanced over to the doorway to see a doctor standing there. Had he said something to her? "Yes?" The word came out in a croak. She tried again. "Yes."

"I'm Dr. Lee." He held his metal clipboard against his chest, a barrier between them. "I admitted your brother."

The doctor studied the monitors, checked Menno's eyes responses with his flashlight, skimmed the bottom of his feet with another instrument, pulled out his stethoscope and listened to his heart and lungs. He turned to her. "Menno's condition remains unchanged." Another blow to Julia's gut. "Are you Menno's guardian?"

From some distant place, Julia could hear herself say, "Of sorts. I'm the eldest in the family. My father will be here soon, but he isn't well. If there's something about Menno you need for us to know, I'd appreciate it if you could tell me first."

The doctor cleared his throat and his shoulders rose and fell in a sigh.

"Will you be taking him in for surgery soon?"

"Surgery?"

"To get the bullet out of his head," Julia said. Just how experienced was this doctor? He didn't seem to know what to do next.

Suddenly she felt herself shaking so hard she had to sit on a chair. She grabbed her elbows and leaned forward, head down. "You think he's going to die, don't you." Julia's voice was a dry rasp.

The doctor crouched down beside her. Then, slowly, in a gentle voice, "Miss Lapp, when your brother came into the hospital, he was already comatose. The brain function is minimal. We've done all we can do for him."

At the window, Julia saw a nurse leading her father, Fern, and Uncle Hank to meet Sadie and M.K. The nurse quietly opened the door and let them file around Menno's bedside. Fern and Uncle Hank stood against the wall. Fern gave M.K. a gentle push to go stand by her brother. Sadie leaned over and whispered something in Menno's ear. Julia heard only the sounds, not the words. It reminded Julia of when they were young. Menno's language was slow to develop, and Sadie, though two years younger, spoke sooner than he did. Her mother used to say that Sadie was God's gift to help Menno along. Sadie seemed to understand what Menno wanted to say before he had words of his own to use. She would whisper something to him, like she was doing now, lean close to him, hearing something from him that only she could hear.

Amos picked up Menno's hand in his and stroked it gently. The doctor quietly explained the situation to everyone.

"But he is breathing," Amos said, "and his heart is beating."

"Yes, because he is on the ventilator," the doctor said gently. "If we turn that off, he won't last long."

Julia stared at the monitors. The steady *beep beep beep*, the snaking lines of tubing, the sucking sound as Menno's chest lifted and fell. Was it true? She studied her brother's face and his arms and hands. Beautiful Menno, special Menno. He had taught them all so much—patience, loving unconditionally, daily reminders to slow down and notice things—to *really* notice. She took his hand in hers, this calloused hand that had gently nursed so many animals back to health, this hand that had built so many birdhouses to shelter birds.

"Stay with us, Menno," she whispered, clutching his hand even harder. "Don't leave us."

Julia saw Sadie lean close to Menno, matching her breathing to his shallow breathing on the monitor. "What is it?"

Sadie shook her head, a minuscule movement. She turned her head slightly, then her shoulders dropped. With tear-filled eyes, she turned to Julia. "He's gone. He was here a moment ago, but now he's gone. He waited until we were all together. He's left us."

The doctor seemed puzzled and examined the monitors. "Nothing's changed."

Julia and her father exchanged a look. Sadie knew.

Julia had to get some fresh air. She told Fern she would be back soon, and went out into the hallway. There was a small garden area for families and patients to sit in, so she followed the arrows leading to it and went out into the dark night air. She lifted her face toward the stars.

So many thoughts in an instant, overlapping, colliding thoughts, thoughts without words.

She sat quietly for several minutes. She was too stunned to cry. She had lost more than her brother, she had lost part of herself. She couldn't remember a time when Menno wasn't there. She rubbed her temples. *What are we to do, Lord?* She didn't even know how to pray for Menno, for all of them. Words seemed inadequate for the pain that seared through her. A deep groan poured out of her soul, a wordless prayer. Was this what the Bible meant when it said that the Holy Spirit prayed for us?

She didn't know how long she had been out there, looking at the stars, praying for Menno, when she heard a familiar voice gently call her name. She looked up and blinked. Was she dreaming?

"Rome!" She flew out of the chair and across the small space. "Thank God! Thank God you're here."

He hauled her up against his chest and held her so tight she couldn't breathe. Her fists gripped the cloth of his jacket and she burrowed into him, rubbing her face against his chest. With that, the tears broke loose and she sobbed into his chest. She tried to tell him what had happened to Menno, but he shushed her.

"I've already been to the room. I heard all about the accident."

"How did you know? Who told you?"

"I was heading out to Windmill Farm tonight to ask Fern . . . never mind . . . long story . . . I'll explain later. When I passed by the Fishers', Jimmy told me what had happened. I came as soon as I could."

Julia wiped her tears off of her face. "The doctor said we need to take Menno off the ventilator. He said Menno's brain is . . . he said that there's no sign of brain activity."

Rome led her to the garden bench where she was sitting when he came in. He sat down beside her. "Julia, there's something you need to consider. As awful a situation as this is, something good might come out of it."

"What are you talking about?"

He took her hands in his. "Menno's heart. It's meant for your father."

Julia felt a brutal slap out of nowhere. She pulled her hands away, but he wouldn't let them go. "You're saying . . . that Menno's heart be given to my father?" Her voice shook.

"Yes." He waited a moment before continuing, letting her absorb that thought. "Think about it, Julia. If Menno were here, he would want you to consider this. I know he would. But he's not here, and I need to do this for him. The heart may not even be a match. I'm not even sure what the protocol is about organ donation, but we need to try. You need to convince your father to try."

Her face scrunched up again and the tears resumed.

More urgently, he said, "We should do what Menno wanted."

She was squeezing his hands now, hard, so hard, but she couldn't help it. She was a bundle of nerves. "I can't make that kind of decision for him. I don't know what he would want."

"Yes, you do. Do you remember, a few weeks ago, when we were in your father's room and he told Menno and Sadie and M.K. that he was dying? Do you remember what Menno asked? He asked him if a person had two hearts, like two kidneys. He said he would give Amos his heart if he could. He said those very words."

Her grip relaxed. "I remember. He did say that." Her hands slipped into her lap.

Rome stood. "I'll be right with you when you talk to Amos. But it needs to come from you. He'll listen to you, Julia." He held his hand out to her.

She looked at his hand for a long moment, then put her hand in his.

Rome watched Amos listen carefully to Julia, and to him, but he could see it was Uncle Hank who made the difference.

Hank put his hand on Amos's shoulder and said, "That boy's life was a gift from start to finish. This is his final gift to you, Amos. You would be wrong not to receive it graciously."

Amos looked at Hank with searching eyes. Hank loved Menno like he was his own. In a way, he knew Menno better than any of them. They spent hours together, hunting and fishing and talking.

"Our Menno would want this, Amos," Hank said. "More than that, he would delight in this coincidence." He held up his finger. "No, he would correct me. He would say that what man calls coincidences, God would call a miracle."

Amos quietly said he needed some time alone with Menno.

Rome saw Julia cross the room and sit next to Uncle Hank. She put her hand over his, and he clasped hers tightly. They remained that way until Amos returned from Menno's room, about ten minutes later. He told Rome to go find that heart doctor, Dr. Highland, the one who looked like he was ten. He didn't need to tell Rome twice.

As Rome hurried through the halls, he felt an awe at God's perfect timing. God was always in the business of redeeming, Fern had told him once, if only we let him. He prayed in the elevators, prayed in the hallways, prayed as he waited for the doctor to be paged. *Lord, let this be a match. And then let them agree to give the heart to Amos. Don't let Menno's death be in vain.*

Dr. Lee took Julia aside to ask if the family would consider allowing other organs for donation. "I realize you have a great deal to cope with right now, but there is a question I need to ask. Would you be willing to let Menno's other organs help save other people?"

They wanted more of Menno? Julia felt a wave of nausea. How could she possibly make such a decision, at this moment in time?

"Julia, your brother can give the gift of life to someone else with his heart, lungs, liver, kidneys. His corneas will help someone see and his skin will heal burns. Medical science has learned of ways to use so much healthy tissue. But, of course, Menno is not of age, so we would need your father's permission. Would you speak to him?"

She didn't answer right away. "Give me some time."

"Of course. But, the longer Menno remains on the machines, the fewer organs we can use."

She got up and slowly walked out of the room, down the hall to Menno's room. She passed the garden where she had talked with Rome, and felt a pull toward it. *Dear Lord,* she prayed, *I can't even imagine life without Menno. And now my father has a chance to live. I don't know what you have planned for my father. I want to believe you will send us a miracle, but if you can't, I know that you will take him home to be with you in heaven . . . the ultimate healing. Whatever you decide, Lord, thy will be done. I only ask that you give me strength to help me through.*

As soon as she finished praying, the word *trust* popped into her mind, the way it had just a few days ago, when she prayed about Rome. Was it just a few days ago? It felt like a lifetime. But maybe that's why God gave her that unique experience. To fortify her for what was coming.

Trust.

A quiet peace stole over her soul, replacing the heavy garment of fear she was wearing. She could feel the tension in her shoulders release and the tightness in her chest from constant worry begin to dissipate. She took a deep breath and looked up at the diamond-studded sky. Was Menno looking down on them now?

She went back down the hall and into Menno's room. Fern and Sadie looked up when she came into the room. M.K. was curled up in a chair, asleep. Amos was stroking Menno's hair. Uncle Hank sat in a chair, head in his hands. Rome was at the window, leaning his back against the sill.

"The doctor wants us to think about donating Menno's other organs," Julia said. "Not just his heart. His lungs, his liver, his kidneys. Even his corneas and skin." She looked down at her clasped hands and swallowed hard. When she spoke, her voice was raw with emotion. "I think we should say yes. I think Menno would have said yes. He's with the Lord. He doesn't need his earthly shell any longer."

Rome's eyes caught hers, his expression tender, sad, amazed.

Sadie went over to her father and put a hand on his

shoulder. "I think Julia's right. I know she is. Menno would have wanted to give anything he could to help someone else."

"Dad?" Julia asked. "It's really your decision."

Amos gave a brief nod.

The door opened and Dr. Highland, Amos's cardiologist, walked in. "The team is waiting to check the viability of Menno's heart. It'll take a few hours. The transplant coordinator has asked the Organ Procurement and Transplantation Network to review factors to distribute the heart to Amos. So far, the blood type is a match, your weight and size fit within the parameters. The chance of rejection is greatly reduced when the organ donor is a family member. And your heart is in such bad shape that you're high on the transplant list. This looks good, Amos. This looks like it might be the heart that is meant for you. If the OPTN gives us its blessing, you'll be transferred to Hershey Medical by ambulance." He looked over at Menno. "It's time to say goodbye."

One by one, each family member gave Menno a kiss and told them they loved him. Then it was time. The doctors and nurses surrounded Menno as they prepared to turn off the ventilator. The family stood against the wall. The machine blew out its last wheezing breath, and the doctor looked at the clock to record the time of death. In a deep voice, stronger than it had been in months, Amos prayed aloud the Lord's Prayer.

Menno Joseph Lapp's time of death was officially recorded as Thursday, October 27, 11:52 p.m.

That was what the death certificate would state. But Julia, Sadie, M.K., Fern, Uncle Hank, Amos and Rome knew that Menno had been taken to be with the Lord over an hour ago, when the family first gathered around his hospital bed.

It was long after midnight. Sadie noticed Edith Fisher sitting alone in the waiting room and went over to sit by her.

Edith looked up and said, "You must think I'm a horrible person."

Sadie made a calming gesture. "No, Edith. I don't think you're horrible."

"I was home alone, and heard the dog barking. Then I heard screaming and I knew that bear was out there—she's been helping herself to my hens on a regular basis—and the boys weren't home so I grabbed Paul's rifle off of his bedroom wall and I just started shooting. I couldn't see much because of the dark, Sadie. I didn't know that Menno was there. Or M.K. I thought the bear was attacking the dog. I just panicked and started shooting." Edith's eyes filled with tears. "When I found out a bullet hit Menno, I just . . . I don't know how you'll ever be able to forgive me."

"We already do, Edith. We know it was an accident. Accidents happen."

"I was always so fond of Menno."

"Everybody was. Menno knew you would never mean to hurt him, Edith. It was God's time to call him home, and God doesn't make mistakes."

Edith's head bounced up. "Julia will never forgive me. Never."

"She will. She will forgive you, because she's Julia." Sadie had no doubt of that.

"What will Paul say?" She rocked herself back and forth in abject misery.

"Paul loves you. No one is blaming you for an accident."

Edith started sobbing again.

"Would you like me to get you something? A cup of tea? A glass of water?"

"Would you. . . . just sit with me for a minute?"

"Everything is going to be okay," Sadie said. She felt Edith relax, as if she believed her.

* * *

Other than that first meeting in the hospital garden, Rome hadn't had a minute alone with Julia. She was constantly being taken aside by nurses or doctors or hospital workers who needed papers signed. So much paperwork.

The bishop and the deacon arrived at the hospital to offer support and prayers. Menno's funeral needed to be planned in the midst of all of this. Rome was so proud of Julia—she was handling the pressure with calm and poise. Her twenty-one-year-old face looked middle-aged and careworn. This long evening of profound decision making had exhausted her. He didn't know how she was holding up, hurting from the loss of her brother and frightened for her father. An hour ago, they received word that the OPTN agreed to the transplant. They had looked at several factors: blood and tissues were ideal matches to reduce risk of rejection, the weakened condition of Amos's heart and the length of time he had been on the transplant list, as well as the geographical convenience of the donor heart. It was a go, the doctor said. There was no turning back for Amos. This was it. They were all aware of that. Amos's last words to all of them, as he was being wheeled away by the nurse to prepare for the trip to Hershey, were: "I will have joy in the morning." Either way, he meant.

As Rome watched Julia down by the nurse's station, an unexpected wave of longing was triggered. Into his gut came that restless feeling of searching, of wanting. Something un-thinkable pulled at the edges of his brain. He tried to push it away, but it only gathered strength. What if Julia had been right? He was letting fear dictate the course of his life. These last few days had given him time to think, to sift through the rubbish in his life that was shackling him.

In that moment, watching Julia, he understood what he needed to do. Maybe it would work, and maybe it wouldn't. Maybe it would take heartbreak to a whole new level.

21

Amos's operation began well before dawn on Friday morning.

Julia had accompanied her father in the ambulance to Hershey Medical. Fern and Edith took M.K. home. Uncle Hank, Sadie, and Rome hired a taxi to go from Lancaster General to Hershey, about thirty minutes away, to keep vigil with Julia in the waiting room . . . waiting.

She glanced at the clock again. Five more minutes and it would be seven hours. Sadie had fallen asleep, curled up on two chairs, with her head in Julia's lap. Uncle Hank paced up and down the halls. Rome sat quietly, across from Julia, hands clasped, head down, his lips silently moving. She knew he was praying and the sight touched her.

At the sound of footsteps, Julia glanced up the hall. When she saw the surgeon who performed the transplant with his face mask hanging around his neck, she rose to her feet and practically dumped Sadie on the floor.

The doctor smiled at her. "I have good news for you. That new heart is beating away like it belonged there." The surgeon's smile looked as tired as she felt. "Amos is in recovery. He'll be heavily sedated for the next day or so, depending on how he responds."

Julia ignored the tears trickling down her cheeks and smiled away. And kept on smiling. She sniffed and nodded. "Thank you." Her father had a new heart. A new life.

Sadie squeezed her hand, sharing the thought. Uncle Hank patted Rome so hard on his back that he almost lost his footing, and they all laughed, a mixture of relief and joy.

"A word of warning," the doctor said as he took Julia aside. "Now we fight the rejection battle."

This warning, sobering though it was, had not succeeded in dampening Julia's pleasure at the operation's success. She had seized upon the positive words the doctor had uttered: there should be no reason why there should be any complications. There was much to be relieved about.

And there was much to grieve about.

The next day, Julia was allowed into her father's hospital room. Already, she could see signs of returning health. The blue tinge was gone from around Amos's mouth and eyes, even his fingernails were a healthy pink. When Julia took his hand, the warmth of it sent spirals of joy dancing up her arm and lodging in her heart. She had seen him for just a moment when he was getting wheeled from recovery to his room and was startled by how cold his hand was. The nurse explained that his body had been chilled down for surgery and it would take several hours to warm up again. Last night, he had been heavily sedated, but today, when she squeezed his hand, she received a squeeze in return. His eyes fluttered open and a slight smile moved the corners of his mouth.

He tried to speak but couldn't because of the tubes running down his throat to allow the ventilator to breathe for him. The surgeon gave him a pad of paper and pen to communicate. Julia hung there, waiting for her father's first words.

Slowly and carefully, with the doctor's help, he scrawled, "When can I go home?"

Julia laughed for pure joy until she wanted to cry. It was a miracle. She could see the vein in her father's neck pulsing. Deep in his chest, Menno's heart was pounding a steady beat.

"All depends on how well you do, Amos," the doctor said. "Minimum stay is usually a week."

Julia was surprised. "That's all?"

"Amazing, isn't it? But he was in fairly good shape when he arrived—a lot of folks waiting for transplants are knocking at death's door, and your father had been trying to stay in shape."

Fern! Julia breathed a prayer of thanks for that bossy, wonderful woman, sweeping into their lives so unexpectedly. So profoundly.

"Besides, we find people heal better at home." The doctor checked Amos's responses, wrote some notes on his pad, and nodded to Julia. "We'll keep him pretty heavily sedated today and see how he's doing by evening. The respiration therapist will be working with him to keep the lungs clear. So far he's handling the anti-rejection meds. There's a catheter inserted in the side of his neck that enables us to take biopsies from the inside of the heart. We'll take samples and test them five times a day. If all goes well, the samples will be tested daily for a while after you return home, then every other day, then every other week." He paused. "For now, though, we wait."

Julia looked at her father, resting there, and couldn't hold back a smile. She was beaming! "And pray. We wait and pray."

On Saturday afternoon, there was a great flurry of coming and going at Windmill Farm as ladies appeared and worked themselves to the bone—helping quietly and without fanfare. The church at Stoney Ridge was like that. The house was cleaned from top to bottom, the pantry and refrigerator were filled with food, the living room was emptied and benches were brought in as scores of friends and neighbors came through to view Menno, laid out in the front room. Fern remained at the house, directing traffic, while Julia stayed at the hospital with their father. Sadie felt almost useless.

She tried to help Fern but couldn't concentrate on her tasks. Fern finally told her to go outside and get some fresh air. Too much had happened, too quickly. She could hardly believe how life had changed, in just a few days.

As she walked down the driveway, she found Annie at the roadside stand, as if she'd been waiting for Sadie. Beside Annie was one of Menno's pups, now about five months old. Sadie bent down and scratched the pup behind the ears.

"It made Menno happy that you have one of his pups," Sadie said.

The puppy wandered off to sniff around the mailbox.

Annie kept her eyes downcast. "Menno was real good to me."

Sadie nodded. She wouldn't cry. She wouldn't cry. Once she started, she didn't think she could stop.

"Sometime, maybe, you could come pay a visit to me. Maybe we could talk." Annie looked as if she wanted to say more but didn't.

"I'd like that, Annie."

"You know, you were special to Menno. You understood

him best." Annie whistled for the pup, just like Menno had taught her, and walked away.

Then the tears began for Sadie.

Sunday was, blessedly, an off-Sunday, and the family had a quiet morning before the taxi driver arrived to take them to Hershey. They were able to have a fifteen-minute, one-on-one afternoon visit with Amos. M.K. insisted on staying at home, despite Sadie's urging her to join them, so Fern volunteered to stay at home with her. Sadie couldn't hide her exasperation with her little sister. She knew M.K. was hurting, but she wouldn't talk about it. What more could Sadie do? Sadie was hurting too. They all were hurting.

When they reached the hospital that afternoon, a nurse smiled when she saw them in front of the nurse's central monitoring station. "Thirty-six hours and no signs of rejection, other than a slightly elevated temperature," she volunteered, "which is common after major surgery. The doctor was just here. He said your dad is doing so well, he'll be dangling soon."

"Dangling?" Sadie asked.

"Sitting up, feet over the side of the bed. Precursor to standing on the floor."

Julia and Uncle Hank insisted that Sadie go in first to visit with her dad. She had only seen him briefly, right after surgery. She wore a gown over her dress, a face mask, and paper slippers over her shoes—to reduce the chance of infection for Amos. As Sadie pushed the door open, she felt her stomach twist into a tight knot. Her father was connected to a network of wires and tubes—some attached to the heart monitor, an IV, a blood pressure cuff. Swathed under white sheets, he looked so small. It was a stark contrast to the rugged, deeply tanned figure of her father that was fixed in her mind from childhood. The lights were dimmed in the room, but the bank of machines that pumped and hissed with beeps of their own were still visible, their monitors casting a soft, diffused light. Her eyes filled with tears, but she fought them off. She needed to get used to this, if it was true what Fern had said—if she was a healer.

"Dad?"

Amos looked up, his eyes unfocused. It took him several seconds to focus. "Sadie?" he asked, his voice a mere whisper, then his eyes flew open wide with recognition.

The nurse stole quietly into the room. Slowly, she raised the head of the bed so he was sitting nearly straight up. Amos gasped as she moved his feet toward the edge, but he sat up with his own muscles.

"No rush now, we'll take it easy," the nurse said.

Sadie laid a hand on his shoulder when she saw Amos quivering.

"Okay, now swing your legs over slowly," the nurse instructed.

Amos inched his heels toward the side of the bed, hanging onto the nurse's forearm. Sadie held her breath.

The nurse scooted the IV line out of the way. "Good, you're almost there. Feeling faint? Don't forget to breathe."

With his feet hung straight down from his knees, fairly close to sitting straight up, he let out a whoosh. "Made it."

"Way to go, big guy."

Amos gave her a thumbs-up sign.

"You did it. How's it feel?"

"Wobbly. I don't think I'll be walking quite yet."

"No, but standing by tonight." The nurse put her stethoscope to Amos's back. "Good and clear. Just what we like to hear." She looked into Sadie's eyes. "You want to hear?" When Sadie nodded, she slipped the earpieces into Sadie's ears and held the disc against his back.

The nurse put the stethoscope back in her pocket. "You got a real thumper there. How you feeling?"

"Like I just plowed ten acres with a stubborn mule."

When Amos was lying down again, with the bed propped back up, he puffed out his cheeks and blew out a breath. "You know, tiring as that was, I can tell I'm getting more air than I have for a long time. I've been weaker than this at times at home lying on the couch." He glanced at Sadie and saw tears streaming down her cheeks. "What's this?" He reached out a hand to her cheek.

"Dad, that's Menno's heart beating inside of you." She leaned her forehead against his and held his hand against his bandaged-up chest. "Menno is part of you."

※

Monday was a very big day. Five hundred and thirty-two people attended Menno's funeral. M.K. counted. It was a way for her to keep her mind away from thinking about the pine box right in front of her that held her brother's body. As soon as the graveside service in the cemetery was over, she waited until Fern's back was turned, and then she ran. She ran as far as she could and didn't stop until she was completely out of breath and had stitches pinching her side. She found the shortcut to Blue Lake Pond and walked down to the shore, holding a fist against her side. She flopped down on the shore and stared at the still water.

The sky was bright blue and the air was crisp, a hint of

winter on autumn's heels. The day was beautiful and it was cruel. It was Menno's favorite kind of day.

Out of the blue, Jimmy Fisher sat down next to her on the sandy dirt.

She scowled at him. "What are you doing, sneaking up on me like that? Can't you see I want to be alone?"

"I wasn't sneaking," he said. "I saw you run off. Thought you might need some company."

"I don't."

But he didn't leave and she was glad. They sat there for a while, watching the water lap the shore.

Finally, Jimmy spoke. "The game warden caught the bear and her cub. He took them up to the mountains. They won't be bothering anyone anymore."

M.K. rested her chin on her knees.

"My mother feels awful bad. A police officer came to our house and had her fill out a report about the accident."

"I don't blame her. None of us do. If anyone's to blame, it's me. It was my idea to take a shortcut through your cornfield. That's the reason your mother got scared. If we were coming down the driveway like normal people, we wouldn't have had to go through the chicken yard and make your dog even crazier than it is. Then your mother wouldn't have started shooting at anything that moved." She rubbed her eyes. "I should've stayed with him. I shouldn't have left him. I knew he got confused when too much was happening too fast. I left him alone. He must have been so frightened."

"The bishop said it was Menno's time. Maybe it was, maybe it wasn't. I don't know how to sort all of that out." He turned his head toward her. "Maybe it was just an accident. Sometimes, bad things happen and there's just no explaining them."

She kept her eyes straight ahead. "That's as hard to get my head around as the bishop's way of thinking."

"Maybe because . . . the problem is . . . you can't forgive yourself."

A single tear leaked down her cheek, then another. Soon, tears were rushing down her cheeks. She started to sob. Jimmy patted her on her back, then finally threw an arm around her shoulder as though trying to impart some of his strength.

He waited until her sobs subsided before he said, "If the bishop was right, that it was Menno's time, then I guess God has something else in mind for you to do."

With a gentleness she didn't think was possible of Jimmy, he wiped her tears away. He looked at her with earnest eyes. "I always did figure God had something special in mind for you. You're not exactly . . . an ordinary girl."

If this were any other day, and she weren't so tired and so sad, she might have popped him one. Instead, she decided that she would ignore that remark. They sat companionably for a while longer until Jimmy rose to his feet.

"Let's get back to the house before you're missed." He reached out a hand for her and helped her to his feet.

She hesitated, almost expecting him to let her hand go so she would fall back, the way she had seen him trick plenty of unsuspecting girls on the schoolyard.

But this time, at least for today, he didn't.

The nurse stood right behind Amos, ready to catch him if he did fall. It was time to walk. Something he had done since he was a baby, and right now, it felt like he was climbing Mount Everest without oxygen.

"Okay, one foot at a time. Put them forward. Keep your back straight, let that walker roll forward, nice and slow."

Amos made it to the doorway before he had to stop. "Whew." He braced his arms on the walker and leaned forward. The nurse braced the walker in front of him and helped him to a chair.

"Not sure how I'll get back up." Amos leaned against the chair. "But I'm up and walking, and while I feel weak, I can breathe and not get dizzy." He drew in a breath and let it out. Would he ever grow accustomed to that wonderful feeling of taking a full breath? He had been intubated for two days. How Amos hated that tube down his throat! He didn't even mind the discomfort from the incision that ran from his throat to just below his sternum—metal stitches that looked like the laces of a tennis shoe on an X-ray. He didn't mind the feeling that he had been hit, head-on, by a truck. But that little tube down his throat? It terrified him. He had to breathe with the rhythm that the machine established. It was hard for the mind to tell the body to let the machine breathe for you. It felt like the final stages of drowning.

When the tube was pulled from his throat, he sucked in his first full breath of air. Bliss! It felt cool. It felt sweet. Only a newborn baby, he thought, could understand the joy of filling lungs with air for the first time.

He stood and slowly made it back to his bed. As he inched into the bed, he saw Julia standing at the door.

"You all right?" Julia asked softly.

He caught a yawn and suddenly felt like a deflated balloon. "Just tired. I start to feel good and then I guess I overdo it."

Sadie brought in a cup of ice chips. She sat next to Amos's bed and held the cup out for him. Julia straightened up the room. The early afternoon sunshine was streaming through the blinds, capturing floating dust particles.

Suddenly, Amos's EKG monitor started picking up its pace, faster and faster. A high-pitched alarm went off and a nurse flew into Amos's room. She brushed past Fern, who was standing tentatively at the door with a worried look on her face.

"What happened?" she asked, checking knobs on the monitor and taking Amos's pulse. The beep of the monitor slowed back to a steady pace.

"Nothing!" Amos said. "Fern walked in and the machine went haywire."

"Oh," the nurse said. Then her eyes went wide. "Oh!" She winked at Fern. "Better warn him next time you're coming."

Julia glanced over at Sadie, a question in her eyes.

Sadie sidled over to her and whispered, "Don't tell me you haven't noticed!"

Amos felt his cheeks burning, as obvious as two circles of red felt. This was quite possibly the most mortifying moment of his entire life.

Rome didn't know how Julia was holding up. She must be exhausted, trying to keep everything on an even keel. He kept hoping to find a moment alone with her. The opportunity came late Thursday afternoon, at the hospital.

"Julia." He touched her shoulder as she left her father's room. "Let's go somewhere to talk." He led her out to the hospital garden and pulled out two chairs to sit in. "Today is the third of November."

She nodded. "I know."

"M.K. said you told Paul no."

She nodded again. "I'm a little surprised you're still here, Rome." She sounded tired. "My father is on the mend. I'd have thought you'd have left by now."

"Julia, I'm staying."

She tilted her head, as if she hadn't heard him right. "You're going to stay in Stoney Ridge?"

He swallowed hard. He managed a jerky nod. He had to do this for her. But he had to do it for himself too. He was tired of his wandering, scared of the person he might become if he kept on like this—a man with a life so small it could fit on the back of a bee wagon.

She regarded him stubbornly. "You thrive in new places. It's putting down roots that gives you trouble."

"You told me I needed to grow roots, and you were right. So I'm going to try."

"Try?" Her voice sliced through him. "You'll try? You either have the guts to take a risk or you don't."

"I won't know until I try." He took her hands in his. "I mean it, Julia. We belong together."

She pulled her hands away, stood up, and walked a few paces before spinning around to face him. She planted a hand on her hip. "And then one morning I will wake up, and you and your bees will be gone."

He walked over to her. "You'll wake up one morning, and turn to me in bed and say, 'Good morning, my wonderful husband.'"

Her bluster faded and her lower lip trembled. "Haven't you tried to tell me all summer that you're not the settling-down kind? Do you think I would seriously consider marrying a drifter?"

"How about a reformed drifter?" She still didn't believe him. *Okay, Rome, it's now or never. Say it. Say it, Rome.* "I love you, Julia. And once you get over being mad at me, I think you'll discover that you love me too." There. He said it.

She eyed him suspiciously. "If you leave, I'm not coming after you."

"Fair enough."

"I need time to think about this."

"Take all the time you need. As long as you agree to marry me."

A shy smile started with her lips and ended with her eyes. All her sass and strut was slipping away. He closed the distance between them in two strides, pulled her into his arms, and kissed her exactly as he'd been planning to do for a week now.

She kissed him back too.

⁂

On the day that Amos was discharged from the hospital, the weather turned cold, a hint of winter around the corner. Amos would spend the next few months making regular trips back to the hospital for biopsy tests to watch for rejection. He was grateful Windmill Farm was only thirty minutes from Hershey, otherwise he would need to remain near the hospital. He was dressed and ready to leave, with the blasted face mask on to protect him from germs, but was told to wait for someone from the hospital billing department to stop by his room.

This was the moment he had dreaded. He would be presented with a bill for eight hundred thousand dollars, less ten percent if he paid cash. It was a horrifying thought. The money from Julia's quilt would be a start, but there would still be a sickening burden placed on his church family. But . . . it was done. And Menno would never want him to think this way. This heart was God's good gift. It was priceless.

Still. Eight hundred thousand dollars. A staggering sum!

He heard a knock on the door and in walked his daughters—Julia, Sadie, and M.K., followed by Fern and Rome. Uncle Hank was watching over the farm. Amos's heart felt full to the point of overflowing. His family had arrived to accompany him home from the hospital, all wearing paper face masks so only their eyes were visible. On their heels was a small young fellow with thick glasses, wearing a suit that looked two sizes too big for him. Where did the hospital get their employees? From a local elementary school?

"Mr. Lapp, I'm George Henson, from accounting." In his hand was a fat file.

Filled with unpaid bills, no doubt, Amos thought, but he said instead, "We're able to pay a portion of it now, and make monthly installments."

George Henson pushed his glasses back up on the bridge of his nose. "Mr. Lapp, I just wanted to let you know that your hospital bill has been paid in full, and a fund has been established for your yearly pharmaceutical needs. And those will be substantial. About twenty-five thousand dollars a year."

Paid in full? Amos was stunned. "But . . . how?" He looked at each one of his family members. The girls and Hank were dumbfounded. Rome and Fern kept their eyes fixed on the floor. Amos zeroed in on those two. "What do you two know about this?"

Fern and Rome exchanged a look. "I admit that I paid part of that bill, Amos," Rome said. "But nowhere near that amount."

"Where would you get that kind of money?" Amos asked him.

"I sold my family's farm." Rome looked over at Fern. "At least, I thought I did. Then, in the mail, the deed was returned to me. Someone bought it from me, then gifted it back to me."

One of Fern's eyebrows twitched. She eyed the small man in the suit. "When was Amos's bill paid off? And how was it paid?"

The man looked ill at ease. "The remainder was paid off by a cashier's check, just ten minutes ago. But that's all that I'm at liberty to say."

She huffed. "I *thought* I saw him down the hall!" She frowned and pointed a long finger at Amos. "Don't move. I'll be right back."

Amos sighed.

Julia didn't know what she felt more astounded by—that her father's hospital bill had been entirely paid in full, or that Rome had sold his family property to help her family. And to think he hadn't even wanted anyone to know! She was touched beyond words. Life was endlessly perplexing. She looked over at Rome as he played a game of tic-tac-toe with M.K. on the back of a hospital bill as they waited for Fern to return.

Not six months ago, she would never have believed it if someone had told her how life would play itself out. To think she was in love with Roman Troyer, the Bee Man, Roamin' Roman! And he was in love with her. It defied logic. It was strange. It was wonderful. It was strangely wonderful!

Rome glanced up at her and smiled with his eyes. Soon—

maybe tomorrow, maybe the next day—she would tell him that yes, she would marry him.

Fern pushed the door open. Behind her came a man wearing a panama hat.

"You!" M.K. said. She jumped up and ran to him. "You're the man who taught me how to play the shell game!"

"You're the one who bought my quilt at the auction," Julia said.

The man stood at the end of Amos's bed, looking sheepish.

"Did you buy my farm?" Rome asked. "Are you R.W.?"

The man gave a slight nod.

Rome was confused. "Why did you turn right around and give it back to me?"

"Why?" Amos asked. "Why would you be spending your money on my family?"

"Go on," Fern urged the man. "Tell them."

The man looked at his feet. "Money is something I happen to have plenty of. I, well, I made a lot of money on building motor homes years ago. Money isn't a problem for me." The man rubbed his hands together. "But a clean conscience— that's something I can't seem to buy."

"What's troubling you?" Amos asked softly.

The man swallowed hard, but couldn't speak. He looked over at Fern. She waited a long moment, then she, too, choked up. The man closed his eyes and tried again.

"My name is Richard Webster." He looked at Rome to see if he recognized the name, but Rome's face was blank. "I'm the cause of your sorrow."

"What are you talking about?" Rome asked.

"I'm the reason they're dead. Your family. Your uncle too— Miss Graber's fiancé. I'm the one who caused the accident. Six years ago. I'm the one." The man pulled out a handkerchief and wiped his face.

This man was hurting, Julia could see that. A strange combination of sorrow and joy spread through her. His pain—she had seen that same raw pain in Rome. She looked at Rome. What was he feeling? What was he thinking? His face was unreadable.

"Have you been watching us?" Amos asked. "Spying on us?"

The man shook his head. "I spend my time traveling around the country in my motor home. I paid a detective to do a little research and found out Fern and Rome were both in Stoney Ridge this summer. So . . . I came here. I just wanted to see . . . if there was something I could do to help out. To make things right."

Rome cleared his throat. "You wrote me a letter after the accident. I read it. I wrote you back. I told you that you were forgiven."

"I did the same," Fern said.

The man shook his head. "You wrote me that one time—but you never answered my other letters. You never let me do anything to make it up to you. You wouldn't accept my offers of money."

"But there was no need," Rome said. "You weren't guilty of anything. It was an accident. I knew that. I forgave you, long ago. So did Fern. There's no need for anything else."

The man took off his hat. "There is a need. I need to know you *truly* forgive me. Words—they're cheap."

Julia could see the shame eating away at the man. Didn't they see what this man wanted from them? It was as plain as day. She walked up to the man and put a hand on his arm.

"Would you join us for dinner at Windmill Farm on Sunday? We'd like to have you come to our home. We'd like to get to know you." She swept an arm around the room. "All of us would like to get to know you. To thank you for what you've done. We want you to know that you're truly forgiven."

The man looked at her, surprised and hopeful. "If . . . if it wouldn't be too much trouble." He cast a furtive glance at Fern and Rome.

Rome walked up to the man. He covered Julia's hand, still resting on the man, with his own. "No trouble at all." He looked at Fern. "You don't mind, do you, Fern?"

"I'm used to trouble out at Windmill Farm," Fern said.

A look of abject relief covered the man's face. "Then, yes, if you're sure, well, I'd be honored to come." He put his panama hat back on. "I'll be off then. Until Sunday."

"Twelve noon," Fern said. "Don't be late."

"I won't, Miss Graber," the man said. "I won't be late. You can count on it."

When his hand was on the door handle, M.K. called out to him. "Mr. Webster, do you happen to like dogs?"

"I do. Been looking for a dog to keep me company on my travels. But it has to be the right dog."

M.K. nodded. "The dog has to pick you."

He looked a little puzzled, but then his face filled with a thoughtful smile. "That's when you know it's right. I've always thought it's best to let the dog do the choosing." He tapped his panama hat snugly on his head.

After the door closed, silence filled the room.

Finally, Amos cleared his throat and spoke up. "Well, if someone isn't going to wheel me out of here, I'm going to walk myself out!"

That broke the spell, and they all laughed. Sadie pulled the door open and M.K. skipped out. Fern grabbed the handles of Amos's wheelchair and pushed. "That's all we need—to have you trip and break a leg."

"At least I'd be close to the emergency room," Amos shot back.

Rome and Julia smiled at each other as the voices faded down the hall. He reached down to pick up Amos's suitcase and held the door for her. Julia looked back to make sure they hadn't forgotten anything. But she knew they would be bringing all that had happened in this hospital room along with them. Memories as real as Menno's heart, a part of every breath.

Life was endlessly perplexing.

"Ready to go home?" Rome asked, holding a hand out to her.

She slipped her hand into his. "I am."

Questions for Conversation

1. You might have found your feelings about a character changing throughout the story. Consider Julia. Did you pity her after Paul called off the wedding? How did you feel about her later, when she told Paul she wouldn't marry him?

2. Take Fern. You might have assumed you had her pegged early on, only to discover there was more to Stern Fern than you first thought. Have you ever found yourself changing your opinion about someone? What lesson is there in that?

3. There were a lot of opinions floating around about the Bee Man before he finally appeared at dawn at Windmill Farm. Was Roman Troyer how you expected him to be? Why or why not?

4. Despite his famous independent streak, Rome lived his life cautiously. At one point, he says, "Things could go wrong. So many things could go wrong." How did that

one comment speak volumes about Rome's reluctance to form attachments of any kind?

5. Avoidance was Rome's method to cope with grief over the death of his parents and younger sisters. Julia tells him that grief is the price of love. "But hearts are meant to mend," she said. "Christ can do wonders with a broken heart, if given all the pieces." What is your response to that?

6. Have you lost anyone close to you? How do you deal with grief in your own life? How do you comfort others who are grieving?

7. Julia was so busy telling God that Paul was the man for her that she forgot to ask if God agreed. She had to learn to give God a chance to "chime in." Have you ever had a similar circumstance in your life?

8. What incident(s) do you think brought about the most change in Rome? Why?

9. Who was your favorite character in this book? Why? What part of that character's personality, if any, can you relate to?

10. The struggle for control was a constant theme for characters in this novel: Julia struggled with it over Paul, Rome wrestled with it over letting himself feel too much, Amos battled with accepting a heart transplant. What lessons did the characters learn about relinquishing control to God?

11. As Amos was being wheeled out to prepare for the heart transplant, he said to his family, "I will have joy in the morning." What did he mean? What does that perspective say to you?

12. What's your personal attitude toward organ donation? Could you understand Amos's point of view? Did your perspective change toward the end of the book, with Menno's death and gift of life to his father? If you want to learn more about organ donation, here's a place to start: www.organdonor.gov.

A Note from the Author . . .

Thank you for joining me on this armchair journey to Stoney Ridge. If this is your first visit, I hope you enjoyed getting to know the Lapp Family. If you're anxious to learn more about Sadie and Mary Kate, you won't have long to wait. The second novel is set for release in August 2012, and the third will release in January 2013.

In the meantime, I hope you'll drop by my website, www.suzannewoodsfisher.com. You can check out my blog, send me a note (I always love hearing from readers), read excerpts from all five of my novels—all set in Stoney Ridge (BTW, more stories of Stoney Ridge are in the works!), or check out my calendar to see if I might be coming to visit your area.

Again, thank you for visiting Stoney Ridge. I hope you had as much fun reading this book as I had writing it and that you'll be back soon.

Blessings and joy!

Suzanne Woods Fisher

Acknowledgments

There are two subject matters in this story that took a great deal of help from others to "get it right": beekeeping and heart transplants. Thank you to Troy and Susan Buuch for sharing their vast knowledge about beekeeping with me—especially helpful was the information about how an Amish person, without electricity or vehicles to transport hives, would keep bees. And a very special thank-you to Ron and Mary Westgate, for telling me the story of Ron's heart transplant. With Ron's editing, I tried to depict Amos's illness and heart transplant as accurately as I could, but this is a work of fiction. Any blunders—or maybe a better way to say it would be "any stretch of circumstances" (such as having the Organ Donation Transplantation Network swiftly agree to allow a recently deceased family member to donate a heart)—belong to me.

And I feel compelled to add a note about the Swartzen-truber Amish in this story: According to Erik Wesner of AmishAmerica, there is only one Swartzentruber church district in Pennsylvania and it is in Cambria County, not

Lancaster County. Another stretch on my part, but remember . . . this is fiction!

A thank-you to a few other people who answered questions for me: Karla Hanns, my Canadian Facebook friend, for her expertise in quilting, and Sherry Gore, another FB friend, for answering questions about shooting bears.

And the entire Revell team who does so much, start to finish, to help my book be the best it can be: editors Andrea Doering and Barb Barnes, who have the first (Andrea) and last (Barb) look at the manuscript. I hope we are sharing this journey for a very long time! And a special thank-you to the art (Cheryl), marketing and publicity departments (Twila, Michele, Janelle, Deonne, Donna, Sheila, Claudia), and the tireless sales reps! There are others at Revell too who have a hand in making a book come to life and get into the hands of readers. Working with all of you is an honor.

To Joyce Hart, my agent, for your professional support.

To my selfless first readers, Lindsey, Wendrea, and Nyna: how can I ever thank you? Your input and suggestions are invaluable.

My heartfelt gratitude to my husband, Steve, for his loving support and encouragement in this author gig.

And finally, to God. What a blessing you have bestowed on me! I'm incredibly grateful for the opportunity to write books that, I hope and pray, reveals you to readers in a new way.

Suzanne Woods Fisher is the author of *The Choice*, *The Waiting*, and *The Search*—the bestselling Lancaster County Secrets series. *The Waiting* was a finalist for the 2011 Christy Award.

Suzanne's grandfather was raised in the Old Order German Baptist Brethren Church in Franklin County, Pennsylvania. Her interest in living a simple, faith-filled life began with her Dunkard cousins. Suzanne is also the author of the bestselling *Amish Peace: Simple Wisdom for a Complicated World* and *Amish Proverbs: Words of Wisdom from the Simple Life*, both finalists for the ECPA Book of the Year award, and *Amish Values for Your Family*. She is the host of *Amish Wisdom*, a weekly radio program on toginet.com. She lives with her family in the San Francisco Bay Area.

You can find Suzanne online at www.suzannewoodsfisher .com.

Meet Suzanne online at

 Suzanne Woods Fisher 🄱 suzannewfisher

www.SuzanneWoodsFisher.com

Don't miss the
LANCASTER COUNTY *Secrets* series!

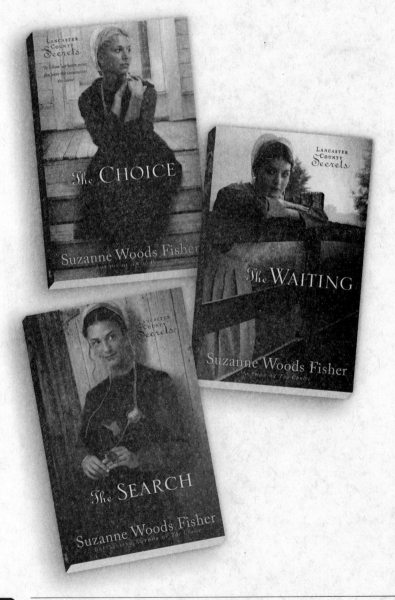

Make the Peace and Wisdom of the Amish a Reality in Your Life

SPRING CITY FREE PUBLIC LIBRARY